61448

LP   Greenberg, Joanne

Gr   Of such small
          differences

Of Such Small Differences

Also by Joanne Greenberg
In Thorndike Large Print

Simple Gifts

Of Such Small Differences

Joanne Greenberg

Thorndike Press • Thorndike, Maine

Library of Congress Cataloging-in-Publication Data:

Greenberg, Joanne.
    Of such small differences / Joanne Greenberg.
        p.   cm.
    ISBN 0-89621-233-5 (alk. paper : lg. print)
    1. Large type books.   I. Title.
[PS3557.R3784O35   1989]
813'.54—dc19   88-32671
                                                          CIP

Large Print edition available in North America by arrangement
with Henry Holt and Company.

Cover design by Michael Anderson.

61448

To Margaret Williams
and Erica Brundquist

Long and Strong

Acknowledgments

I have a profound debt to those in the Deaf and Deaf-blind communities and to those who hear and see but are part of those communities as friends, guides, and interpreters.

My special thanks go to Bob and Michele Smithdas, Bob as catalyst and antagonist, Michele for her example of grace under pressure. I thank Rod and Ele McDonald for their courage and honesty in letting me in, and Therese Smith, whose generosity of time and advice was invaluable. It was also Therese who gave me Frieda Le Pla's excellent book, a memoir of her experience as a Deaf-blind person.

Thanks to John Washington, who walked on water, and John Foley, with whom I also walked, and to Lorna Purdy, who made basic good sense. Thanks to Regina Wilkuzenski, the first Deaf-blind person I ever met, who took away my fear of Deaf-blind people, to the American Association of the Deaf-blind for the assistance of its membership, to

Mitchell Turbin for his arguments, Len Siger for his input about body-language, Martina Milan for her insights in Deaf and Deaf-blind interaction, and to Bambino (Bambi) Marcantonio, who changed for me the meaning of "the blind leading the blind" and whose contributions to Colorado have made her name shine in this state.

Most of all, thanks to McCay Vernon, enabler and catalyst and supportive friend.

Before you love

Learn to run through snow

Leaving no footprint

Zen saying

ONE

He stood in the cold outside and to the hinge side of the door so other people could move past him. His hand against the door frame, he felt the pulse of steps; then the door came, went, came, went. He touched his watch. Late. Sam was late. John sighed heavily with impatience, and then there was hint of someone, guess at a shadow near him, next to him, less than a guess in this cold, with a coat between him and the air and the thing he called shadow. He sighed again with frustration. Someone? There was no evidence he was being spoken to. Maybe his sighing had gone to sound. He carried a card in his pocket, but he didn't want to get it. They saw the cane, but they didn't know he was Deaf, too. The person was still there. "I'm deaf, too," John said. A big shadow, and close. Trouble, someone. Sam's quick Sign against his cheek. "What?" John took his hand out of his pocket. In the cold he could barely read Sam's Sign.

11

"You were yelling again. The man said you sounded like a wounded rhino."

"What is a rhino?"

"Like an elephant."

"I told him I was Deaf."

"He said you sounded like yelling for help. He didn't understand."

"Maybe I didn't spell Deaf with a capital *D*."

"Funny. Funny."

Sam Signed it the Deaf way, bringing John's hand up against his own nose — the Sign for *funny*. Then John went caning efficiently on the way to the van, although he didn't need to; Sam would have led him. "Where?" It was too cold for spelling. Sam indicated with a little tug. John moved so he could cane the near wheels of three parked cars. Double parked. Sam had taught him. "OK, OK," he said.

John liked Sam, who got extra money for driving the van to the workshop, besides what he was paid as guide-interpreter. Sam was not crazy-funny like Martin, but he was better than Kenneth and certainly better than Hillary, who had been punishing in some ways and was religious and had said that Christ had died for John's sins, and when John had asked what sins, Hillary had said lying and blaspheming and masturbation. Then John had said, "If he *died* so I can masturbate I better do it all I can." Hillary gave no extras after that, only picked him up and interpreted what was required, no added explanations, no jokes, no reasons. Reasons make the world.

Around the car, parked. He passed it, handing it behind him. The van. Sam guided lightly, a kind of friendly hand because John certainly knew the van by now, edging the door. John's shin found the first step. Up and in. Hands were there. He sat in and got the taps of their identity from the others. They all worked at the workshop, but he was the only Deaf-blind one.

He sat, relaxing in the familiarity of the trip. The first part went morning-sunward, face warm, in summer, then north, which is sun's left hand. They stopped at certain times, or being lucky, not stopping. No stops this time. Sunward again and then in the circle that bent them all way over right-hand side inside the van and two more turns, then away from sun a short way, that turn a sign they were at the workshop.

John got out of the van quickly because there were others after him needing help, and when he was slow they sometimes pushed at him with their fingers or their canes. As he went up the ramp toward the doors of his work, he was thinking about a poem, something new for which there were not yet words. He should not have been thinking about it, but since waking it had been forming itself and all during his ride to work it had been walking around in his mind. He was trying to remember something from long ago, something he had thought or been told, and he wasn't caring this very familiar place and suddenly, he was collided, knee, shoulder, with sudden unknowing, and he went down. Then, he found parts of someone entangled with his own arm and leg, a flower smell, familiar but not nameable, and it was all moving, struggling, so that he tried to grab for the arms to find the top of him — *her*, the mouth, the face, to see if she was hurt or crying or if her eyes had disappeared in pain. He began to breathe, to vibrate, hoping it was not too loud or unpleasant, by which he could ask forgiveness, since she must be Hearing. With all his winter clothing and hers, he couldn't seem to unwind himself from her, to know whose clothing was whose.

Suddenly arms were at his shoulders and then under, lifting him, and he was pulled bodily away and hung like his own clothes in the closet, straight down, and Sam was Signing into his ungloved hand. "Stop it. You're howling like a slaughterhouse." Then, "If you want to make love, do it upstairs where

14

you can take your clothes off."

"A woman?"

"Yes."

"Where is she? Is she all right?"

"She's all right now that you stopped beating her up."

"Here." He put his hand out and touched. "I'm sorry," he vibrated.

"Stop yelling," Sam pounded into his other hand. "Come inside. We'll all go inside."

Glass. The door. Pull the handle, turn the glass, around the glass and inside to the familiar smell. He took off his coat and hooked his gloves to the collar so he could tell it from the others and hung it with the others on the pegs-right-wall. Sam stood with him. "Leda Milan. Here. She wants to say she is sorry."

"I am sorry." He spelled it into the air.

"Don't waste your time; she doesn't Sign or spell."

"Tell her — "

But a hand stopped him, a cool, active hand, quick and vigorous. He took the hand, and the woman allowed him to move up her sweatered arm. His fingers went up and to her shoulder and neck to her chin and cheek. A woman she was, whose head would top at the level of his eyes. She was standing very still. She let him use both hands, tracing lightly the lines and hollows of her face. It was a strong

15

face — not pretty the way pretty is supposed to be. Her nose came from her forehead without the dip, straight down, and her chin and upper jaw came forward a little more than pretty was supposed to be. Of very small differences beauty and ugliness are made.

"Interesting face," he said to Sam, "not pretty, but I like it."

"Your honesty has won her heart," Sam spelled, "she says go ahead."

Ears, hair. The hair was exceptional, handfuls of it, bearing the perfume of the outside. Strong, coarse, it was heaping down her back. "Where was this?"

"Under her hat."

John had gone to a very good school. Because he had been Hearing until he was nine, he spoke, and had learned to modulate his voice for the Hearing. He had been told his speech was good. Since he could not hear it, sometimes he got too loud or too soft, but he was used to using it. He moved closer and smelled in her hair the warming oils of her body, her smell. When he had finished he stepped back. Breath-puff. "What?"

"She's laughing."

He touched her face and felt her vibration. It was true.

"This was very pleasant but it's time for me to go," Sam said, interpreting.

"Yes," Signed John, with a bobbing fist. "Thank you for letting me touch you."

"I hope to run into you again (that was a joke)."

"Yes, I know it. Very funny."

She was gone. "How old is she?"

"About twenty-five, about your age."

"Pretty?"

"Face is too strong, and she has too much rump, too, for me."

"Ah."

"Funny thing — she wanted to know things about you, too."

"Oh." He had his hands up and waited without saying anything, and then he said, "Sam, am I good-looking?"

"Yes, darling."

"Be serious."

"I suppose so. The secretaries say so."

"Really? Do they?"

"I'm going to puke in a minute."

John's most recent job was in the furniture section. He followed the stripping of old pieces, making sure that all the old finish had been removed from the wood and sanding off what remained. He had worked in many different parts of the workshop, the subcontracting and sorting rooms, and now in furniture.

He was going to ask for a change soon. He liked the work, but by the end of the day the sandpaper had often worn his fingers, making them painful, changing their sensitivity. He went slowly, paying attention, this time, to his place. The fall had unsettled him.

In spite of all the clothing he had been wearing, the fall had also hurt John, had wrenched something in his knee. Whenever he bent down he felt it all during the day. It made him think of that girl.

Glass, water, metal, stone
Shiver, winter, all alone.

It was what they did in school, rhymes like that, to play to. He remembered the excitement of it, Mrs. Lewis's class. She used his touch of such things to teach him some Deaf Signs and fingerspelling. Later, he found out that she had fought to keep him in the class, even though he had been deafened that summer and should have been sent somewhere else, since his school was only for the blind. She had shown him, when he had first come back, how to stay close to Matthew, to feel his body and do what he did without the oral instructions, and they had jumped where there was a rope turning, he with all the other kids running in at a signal and out. "Good for the balance," she said, spelling then Signing into his hand. "Good for the rhythm."

Thank God for rhythm, because rhythm is time and time is the space traveled in the time it takes. Rhythm is heartbeat, blood-beat, legs moving, left, right, the rhythm of the jump rope. These saved his life from despair then, and later they brought him his poetry. He learned to measure movement, time, distance, by the pulses he felt in himself. Voices, the memory of sounds slipped away. Vibration, shape, and rhythm stayed. He learned Braille, and the deaf kids taught him more Signs.

Glass, water, metal, stone
Shiver, insult, all alone.

Again, like yesterday, his mind had gone away from his present work, a dangerous thing for a Deaf-blind — his teachers and interpreters had told him often. He came back when Bernard, in his wheelchair, came by and hit him on the backs of his legs. It was a friendly touch, identification.

"Hello, Bernard," John said. Bernard did not spell. There was only the tap. John worked on. This was a rocking chair, small, with what they called a ladder-back, and even after two sessions in the stripping solution, it

19

still had big globs of old finish on it. John was sanding them out, using gloves. Hand at his back. He took off the gloves and turned. Mr. Bisoglio.

Mr. Bisoglio usually stopped by at least once a day. John might feel his hand and then turn, full of the smell of wood and leftover solvent and old varnish, into Mr. Bisoglio's smell. Mr. Bisoglio was head of the workshop, but he didn't Sign well and his spelling was slow and clumsy. If John needed to speak to him, he answered the single back-pat with a pat on his own shoulder. Mr. Bisoglio would leave and would come back later with his secretary to interpret.

The first time this happened had been upsetting for John. He had clung to Mr. Bisoglio, wanting him to stay. He had not understood when Mr. Bisoglio put John's hands away in denial and then left him. The loss was a familiar ache-anger. John had pounded the table in frustration. People often left in what John thought was the middle of a conversation. He would reach out and they would be gone. Their disappearance hung him in confusion and anguish. He had sometimes had violent thoughts in that anguish, wanting to strike out at whatever he could touch. When Mr. Bisoglio had gone away that first time, John had pounded on the workbench, half-unbalanced between an unknown number of people and things and the defeat of the job he was doing, eating the rejection and swallowing it only to the level of his throat. As he had stood he had felt something near his thigh, a hand he knew. Bernard, in his wheelchair, trying with gestures to say something, and John had let himself be calmed. It had been a good thing, too, because the social worker had told him later how important it was that he keep this job. It was a good job, she said, and important to show agencies how well Deaf-blind could work at varied workplaces, and how easily they could be trained and retrained to adapt to changing requirements in the shop or factory.

Now, he and Mr. Bisoglio understood each other. He had been at this workshop for three years and was comfortable with the way things were. The second year, Mr. Bisoglio had gotten a secretary, Carol, who had some Signs and spelled a little better. Sam was there, too, sighted guide-interpreter, although not most of the time. He got special pay for taking John to different places. John enjoyed Sam's company very much.

A little before lunch John felt Mr. Bisoglio's hand again on his shoulder. Now Carol would be with him. John stood up. He was still working on that rocking chair. He put the sandpaper carefully on the seat of the chair and rubbed his hands, to take away the dust, on a rag he had tied to one of the arms. Instead of Carol, the expected hand, the hand was Sam's.

"For your poetry, Mr. Sherline comes tomorrow."

"Fine; yes, I know."

"Lunchtime."

"Yes."

"Another Deaf-blind is here."

"Where?"

"Repair assembly."

"Man or woman?"

"Woman named Kaminska. New. That's why I'm here."

"What kind of woman?"

"A looker," Sam said, "a blond."

They talked about sex a lot, interpreters. It had always puzzled John that their unofficial words were about girls, their looks, their availability. Turned somewhat away from his place with Sam and Mr. Bisoglio, John had a hint, one breath of a flower smell. "Who just passed?"

"The woman you jumped this morning. She works here, driving another van."

John nodded. The smell, the woman, had gone.

Mr. Bisoglio was tired. John had felt that in

his touch. Sam took over and talked for him. John asked for a transfer out of furniture stripping and into something else. When he gave his reason, Mr. Bisoglio agreed. What would he like to do? they asked.

"Furniture assembly?"

"No room there." He said he would let John know when something opened up. What else?

"The sewing room."

"No, not that. There are new federal regs prohibiting that for Deaf-blind without special equipment."

"Small assembly?"

Mr. Bisoglio said it was all right and that Sam would come one day next week to interpret the learning of the job.

"Maybe she, the Deaf-blind girl, could be moved there, too, later."

Sam's posture changed slightly, and his weight, from foot to foot twice. His spelling became official as the quick words went from Mr. Bisoglio to him. It was against policy to let Deaf or Deaf-blind work together. When they did, they communicated all the time instead of working. It had happened before, and the two or sometimes three had had to be separated. John might see the woman before or after work, but not during. It had happened before. It was policy.

John tried to keep his voice from over-vibrating. Of course they would want to talk, he and a friend. Friends talk. Why was it policy? He wanted to yell but adjusted his voice carefully to where it could no longer be felt — "Why was this done without our agreement? Friends talk but friends work, too." That was a strong statement, he thought, but there was more. He hoped no one else was talking. They hated that, the Hearies. "The Sighted-Hearing go to school," John said, "then they get out. For us, school rules are as big as the world is."

"They're changing your job," Sam said, not interpreting, "and I'll see you get to meet the girl, maybe even this lunchtime. That's what I stayed over for, to interpret *her.*"

"Where is Mr. Bisoglio?"

"Oh, he left."

"Was I facing him when I was talking?"

"Actually, no."

"Why didn't you let me know?"

"He was gone by then."

"I wanted you to — "

"I'm not officially interpreting for you now, professionally; not in this situation."

"I wanted to let him know how I felt."

"You got him to change your job. Why get him upset over something that might not work out? You said yourself you hadn't met her yet."

John did not have the words to describe why he felt the way he did, the school feeling, the armless feeling. He had made his strong statement to empty air. He wanted to kick something, to feel it break, to hit something and feel it give at his hands. He had been told many times that his having this job was special, important, that because of him, other Deaf-blind would or would not be working in jobs like this. In case anyone was standing nearby, he said, "I have to go to the bathroom," and then took his cane and tried hard not to cane away enemies from his path. There was a bathroom on this floor, but he wanted to walk, to vibrate the stairs with his feet, so he went to the one on the level above. It was in the small-parts assembly room. He had worked there before. On the stairs he caned and vibrated and slammed at the walls going up and going down, trying to tire himself out of his school-anger.

And they were right in the end, Sam and Mr. Bisoglio. He had hit walls and doors for nothing. The girl he met later was Deaf-blind, but she was retarded also, and illiterate. There was a big meeting at lunch, self-conscious and unnatural, and far too well attended: Sam interpreting, a rehab counselor, and Mr. Bisoglio's secretary, Carol. Someone else, that flower-smelling woman, moved back and forth at the edges of his sense of her. The Deaf-blind woman was young, maybe even pretty, but her hands were limp and slack, her mismade Sign repetitive, without information or spirit.

"How are you?"

"Yes."

"What's your name?"

"Alm . . . Alm . . ."

"Where did you go to school?" Nothing. He tried again, "School." She hit his hand several times. It was probably some kind of made up home-Sign. It was furtive; like a scrabble. "Do you belong to the church group?" Nothing. *Church?*

"No."

And on and on without any receiving from her, any statement of preference or wish. He was glad when it was over.

Carol was all fingers and eagerness. ". . . wonderful to see you people together — so much to share —"

"She's retarded," John said, "she uses home-Sign."

The other woman spelled to him, persisting, "But she appreciates so much, flowers and music — she picks up the vibrations from the floor . . . it's wonderful."

"I know." Every Deaf-blind John knew did that. It was not *communicating*.

26

"You should come up to see her and have lunch up here, and after work."

John breathed out and then said, trying to keep his voice from vibrating, which made it too loud, "When you talk with her are *you* interested?"

The woman's body changed, just that little shift in weight the Hearing get in discomfort. The hands went wary and cautious. "We do want Alma to socialize. It's very important to socialize; you know that yourself."

"Are you an interpreter?" John asked.

"No, I'm from the state school. I'm the rehabilitation counselor. She's a placement."

John wanted to laugh. The term made the poor retarded girl sound like a fire hydrant. He had tripped over those enough times. No shadow where you felt for shadows. "Don't place her with me," he said.

This had often happened to John since school, that people assumed a handicap to be the strongest link between unlikely people. The worker was persistent, "But she's like you in so many ways. . . ."

He sighed and let it vibrate and felt her leave him. "You're a pistol," Sam said a minute later.

John was surprised. He thought Sam had gone. "Who else is here?"

27

"Just us. You shocked that rehab woman."

"I thought you were interpreting Alma."

"Bisoglio asked me to come."

"Where's that woman?"

"Which woman?"

"The woman who smells like a flower."

"The one you bumped into?"

"Yes."

"I guess she might have gone by; I didn't notice."

"You can see, can't you?"

"Seeing doesn't mean a person notices everything. I might have been looking the other way."

"Don't they give you some kind of training in it?"

"No; they just leave us on our own. Time to get back to work —"

On Friday Mr. Sherline came to get the poems from John. John had been waiting since lunchtime, but Sherline didn't come until it was time to leave, and John had been worried. When he came, Mr. Sherline shook John's hand and then got his assistant to spell into John's hand by using the manual alphabet. They would use two of the last week's poems, but it would be better if John got some new subjects because he was beginning to repeat himself. Handicards had gotten two new artists — one crippled woman who held the brush in her teeth and one retarded man who was able to reproduce perfectly on paper any three-dimensional form he saw. The sales were up, and at thirty dollars apiece, John should be getting a check for a hundred and fifty dollars for the month, but because the poems were so good with the new paintings and because stores wanted reorders, Mr. Sherline had decided to raise John's base to fifty dollars. Today's check was for two hundred and fifty dollars. Oh, yes, they would need a picture. Handicards was going into a boxed set, and in each box there would be a picture of the handicapped artist and handicapped poet.

So they posed him in Carol's office, sitting at a typewriter. When John said it wasn't a Braille machine, they said it didn't matter. They took pictures, making him sit this way and that, telling him to try to look as though he was thinking of a poem. When he did that, they stopped him. "Don't keep moving your hands and face. Sit still."

"You said you wanted — "

"Just sit still then and put your hands on the machine." So he did, and they got what they wanted.

Later, at home, John thought about the money he had now. Soon it would be enough to go to Aureole for a weekend to visit his mother, his brothers, and sister. Then he had an idea. Perhaps Mr. Sherline could send a box of cards to his family. Monday he went in to Mr. Bisoglio's office and talked to Carol. She said she would talk to Mr. Sherline. Later she came to John as he worked and got the address in Aureole.

John quoted the address of his mother's house, an address whose numbers he had had so much trouble learning. He remembered having been astonished that there were so many houses in the town that people had to number them. Numbers in general had been a problem for John until he went to Blind school and the teacher had poured through his hands numbers of marbles, ball bearings, cinnamon candies, kidney beans, and made him sort them by touch and smell. The number of houses in Aureole was more than all the marbles, beans, and ball bearings in his sorting bag. Later he learned about the populations of the world. That was still a number only; he had no sense of it. Martin, one of his guide-interpreters at school, had told him that this was because he was Deaf-blind and could not see or hear a crowd. There was no way for him to perceive what a crowd was, or even what a billion stalks of wheat looked like in a wheat-field. "You get things," Martin had said to him, "people and cars, one at a time. It's the way things should be. We see too many crowds and it makes us callous." John had known the word; it was a word applying to feet.

"Callus?"

"Our souls get thick like the soles of our feet; slow to feel."

Martin — how he had hated Martin at first, the smell of sweat and the big cigars Martin smoked, and now how he missed him since . . . Twice on the street, smelling cigar smoke gone stale, sweat and greasy food together, he had run at the bearer of the smells crying, "Martin!" only to be pulled away; not Martin; never he, maybe never again.

His memory was interrupted by Carol's hand. "Do you want me to write something to them?"

"Yes, that I will soon be visiting with them."

"I will."

"They write to me once a month," John said.

"Really."

"Sam reads me the letters. I write, too, every week."

"What are you waiting for, more pictures?" It was Sam, joking. "What a ham! I've been holding the van for you." The joking was also in Sam's fingers, playful, and not angry. He must have come in while they were talking.

"Why do they call it 'ham'?"

"Because a little goes a long way."

That smell again, there was that flower smell. John was being light with Sam, spelling and signing with quick fingers, but he stopped, midword, his hands before his face. The scent came stronger. She was close. He had often felt people walking on this level of the workshop. They had put carpets down, which had changed the vibrations in the air but not in the floor; she was passing, coming. Then he felt something, someone on his left, and he reached out and she guided his hand in to touch her, a rough garment, collarless. He had read somewhere about slaves wearing such things. It got his concentration off. Her hand caught his and slowly stumbled through a salutation. "Hello; I'm Leda ... we met before."

"You are the woman I bumped into last week."

"How — ?"

"Your smell. You dress like a slave and you smell like a princess." He could tell she was laughing, but not by breath-puff; he did not know quite how he knew, but he had the idea for which he searched, all of it, including the long hair. "Like the goose-girl. I read it when I was learning Braille."

"That story," she said haltingly, her hands fluttering — mute until she remembered the lost letters, "princess cannot speak either."

He took her hand with his left and spelled in the air with his right. "And in this story, the princess knows but cannot Sign." Breath-puff. She was laughing. "You have been passing by here all week," he said with his voice, "why didn't you stop?"

"Smell again?"

"Yes."

"Is damn perfume too strong?"

"Most is; yours is strong enough. I like it. Why didn't you stop?"

"I didn't know manual alphabet. Had to learn."

"To work with Deaf-blind?"

"Helpless when I bumped into you."

"Now you will be able to say, 'Watch where you are going, Tanglefoot.' " Her laughter was hearty, not the polite laughter for form he sometimes felt, barely stirring the air, barely present against his hand, or felt, forearm-to-ribs if he was being guided, or through an interpreter — ha ha.

"I have to go now," she said. "Drive van."

"I know. The other one."

"How do you know?"

"I asked."

"See you again . . . oh, sorry!"

"No. I *see* you, only in another way."

"It's all right?"

"See you."

"See you."

On the way home John asked Sam about being an interpreter at church. Every third Sunday the Deaf had an interpreted service and Deaf-blind people also came and sat through the time in order to enjoy the meeting afterward. It was an event he looked forward to all month because Deaf-blind friends came from everywhere in the area. Lately, they had a new pastor, and his sermons were so good that people were asking for interpreters and not only the guides the church provided.

"Sorry, I'm busy Sunday. I have a date."

John said, "Could you take a weekend off soon? I want to go to visit my family in Aureole. Could you come as guide-interpreter?"

"I would have to charge. It would come to quite a lot of money."

"By spring — May or June — I should have enough. Are you interested?"

"I'll think about it and let you know."

John wanted to ask about Leda. Sam's kidding was too hard for him in this. His thoughts about her, questions about where she lived and what she liked to do were secrets he wanted to keep, especially from Sam's laughter.

Two

Once a week Sam or another interpreter took John shopping. The state agency paid for that. John knew it was expensive because Sam had told him and so had Mr. Bisoglio. Before that, volunteers had brought him food from a list he made. He liked shopping trips with an interpreter. Then it was more interesting, informative, and fun: samples, new foods to try, aisles and aisles, pushing the cart while Sam described what there was to eat or to clean the house with — the rugs, the toilets, the refrigerator. "Buy light bulbs," Sam said.

"Why?"

"You should be turning lights on when you come home and off when you go to sleep."

"Why?"

"To let the robbers know you are there."

"Can't I just put up a sign that I'm in, the way doctors do?"

"Very funny. How do you know doctors do that?"

"Martin told me."

"The one who went to jail?"

"Yes."

John was sorry he had told Sam about that. It was Corson who should have been in jail, not Martin. Martin had been arrested for reasons John had never been able to learn or understand, something to do with the stops they made on their walks all around the city, but what could the trouble have been? Martin was generous, humorous, and wise. He worked for the school; John loved his mobility training with Martin, who would announce it in the hand like a bunch of flowers: "Mobility now — let's blow this place."

"Blow?"

"Because of the wind we leave, wind of our fast passing."

"Wind-edge?"

"What's that?"

"Oh, the wind *things* cause — cars in the street, trains, big things: like this . . . " and John made the shape in the air. "There is a change in the wind off its edge." (It was a valuable thing Corson had taught them.) How John missed Martin's thick, ugly fingers, Martin's once-disgusting, now longed-for smell. . . . How he had grieved for Martin. When he went to the jail to visit, and that after months of pleading, they let him "see" Martin but not touch him. They put him before a "window" and gave him a "telephone," both useless. No touching. John had cried with rage and hated his humiliation for crying and covered his face and vibrated at the top of his power to vibrate, knowing they hated it, remembering from his hearing childhood how loudness hurt — the way train whistles and explosions hurt him now.

John and Sam always went out after their shopping and laundromat chores to McDonald's or Burger King, and each time they ate something different. John paid for these lunches now with his poetry money. Coffee with, coffee without, Cokes, Sprite, Dr Pepper, McNuggets, McMuffins. John knew them all. "You are a veritable gourmet of junk food," Sam said.

"If it's grease, it's peace," John answered.

"After this," Sam said, "Taco Bell, Tokyo Bowl, Eggroll Express. No limits in life." It was these adventures and the spiritedness of Sam that made John like him so much. Unfortunately, other Deaf-blind people, some of them friends of his, liked Sam, too, and asked for his services, so Sam was often busy.

Sam was busy on Sunday, so a volunteer took John to church. The ride was in a car, not the two buses and four-block walk John would have made if he'd gone with his interpreter. The volunteer wanted to bring him home right after the service. John explained that his whole purpose in going was to be at the social hour, which, when he said it, angered the volunteer.

"Don't you care about your immortal soul?"

"Immortal means lives forever . . . "

"Yes."

"Then it's got lots of time."

The volunteer told John he could have half an hour.

"Can you leave and go home and eat and then come back?"

"I live on the other side of town," the man said.

"Can you find me a ride home?"

"I'm doing this as a favor in Christ."

"I know."

"You people always want extra favors."

"That's true."

"Half an hour."

It turned out to be no sacrifice because John's better friends were not there, but he talked to Swede and Madonna for a while. Swede was deaf and Madonna was Deaf-blind; they were married. John envied them their happiness with each other.

Sunday afternoon was the time John liked

best because he read and wrote his poetry. This Sunday the weather was pleasant, so he took a walk around his block before he went in to his lunch and reading. The people on the block knew him. There would be, on days in the spring and summer, familiar touches on his arm as he went, and Mr. Aberdeen wrote things into his hand. He had these friends because, when he had first moved in, he had gone with Kenneth, his former guide-interpreter, to meet everyone in his apartment building and neighbors up and down the block, shaking hands and being introduced. It had taken him a month of weekends to do this, but it had been worth it. He had been helped on walks and now and then given rides to various places. No one was out today; it was too early in the year, but he liked the walk, the exercise and the air on his face, the sense of freedom, and the familiarity he had with the streets. After his walk, he went back to his door, up the steps, and into his own place to work on his poetry.

Mr. Sherline was right; his work was getting repetitious. Fourbuds, his cat, sat in the poetry box while John read his collection of poems, his hand light on the Braille-punched paper.

He had read poetry for many years before deciding to write it. Much of the poetry he read lately was pulseless, or its rhythm was subtle, like a body pulse felt under clothing. He admired the light-pulsed poems but felt more secure with rhymes and pulses, and Mr. Sherline said those were what he wanted. Sometimes, John liked to try other kinds of poetry for practice, once a series of personal definitions that were different from anything he had written.

John's problem now was subject. He had written about all the poetic things he could think of: cats, Christmas, friendship, trees, flowers, the sky, the stars and moon, gardens, mothers and babies, the seasons. Maybe an idea would come to him tomorrow. He spent the rest of the afternoon reading *Moby Dick*.

The story had great force and power even though many of its words were unknown to him. Some he looked up dutifully but most he skipped over with his fingers, stopped and went back and then let them fall into the sea where the boats sailed and the whales swam. He had been told about the sea many times and had been taken there twice, to the edge of it, on a special school trip. What amazed him about Mr. Melville's book was not the part that described nature, spoke of the water and the sky, but how he described the courage and heroism of the men, the power and command of Captain Ahab, and the force of his

40

quest. John decided to write a poem about Captain Ahab. Maybe he could write poems honoring other people in the books he read; it would be a way of talking to them in poetry. The idea excited him, and in thinking about it he almost went past his dinner hour.

When he realized this, he got up and began preparing his usual Sunday meal, warming the stew he had made on Saturday and making corn muffins that he would keep to eat Monday and Tuesday in his lunches. He smiled when he remembered Mrs. Pfansteihl at school. Her spelling and Signing were forceful and almost angry. "Just because you are Deaf-blind doesn't mean you can't take care of yourselves. Deaf-blinds' diets are terrible, junk food and bad eating habits. Not for you. Not for you." And she had taught them cooking and baking. "Timers have set you free, but don't forget your own fingers, lips, and noses." Now he thought: Mrs. Pfansteihl was like Captain Ahab, and he laughed, vibrating deeply back in his throat. When his dinner was ready he sat down at the table and ate and then began to get ready for the next day, washing the dishes, drying and putting them away, making his sandwich and packing the apple and corn muffin for his lunch at work.

This, like all routine work times, could be

dangerous for John. If he allowed himself, he found he drifted dreaming-awake about what he had read or written, about his conversations with his friends or Sam or with Martin, with whom he held conversations still, in his thoughts. Then he would find himself speaking his part of the conversation, swimming in the daydream. That was when he might forget to fulfill some requirement of his routine, which would confound him later. Once he had left a carton of ice cream out, and it had leaked all over the counter and made a sticky mess. Sometimes if he went drifting he would put things away in the wrong places and then have trouble finding them for days.

So John forced himself to the work at hand, knives with the knives, pots and pans, the lunch made, the towels hung, and Fourbuds's dish of water filled and her area cleaned. Was the cover on the garbage can? If not, the cat would get into it and drag bits of bone and fat all over the place, on which John was sure to walk. The drifting still tempted him. It had been the drifting that had made his school life so difficult. He had hated the change, hour after hour, of subject, rhythm, place. Interested in his wood project or his walk, he was continually being changed, moved, turned from one idea to another, and so he had drifted until the hour bells vibrated the floors.

Floors — years of floors.

Martin had ended that when John returned to his old school as a special student. Martin would come in the afternoon, his cigar odor announcing him well before the feeling of his tread, which John learned to identify. He would catch John's hand and shout, big-fingered on his arm or hand, "MOBILITY," and off they would go, ranging all over the city, talking about everything and anything, about history, geography, the news of the day, and all the people they knew. He had thought Martin's smell — of cigars and sweat and booze — would make him permanently sick, but he had begun to be taken by Martin's wit and spirit and he began to wait for Martin eagerly, thus for the smell of him, so that the smell became good, and soon he began only to remember having hated it.

There was something about the stops they made, going all over town, and there was trouble, and questions by the school principal, and then Martin was gone. It still ached in the memory, low and mean like a backache. It was Martin who had said to him, "You're a poet. You see things the way poets do . . ." and it was Martin also who got a Braille typewriter from some back room in the school, an old manual one, and brought it to John. "Here, poet, make me proud." John ordered all the Braille books on poetry he could find. He had always loved words and reading. Now his reading had a point beyond casual interest; he began to study.

At first, studying was like walking alone in woods, branches caught at him, the ground was treacherous, sudden troughs, sudden rocks, no ways made and no people to help or guide. The words resisted. For two years he read every kind of poetry he could all the time he could. His writing changed and changed again. He read and argued with his teachers, he read and argued with the poets. He read with a dictionary and without one and with one again. The rhythm, the heart-pulses in him, the vibrations of his walking, of his breathing, were parts of a poem — question-answer, in-out-back and to, long and majestic, short and intense, as it was with the heartbeat in his hand at rest and at his throat when he ran.

He read about sunsets, which he had never seen, and music, which he had heard long ago and heard no more and had forgotten, of fields and meadows, which were poetic truths to him but not real ones. His teachers praised the poetic truths he produced. His poem "In the Mountains" was read at the school commencement and his poem "Trip to Town" at a parents' meeting. He wrote that poem after

44

the senior class and he, as special student, had gone for a day to Denver, and people had praised his poem for days after. *My soul sings the song of the city*, it began.

These poems were the ones someone remembered after Martin had been arrested and was in jail and John's two years as special student were over. By then he had the job in the factory, and although he read more, he was writing less, why, he did not know. One day an interpreter came and began to talk about Mr. Sherline and Handicards and said that people would be interested in the poems he wrote in Braille, which could then be translated into flat copy. If Mr. Sherline liked these poems, he would see they were printed and illustrated by an artist also handicapped. They would be poems on subjects people liked best. They would find out which sold best.

But the subjects, as Mr. Sherline had said, were narrowing. He thought he might sit down later and type up a list of new subjects — something to help him get new ideas. It would be very pleasurable to write a poem about Moby Dick or Captain Ahab. . . .

His concentration had been broken. He stood in the middle of the kitchen with his sponge in his hand, wondering if he had finished his job. With a vibrating breath-word, he had to drop to the floor to feel if he had given Fourbuds her water and if there were bits from her dinner around her bowl. Then he washed and inspected the area. There were knives and forks on the counter that he had neglected and the refrigerator door was open.

When his kitchen work was finished, John went to where his couch-bed was and took off its cover. He got ready for bed, wishing he could go out in the air-thick night-cold streets. He had always yearned to do that; everyone said it wasn't safe, that criminals lurked there. The quality of the vibrations was different at night, a strange air prickled his skin at that time; something fascinated, a feeling that the earth was drifting, dreaming as he did. He wondered if he had truly experienced this or if it had been told to him or if he had read it. Some day he would just get up and go out. To know the freedom might be worth whatever suffering he had to endure from street people. John never thought of himself as handicapped except in that one way, the grinding daily need to be taken and brought back, interpreted, explained to, bordered, bounded, made to go and come by other people's needs and laws. It was too dangerous here, there, at night, in winter, in the woods, at the seashore. His whole life was continually being defined and interpreted to him because direct experience was too perilous to dare. He breath-vibrated. Was it to be tonight, that escape from rule and law? No, not tonight.

So he went about his routine, putting out the next day's clothing, doing his teeth, washing up. He let the tiredness come as it usually did, in the routine of his preparation for bed, closing up the day, tying it string by string like a garment he had worn in one of the schools years ago.

In all the schools he had been told not to rub himself — that such rubbing only made the desire more and more. Sometimes he and the boys from the Blind school did it to one another, but he had not liked that — too rough and angry. Once he had been used by some of the older Deaf boys, a day of awful memory. They had taken him out beyond the places that were familiar and they had rubbed him and then used him and then they had left him. It had taken him hours to come back and he had been scolded for having willfully gone away. "Serves you right," the school nurse had Signed in his bloodied hands. Still, sometimes now he rubbed himself until his need broke and then he thought for a while and then he slept. This he did and lay at rest, thinking of himself as a whale in the water, Moby Dick, moving in another element, an air thick as nights in rain. Man's way is direction by two elements: a hard element, feet on ground; and a soft element, a leading through air. As a whale, his whole body was unimpeded by ground. Let him break free; it was a freedom like flying, but direction was close as his will and all his body long.

Then he slept, and in his sleep he dreamed he had sight. It was not uncommon for him to dream that he heard or saw. The sight consisted of a kind of certainty about streets and people, and he went everywhere without bumping into anyone or anything or being guided or interpreted. Touching, when he was awake, gave him the security of location. Now that he could see he went everywhere without needing a guide. Then he could hear, too, which meant he could automatically tell what people were thinking; by sight and hearing. Everything was understood, complete. In his dream he went to see Martin at the prison and he put his hands up to the window, and through the window he could feel Martin's face with his hands, and, putting his ear to the window, he could tell what Martin was thinking. Then they communicated, thought to thought in so pleasant and happy a way, he and Martin, that the whole day went by and they didn't want to stop. The guard came and Martin began to think about being in prison and he put his chain up to the window and John felt its links through the window, the steel cold and greasy to his hand, and then it was gone because Martin had been taken away.

John had never been told what Martin had done. He knew from his books that prison was a terrible place — all the books agreed on that, but he knew that Martin was a good man — a very good man and his friend.

He had never been able to get an answer to this puzzle, a reason for this dislocation, and because of it, when he dreamed of Martin he always woke to a dull pain, like the pain of overeating, and to a dull fear, like the fear of being alone on an unfamiliar street.

THREE

In March, on Madonna's birthday, her family always gave a party for Madonna and her friends. John had been to three of these. One year he had been taken to the museum and had gone through the rooms where there were statues and things to touch. There had been four friends, the next year seven, but Louisa and Martha had gone to Arizona and California with their families, and so last year there had been Madonna and Swede, Eleanor, Luke, and himself.

Madonna had met Swede at church. John had been there when they met, and over the months knew how the romance was growing, Swede was Deaf but not blind. His family was in Nebraska. They were upset about his choice and came out to try to persuade him not to marry someone who was Deaf and blind. There was also, Louisa told John, a racial issue, because Madonna was not white. John knew there was something disturbing

50

about black people but he didn't know what it was. He had met them in school and had not been able to learn the secret. Some people said attitudes about black people were a shame, and when interpreters and others spoke of this, their fingers hesitated and went careful, censoring what they told him. Sometimes he all but danced in frustration. This censoring was about many things.

But Swede and Madonna did marry and they lived with Madonna's parents. Swede told John that her mother wanted him to quit his job and spend all his time helping Madonna. Swede made good money and they were saving for a place of their own. John's being able to live independently was a strong argument for Madonna and Swede. John knew that this meant they depended on him to succeed.

Another of John's friends was Eleanor. She was a tiny lady, very frail and old. She was of a vanished way, privately taught; she read Braille with the speed of rain, in three languages, caned, used Signs, used the manual alphabet, and also Tadoma, the system of feeling words by holding both hands over parts of her companion's face, mouth, and throat. Her own Sign was modest and elegant. She had had private tutors and companions all her life. No one John ever knew was as privileged as

Eleanor, but she had once said to him, "I am like a diamond ring closed in a velvet box and worn only on rare occasions. That is a toy. Your life is finer than mine. Your life is not a toy's life."

John's best friend was Luke. They had met the last semester of school, after Martin, after Corson. Luke was from Minnesota, and when his father had a stroke, his brother, Fred, had taken him to Denver. Like John, Luke had endured years of idleness after school. Unlike John, Luke was not interested in reading and he did not do it well. He had never mastered Braille training and did not have the great patience it took to go back and practice the missed word, to practice and practice until the words came. Luke had become Deaf-blind all at once from an illness when he was five, so he only learned his Signs from Deaf kids at school. He said he remembered everything, sight and hearing, from before his illness, but John did not believe that. Since he never told this to Luke, they got along very well.

Luke had been looking for work ever since they got out of school. He was always checking back, getting people to take him to the rehab office to see if there was a job for him. He had once worked wrapping packages at a department store and was good at it until the store decided to expand the job to include mailing and let him go. There had been other jobs, too, for weeks or months, but the business would change hands and the new people would be afraid of a Deaf-blind man working near machines, or the process would change to one that required sight or hearing. The sheltered workshop was full, although they had just hired Alma. There was no explanation. John had asked again and again.

John liked Luke's humor and sense of adventure. With his Braille maps and packet of bus schedules and a catalogue of cards — I AM DEAF-BLIND, WILL YOU TELL ME WHEN BUS #25, 6, 46 COMES? (pointing to the one he wanted) — Luke had traveled here and there in the city. He had even, on occasion, come to John's house. He had many stories about going around town. John was familiar with a six-block area, his apartment building in the middle. There was an ice cream place where he went on Saturdays, too, when the weather was good, and a 7 Eleven where he was known and where, with a list, he could get his casual articles of food and personal use. Every two weeks after work, John went there for some little item because the personnel turnover at the store was so high that he needed to keep making himself known and recognized by whoever the new person might be. There was always someone there who would write in his

hand and someone to spell the manual alphabet to him. Once or twice he had even had
someone Sign to him.

His friends, Luke, Madonna, Swede, and
Eleanor, were like a family to John. His own
family lived in Aureole, a town in the mountains about 150 miles away. He wrote to his
mother once a week, short letters with news of
these friends and his latest activities. Now
that Mr. Bisoglio had told him there was an
opening in the assembly room, he would be
able to write about that, too.

Carol and another man, a foreman, were
teaching John the assembly job. The products
were, Carol said, two-way radios that the
county and three neighboring counties wanted
fixed and "retoned" for all their police and
rescue people. John's job was to unpack and
dismantle all the radios, making an orderly
pile of the parts of each on a conveyor belt that
he would move by pressing a lever with his
foot. This, too, was hard on his hands, but
not nearly so bad as the caustics and sandpaper had been, and he soon learned to avoid
the jagged edges of the radios and the open
boxes. He learned also which screws were
rusted to the receiver-bases, and waiting at
the van Sam told him interesting things about
rust. John was excited. When he knew more

about this and had worked hard on understanding the ideas of it, he would like to write about it. The smell of rot, for example, was very unpleasant; the smell of rust was pleasant, and while the healthy metal was smooth and slickly cold, the rusted, rotted metal was rough but warmer — not so proud.

On the third day he was there, Leda came. He was using his implements to open more boxes, a short, curved knife and a flat, round-end blade he put under the heavy staples to pry them up. He had opened a box and had both hands in it, sorting to get each unit separately out of the pile, when he became aware of that odor, very faint but there, and then to his surprise a kind of rust was on him, a warm roughness as though the air around him had gone faintly caustic or as though all his body had been sanded by sandpaper and the ordinary air had become too harsh for it. He was, for no reason, embarrassed. She might have been standing for a while near him, but not so near that he was conscious of her. Her hand came on his back. She was trying to write something on his back but he couldn't make it out so he turned and took her hand, which said, "Let's eat lunch together today. I'll be up here at noon."

"I don't go to the coin-op place. I eat here. I bring my lunch and I like to drink a Dr

Pepper from the machine."

"I'll see you here, then."

He nodded and she was gone. He had not liked feeling that rust-feeling. It seemed to make the air an enemy. No wonder rusted metal closed its screws against invasion, going deep and secret.

When lunchtime came, John felt the bell's shadow in the air and there was a stopping of machines somewhere, too, a difference in the floor, and then he began to wait for Leda, sitting against the wind-coming-wall where there was a long bench. This building, Sam had told him, had been used as a factory long ago but as a different kind of factory, and its wood and metal were heavy and thick and smelled old. He liked working in the building and had once made Sam take him all around. Years ago, when he had learned what a room was, he had gotten in the habit of doing such rounds. When he had come to work here, he had asked for a long room-stick, ready to define the height of the walls and the presence and height of the ceiling. "Forget it," Sam had said, "the sticks are too short. This ceiling is eighteen, twenty feet high."

"Ha — I thought something was funny about the air here. It's like — I forget where, but where we went once on a trip."

Learning the great room, he had enjoyed its

56

aspect — the direction it faced, not directly wind-coming-wind-going, it had been aspected in an interesting way so that the late warmth came in at the corner. He looked forward to enjoying the changes of heat from the various changing directions, sun-change within the subtle area of direction as the seasons moved. If he was in a place for over a year, he could tell time and season by the heat of the sun through the windows and where on his body the heat moved through the day.

Where was she? He had been sitting, waiting, actively, but unwilling to open his lunch. What had he said, done? She had been angry or embarrassed. Maybe Bisoglio had said something against him, one of those strange things the Sighted seem to pull out of stored bags of criticism to use later. His belly was tight. He went through the room to the Coke machine that was past the first opening where the shadow made him know the go-through was smaller. He got (third button) a Dr Pepper. At first, he had had to drink all the drinks to learn the position of each. Sometimes they changed the positions of the drinks and he would get one he didn't like. So he tasted this one and smiled. Dr Pepper. The sugar in it heated his mouth; the bubbles cooled it. This time, his tension gave the flavor a metallic tang. He came back to the meeting place and waited.

When he was a child he had believed the Sighted were magic. Though he could almost never find them, they could always find him. When Martin told him that people were called Homo sapiens, in the language of science, and that "sapiens" meant knowing, John had nodded, the way he had felt his mother and father nod. Yes. True. They were sapiens, knowing. "What do they call *us?*" he had asked Martin.

"The same."

"Not true."

"True. It is." But he had not proven it to John.

Where was she? Then she was there, sapiens-magic, hand on his hand.

"Sorry — held up."

"Robbers?"

"No, Bisoglio — maybe the same thing."

"Do you want some of the Dr Pepper or this good sandwich?"

"No. You want some of mine?"

"If you will eat part of my corn muffin."

"Homemade!"

"Correct."

"Your landlady?"

"Me. Myself. I live independently," and his pride bore a memory of Mrs. Pfansteihl, the smell of her, off-sweet like old apples, and a slight tremor in the very long, bony hands (by which he knew she must be quite old), spelling fussily. "Everyone must make his way in independence."

They ate. He sensed impatience in her; sitting close he felt her positions changing and moving the air around her. "What?" he asked.

She paused before answering. "I never realized — you can't talk and eat at the same time. Frustrating."

"Meaning of that word?"

There was a long pause. She said, "Eat," then grabbed his hands and held them so he couldn't. Then she stepped on his toes and spelled into his hand, "Move your feet," and then she spelled, "Get up," and held him so he couldn't. "That's frustrating."

"Ah!"

When they had eaten, she said, "Damn eating took all our talking time." Her hands were quick as Fourbuds's heartbeat, but restless. Her posture changed, moving, arranging itself; she breathed and he could feel the change it made in the slight rise of her hand. She was excited and exciting, trembling-alert; she pulsed with life.

"Sorry; I'm a slow eater. Do you work with the handicapped?"

"No. Actor out of work. Here between acting jobs." She tried to steady her spelling. "With this job mornings free when offices are open. Can rehearse most of the midday. If I have performance I can finish here — four to six-thirty — go to theater for eight o'clock curtain."

Her statement amazed him. The busyness of what she did, the travel, the jobs, the sapiens. "What is it like being actor?"

"A lot to it — when I'm better speller, I'll tell you."

"How did you learn? When I first met you you did not know."

"I saw you and Sam; I thought it was interesting."

"There are two of us here, Deaf-blind."

"I know."

John breathed, trying not to vibrate his sigh. "I'm supposed to help her."

"I know — was there for the introduction. Why are you supposed . . ."

"Because she is Deaf-blind, too. Lunchtime; they want me to use my lunchtime."

Her position changed, her air stirred as she moved on the bench. "Yes, I had that idea."

"I smelled you. You went past."

"Yes."

"Why didn't you stop?"

"Too much fuss," she said, "if I'm on stage I want it in a play."

He grinned.

Suddenly he began to have tinnitus. It was

like a fly vibrating inside his head. Dr. Alonso had told him years ago that most Deaf have some kind of head-sound inside now and then; most of it sounded like John's memory of dripping or rushing water or pissing. Sound, John knew, happened when one thing struck another or brushed it. "What hits what to give me this inside my head?"

"No one knows. We would have to take your brain apart while you are still alive to know that," he said.

John had learned to have the tinnitus without mentioning it to people. It made them think he was crazy. There was always some sound, but when *this* came it usually went huge behind his eyes. In an hour or so it would be like an airplane inside his head.

Leda said, "Can you tell people's emotions by touching their faces?"

"Only one or two will show it on their faces and let me touch. The mood is in their hands, their skins, their air, their change of body-place." She took his hand and put it to her brows and then moved her brows so he could feel their muscles moving under her smooth skin, pulling the two halves close with a slight twitching like Fourbuds moving on top of his blanket.

"Now you know it's in their faces, too," Leda said.

"And in mine?"

"Well, yes, it should be. We want to see when a person is happy or sad or angry."

He sighed. The tinnitus was getting worse. His sigh vibrated.

"Don't!"

"Why?"

"It hurts my ears. You sound like a lovesick moose."

He didn't want her to know about the pain. He changed the subject. "We went to the zoo a few times. Missed the moose. What is it like?"

"I'll take you where they have one. You can feel to your heart's content."

Heart's content — the contents of the heart; ingredients. "I write poetry," he said.

"Really? I read poetry quite a lot."

"You should; your name is very poetic. Leda was a person in mythology."

"I only found that out a year and a half ago."

He could feel as he nodded, slight vibrations on the floor. People were coming back to work. He wanted to tell her why he didn't want to be with the other Deaf-blind person; he wanted to talk more to her, even through the mounting vibrations in his head. "What about Saturday?"

She said, "Saturday?"

"To see the moose."

"Oh — yes."

"Do you know where I live?"

"I'll find it."

"Car?"

"Bus."

"Good."

"Why?"

"We can talk."

"I never thought of that."

"Clever me."

"What time?"

"One OK?"

"Yes."

"OK, then. One. Goodbye." Her goodbye was said with a final flip against his hand and it made him twist with pleasure. He would have laughed, but his tinnitus was increasing and also he was afraid of vibrating.

He did not work very well after she left. His tinnitus was now painful. The pain did not start in his ears, which it should have, being, as Dr. Alonso said, a sound; it started on the front of his head like a cap pulled too low by an angry mother. Years ago one of his Deaf schoolmates had talked about a blinding headache and he had laughed and said, "I'm blind already." Recently he had had to beg pardon of that schoolmate in his mind.

The pain began to dance inside his eyes and

make a heavy rain trying to break his skull. Sometimes this happened after tinnitus, but it had not happened for a while, and luckily it could be eased with three aspirins. The pain made him grope instead of walk purposefully. He got downstairs, caning, in the head-roar, to Bisoglio's office. He had found that if he held his head a little to the right, the pain moved back slightly. The desk. No one. He tapped it again with the cane. Waited. No one. He tapped again. He did not know what else to do. Sam would be gone now. Who could help if this secretary was not — A hand was on his arm. He turned inward. The other hand took him and the first: "What's the matter? Why are you banging around?"

"Hurts. My head."

"Lie down."

"I need aspirin — three."

"I can't."

"Why not?"

"It's medicine. Not allowed."

"Please. I need it."

"I'll call Mrs. Ansley."

"Who?"

"First-aid woman. Sit here."

Time went by; the brain-beating continued no worse and no better. John was afraid of losing his special senses because of the pain — his direction and position. He sat, then lay miserably on the chair to which she had guided him. His head roared. At last the woman came. Question and answer, interpreted:

"Where?"

"Here and here."

"How long?"

"After lunch."

"Sharp or dull?"

"Dull, like rain."

"Vomited?"

"Feel like it. I know what cures it. Aspirin pills. Three."

"We can't."

"Why?"

"It's medicine. Must be prescribed."

He could barely read her fingers in the roar. "You give them to friends. I know of this. School secretary to Martin, three, four times."

"Yes, to friends, not me to you."

"*Why?*"

"Different. You are a client. That's medicine. There could be a lawsuit. Forbidden by law."

"Hurts. Hurts bad. *Please.*"

Nothing for a long time. Perhaps they had gone. He moaned with pain. His hand was taken. "Stop the noise."

Oh, God, they were talking about it, over him, as though he were a chair. He remembered Leda saying that they could see this pain, that knowledge of it was made on the face. He also knew that seeing was in some way directional, like walking, this and this, in a direction, not that and that, which was in the other direction. So he had to tell them. "Here," and he vibrated to get their attention, "here," and pointed to his face so they would see the pain. More nothing. The air jumped for him but he couldn't tell if it was his pain or theirs.

The hand: "Do you want to go to the hospital?"

"When?"

"When Sam comes."

"When Sam comes I can go home and get three pills. They are in my home. I will take them in my home. Why not here?"

"We *can't!*"

"Can I have a taxi drive me home now?"

"No."

"Why?"

"You are a client. We could be sued for letting you leave in case you have some bad trouble during working hours."

"What then?"

"Stay here."

The new woman took his pulse and blood pressure and rubbed his neck and felt his forehead. Then they took him to a place where there was a smooth-slick couch with knobs making hills in it, and they set him down to lie the afternoon away, abject and humiliated in the raining pain. He had begun to wear it out the way a person who is fighting hits when he gets tired, the rain of blows now a dull thump, thump. But the victim was tired, too, and could not fight anymore. Direction went. Position went. John now did not know which way he was facing. He could no longer determine whether he was facing straight on. Long later, Sam came.

"Take me home," John said into his familiar hand. "I'm Deaf-blind, really now, really Deaf and really blind. I can't do a straight line. It hurts, Sam — it hurts so much!"

"My God, what is it?"

"It's a tinnitus headache. Three aspirin pills — "

"Just sit there," and a minute or so later Sam was back with aspirin and water, giving John the trembling paper cup, fragile as long ago's heavy-headed flower on a long stem. "Here."

John held his hand open and the three dry-drops hit his palm. He put the pills into his mouth and drank the water. "I — "

"It's OK. Let me guide you. You're breathing too fast; it's making you dizzy. Here — quiet down a little."

They got up. John almost fell over. "OK, it's OK."

"Where?"

"Here. I'll guide." And they went somewhere, maze-walking, as though John had never been led here before. Coat. Outside. The van. Even then he felt no intimacy with his surroundings, no position, no direction. He had wept with pain and shame and now his nose was running so he couldn't even smell. The trip was a trip in the true dark. He had no idea.

Later, when he was home, he began to clear a little. Sam had had to bring him to his door. The shame of it was terrible. "Are you sure you'll be OK? Do you want me to send someone — check you out?"

"No! I'm all right."

"But if — "

"I'll stamp on the floor. The neighbor knows. One if by land and two if by sea." He was trying for normalcy with everything he had; he could only barely sense direction.

"Poetry. Very funny."

"I read it years ago."

"Ah — "

He lay on his bed and let himself weep. He tried not to vibrate because when he had vibrated sorrow at school they had told him he was too loud. Then he remembered he could vibrate as hard as he wanted if he had something in his mouth. He thought he might put some water in a plastic bag and put that in his mouth and pull his body into one huge vibration, but the planning of it took away the desire and so he lay back and wept with unvibrated shame, giving himself over to it like a tired child to sleep, and then he did sleep, still in his coat and shoes.

He woke groggy and thick-tongued. Dinnertime? He had no appetite, so he drank some juice and felt much better, took his coat off and began to get ready for tomorrow. Not eating had saved him cleaning up. More time to read if he wished. Read in bed. It was a luxury he sometimes allowed himself. He was brushing his teeth when the knowledge struck him — Leda. She would hear about his sickness, his weakness, his dependence. Sam already knew. Soon it would be all over the shop the way mistakes and embarrassments went all over school, everyone knowing who wet the bed at night and who didn't wash with soap; and who left his towel dirty. He knew that They judged, were impatient, laughed. Ordinarily, it did not bother him because when They were out of the range of the farthest reach of his arm, he was no longer aware of them in the same way.

But Leda, who had talked happily with him, Mr. Bisoglio, who was judging him, maybe even Mr. Sherline, and all their secretaries and the interpreters, and Bernard in his wheelchair might — would — soon know that he had been sick, weak, dependent, reduced, humiliated, weeping, pleading, begging, pounding his pounding head on the couch arm.

So it was that instead of reading in bed, instead of a special treat of cocoa, which was a sick-in-bed even at school, he lay on his bed in the misery-shape: knees to chest and arms over his head and chewed back his vibration, swallowing it so no one would come and laugh at him here as he wept again.

FOUR

She had promised to take him to see the stuffed moose and heart's content. Or *had* she promised — or had she only *said?* He tried to remember exactly what she did say. "I will take you." It had been told him many times and usually it didn't happen. He had asked Martin about that long ago, why They promised things, said things, and didn't do them. Martin had told him that the Sighted world was no different from the Deaf-blind one; that in both worlds there was intention and there was execution. The Sighted and Hearing have a long corridor to walk down every day and what Martin called diversions waited all along that corridor and made them forget what they had said at the beginning. "But they promise . . . "

"They *intend*. They are saying they intend."

"How?"

"Their seeing and hearing makes them busier than you are."

He hadn't understood then, about the busyness. All of his day was full. He was either working or at school, walking, training, eating, reading, writing, getting ready for something to come or cleaning up after something he had been doing. Could there be any more than *all?* Sam had tried to explain when they went to the rock concert in Boulder. He talked about what he called conflicting choices. "I'm taking you here because I want to go. You pay my way and I take you, but I have more choices — things I could do."

"But you *can* do only one thing at a time."

Sam had laughed and said true, and let it go, but John felt there was more Sam might say, explaining, but he never did. Most things stayed half-explained.

Now that she would know how he had begged and shamed himself, her intention might move from closed to open, becoming like water when a plug is taken out of the hole into which it fits. She had said Saturday. He had no way of contacting her. She had to come to him or not come to him. For him, there was only waiting, and in the waiting, fear-stories of what she must have heard about him and why she would not want to see him.

Then there was the time; *he* remembered they had said one o'clock. This anxiety of his always made waiting an agony for John. He

72

could not read or think or do his poetry.

He had risen, washed, checked the bathroom, dressed, had breakfast, and cleaned his plates. He tried to read, but his fingers refused to make words, so he fidgeted, did a little dusting, ran the sweeper, sewed a button on his coat, tried to read again, played tails and paws with Fourbuds and was, by eleven, exhausted.

He fell into a doze. At a quarter past one his special door buzzer vibrated. Fourbuds, resting on John's chest, leapt off and alerted him. He went to the door and opened it. She first took his hand and put it on her face and then spelled into it. "Sor — sorry — I had a call. Appointment with a director."

"A director?"

"About acting job. TV. Commercial."

"Did you get the job?"

"Don't know yet."

"I wish *I* could talk about TV; it interests everyone."

"Better out of it. I think about it too much. Too much depends on it, if you act."

"Will you come in?" They were still standing in the open doorway. She put his hand on her throat and vibrated laughter, nodding her head. "You like some coffee or tea? I have cocoa, too."

"Yes, coffee. Then we will go."

Instant coffee. He made it carefully and brought the cups to the table. "I have fudge. I make it."

"Yes."

"Are you wearing your slave clothes?"

"Yes and no. You are overdressed for where we are going."

"Do you want me to change?"

"No, but sweater instead of jacket. It's warm out."

He had decided to find out how much she knew. He took a breath and said, "I had a headache on Wednesday, late."

"Too bad. I get them from nervous tension."

John smiled. His noise had retreated to the bearable sound of his still-remembered mother noise. "Shhh." John relaxed into the day.

They had the kind of trip he loved — Martin many times, Sam, too. There was a feeling of wideness and freedom, adventure and surprise. First they took the walk to the bus. He did not cane; instead he taught her how to guide. On the bus she talked about every subject: TV acting, the workshop, Mr. Bisoglio. He told her about his writing poetry, about Handicards and what Mr. Sherline had said. They told jokes and she described a few of the people sitting near them on the bus.

"I called the museum," she said, "told them imperative you be able to touch and understand the moose."

"Will they make the moose's call?"

"I guess so, but you won't be able to hear it, will you?"

"I will if I get a balloon."

"What?"

"Can we buy balloons?"

"I guess so."

So they made a stop at a store and went in just as John used to do with Martin. He loved the smells of convenience stores, five-and-dimes, clothing and hardware stores. The big food stores all smelled bad — of drains, standing water, and refrigerant — but he liked even the bad odors because odor is location and location is direction and direction is a wonderful sense. Besides, there is a story in a bad smell as well as in a good one. He told this to Leda as they waited at another bus stop. "I wish you could meet Martin. I wonder if he is still in prison."

"Prison?"

"I'll tell you later."

"Yes; now this silly balloon."

"Don't worry. I'll put it in my pocket until we need it. Hillary told me about the vanity of Sighted people."

"Vanity?"

"He said they don't like walking with Deaf-blind because people will think it is strange. They are always afraid of seeming to be strange, of seeming — " He was about to go on confidently, but he remembered his own shame that she might have been told about his headache.

"Well?"

"Nothing." This he Signed off his neck with one hand, the Deaf way.

"What's that?"

"A Sign."

"Lots to learn."

"It takes time. I guess I have five languages."

"Which?"

"English, manual English, Braille, ASL, and Swedish Sign, a little. I can swear in three more." He felt her body move next to him. She was laughing; not close enough for breath-puff, but he felt it in her body. "What?" he asked.

"Just talking about vanity," she said, her hand in an odd position, "wrong to laugh — I never knew about those languages."

"Manual English is not really a language; I was trying to impress you."

"Why should you?" She was uncomfortable; her air vibrated, almost. "What's the matter?"

76

"Nothing." But that was not so.

They were surely very strange, the Sighted-Hearing: vain and sensitive themselves, they seemed thoughtless and forgetful of others, moody as cats, and sudden as open closet doors. They got on the bus and John sat without giving or receiving for a while, saving his energy, content in the vibrations of the bus, its changes of balance and direction.

"Lots of traffic," she said.

He didn't want her to know that he had never understood what traffic was. It was an excuse everyone used, but they never explained it. He did know that traffic contained air pollution, which he did understand because it changed or covered other odors. In all this there was the consciousness that Sam, and even Martin, and the others had been paid to do what they did. Some did their jobs in a friendly way, giving favors and offering extra knowledge of the world, but their trips were employment still. This was friendship only; Leda was here because she wanted to be. The thought warmed him, expanded him. He said no more, resting.

When their ride was over she signaled him and they got down from the bus. She wanted to help too much. He had to tell her to let him do what he did his own way, caning, or letting her accompany, not being led. They walked along. It was very hard for her to fingerspell and walk at the same time. He, too, felt the pressure of time because of her need to talk in the slower, less-efficient language of finger-grappled letters, using few Signs because she knew very few. Her spelling was still clumsy; part of her charm, freshness, and impatience, hand like a bird, used to sifting wind in its wing. He had held one once, a homing pigeon, heartbeat quicker than a baby's, the eager wing and the smell of sky. Like all of Them she included unnecessary words and letters and excluded others. He had said, "I hope you soon get rid of your Hearing Accent. We will talk better then." Her frustration made him nervous and being nervous drained his energy. He had hoped so much for this day. Now he found himself removing his awareness for long minutes, resting, saving his strength. It meant that sometimes he only nodded and did not truly take in what Leda was saying.

The museum: she said she had called the people. They went through the doors and the air changed three times as the inside opened and closed. The largest air had a third kind of vibration — one without direction. "This is the main space," Leda said.
"I knew *that*. Where is the moose?"
"The moose awaits."

A door — thin wood, risky. A thin, somewhat bouncing floor. "Temporary," Leda said, interpreting. They let him feel all over the stuffed moose, telling him where to step very carefully because they had many animals together. "Special," she said, "they are remodeling."

John had touched and handled many small and some large animals on visits from school to the petting zoo when he was much younger. He knew snakes, dogs, cats, horses, rabbits, but the moose, with its four ears and face like a swollen horse's, was fascinating. John went carefully over all of it, learning it — the face, soft parts; the body, like a chair. The moose was its skin, as they explained, on a frame; only shape and texture were exact. Then they began, when they saw he was careful and interested, to move from animal to animal, and he felt them, putting his hands on lions, tigers, a brown bear, a polar bear, a buffalo with a huge, neckless head, sea lions, walruses, a dugong, eagles, hawks, a condor, a hummingbird. There was a woman there who Signed-spelled fairly well and she described certain living habits of the animals, which John had not read about. He asked her if the museum had recorded the cries of these animals. "Yes, we have; we have a jungle-sounds tape, a savannah tape, and a tape of mating calls." John took the balloon out of his pocket and blew it up. The museum lady told him she understood. Holding his balloon, he felt the vibrations of the jungle sounds as they came through the air. It was a strange and exciting series of rhythms, like hard rain in soft rain against his fingers. He put his cheek and then his lips to the balloon and let the quick pulses, the slow pulses, the tingling feel before the throb almost slow enough to count, come to his face and his hands. Then there was the savannah with the vibrations of what the woman said was lions calling. "Thick," he said, "dense, like explosions in the snow. I remember that from when They were building a highway near the school."

Wait until July Fourth," Leda said, "I ve got a treat for you."

"Don't think so. I tried it once and it made me sick. Explosions are worse for me than they are for Hearing. I don't know why." As he went from animal to animal, he had the feeling of shadow, a thickening in the pressure of the air against which his vibrating went. "There are people here, aren't there?"

"Yes."

"Many?"

"Quite a few."

"Where?"

"In the room."

"Ordinary visitors?"

"Yes, but they are watching you. Do you mind?"

He did, but he said, "I guess not."

"How did you know they were there?"

"Low shadow. It wasn't there before."

"Shadow?"

"A kind of thickness in the air. Some of us have a sense I call shadow. Low shadow means lots of people."

They decided to go out to eat afterward. Leda said, "What should it be — late lunch or early dinner?"

John told her about the differences between a Shakey's and Pizza Hut pizza, a Big Mac and a Whopper. "When Sam and I go, he chooses and I pay."

"Sounds fair," she said.

"What I mean is that we should do that. I'm hungry — I — " He didn't want to tell her in what awful tension he had waited for her or how tight his stomach had been.

"I'm going to take you to eat something different," she said, "and we'll go Dutch."

"A Dutch restaurant?"

"Indian," she said.

The aromas were strange and wonderful. Over the subtle standing-water smell of drains and disinfectant, present in almost all public places, John felt his mouth melting and running with the tang of them. They sat down and Leda said they should order two different plates and share everything. John told her how to tell him where the food was and how it was placed. He was nervous about its form — rice spills, meat must be cut. It was difficult without touching to know how it should be approached. A spoon was best. "We're sitting in the back," Leda said, "and it's too early for lots of people. Do what you need to do."

The flavors were astounding — new ones and old ones in new contexts; clove and cinnamon in meat, ginger not in cookies but in shrimp, salt and sweet together, weeping-hot things and strange pancake-bread to come between and calm the tongue for more. The tea tasted the way flowers smelled.

They ate, and between dishes they talked. Martin had told John what the ease of air from the mouth was called. When he had one she said, "Good Lord, hand me the balloon."

"Does that vibrate — have a sound?"

"It does! Ten people thought they were shot."

"I used to hear — I guess I forgot. The other also. I think I remember that one. Air from the bottom."

"Yes."

"How does that sound?"

"I can't — it's embarrassing."

"Sorry, it's natural — why should it embarrass?"

"I don't know."

"You can hear."

"Does not mean I understand everything."

John was worried about keeping his hands clean for speech. She seemed to want to talk and he could feel her frustration at having to use her hands for eating instead of talking. As soon as he finished with each portion of something, he cleaned his fingers carefully and rubbed them completely dry and warm on his pants. He wanted so much not to offend her.

They ate more. There were foods heating in the mouth and others sweet-heating together, head-tang, throat-tang in bursts in his mouth, and some heat long and slow like sun on the face. "Can people die from too much food?"

"Yes."

"Let's try."

"How can I show you I'm laughing?"

"Hit my hand, like this," and he brushed across the top of her hand as though it were a breath-puff.

She said, "I always thought laughter was for the benefit of the person laughing. You've taught me better. I wish you could see the expressions on my face, to hear my laughter, or see it. Without some sign my laughter seems incomplete, insulting, almost."

John told her about breath-puff, about how, when he was touching someone, even holding hands, laughter came to him through the body like the ripple on Fourbuds's throat when she laughed.

"Fourbuds?"

"My cat, the cat in my home."

"Why that name?"

"You feel the bottom of her paw on your face or in your hand. It is like four buds on a branch in springtime."

"I'll have to try that."

"You never did before?"

"We look, we spend all our time looking. Feel comes so far behind look we don't notice —"

"You would if you didn't have it."

"Touché."

"Fencing."

"You know the word?"

John told her about *Captain Blood*, which was Martin's favorite book and had been made into Braille years ago. Dukes and kings and ladies, in veils and in trouble, and swords and midnight pirates and flags. He had had a lot of trouble about that word, *fence*, thinking he knew what it was. "I did it with Corson before I knew the word for it."

"You *fenced?*"

"Yes."

84

"With swords?"

"Yes. Foils, they are called. Corson was at the school, tutor-interpreter before Martin, before Rahner, too."

"He *fenced* with you?"

"The idea was good, fencing. From Corson it was bad."

John told Leda about Corson, a little, only a very little, about his ideas on freedom and about how he had secretly hated the Deaf-blind students, how he said he wanted to give them independence, but how he kept taking them into bad situations — stick-fighting with one another or playing toreador with trucks in the road. "He didn't do it for freedom, although in it he taught us freedom. He did it because we were damaged and he hoped we would die."

She didn't change position but her hand stiffened. He thought he smelled surprise on her air. She said nothing and then, "How did you know?"

"He told us — told me, anyway, and Harold, Deaf-blind also."

"Why didn't you report him?"

"No one would believe that. You never tell. He taught us a lot, and we did not die, after all. I would rather have him than Rahner, who came after, who was like a nurse. Rahner wanted us all safe in the cage and taking no reality for ourselves. Corson used to trip me, and now and then he would leave me in traffic, but I learned shadow from him, and shadow is another sense."

She said nothing for a long time. Then she said, "Do you see shadows?"

"Yes. Corson taught me that and I developed it." He felt air-change near his face. "That's not shadow; I feel the warm of your hand, and there is your rose smell a little." Something else had changed. "What?" Her hand was trembling. He touched her lip to see if she was speaking or smiling. Her upper lip was wet. "What is it?"

"Nothing."

He touched her cheek. It was wet. "Are you crying?"

"Yes."

"Why?"

"Aren't you ever . . . Don't you ever get angry?"

"About what?"

"About being Deaf and blind? What's been done to you."

"What was the word you taught me?"

"Frustrated."

"Yes, that."

"I mean angry, at Corson, people like him?"

"I just told you, he gave me more than he thought."

"Aren't you angry at a society that allows people like him to be in positions of command over you?" She felt this was so important she did not shorten the sentence for convenience.

"We depend on people for a lot."

"For too much, I think . . . "

He told her a little bit about the help he needed to live, to get to his job, to be taken to shop, to sort money, to buy clothing.

"Dependency," she said. Then, "In China you could walk to work."

"And in the winter, in ice and snow? In China do Deaf-blind work side by side with Hearing and Sighted people?"

"I don't know."

Why did she think it was wrong to need help, or to give help? Was that dependency a bad thing? "Rahner wanted to make us more dependent than we really were. Corson was cruel like cold water. Martin was the best, the wisest and best, but he got sent to prison. For that I sometimes get sorry because they keep so much from us, those helpers of ours."

"Prison? Why?"

"That's what I don't know. They never told us, even when we begged them."

"Tell me," she spelled, "tell *me*."

He told her things about Martin, how Martin came to work at the school and how good he was, how quick and good his Sign was and how witty and knowledgeable. He told her how Martin had started the mobility walks in the city for the two Deaf-blinds twice a week and then four times and then every afternoon, taking John one day and Herbert the next, here and there all through the city. He told her how all his senses had improved: location, direction, shadow, even smell and taste. "Caning away — he follows me but I do it all myself, all weathers, all directions, until I know the city. I am *here* three years and I don't know a thing — cars aren't mobility, not for one of us, not independence, like caning." He told her how one day Martin was not there. Was he sick? No one told. The two Deaf-blind students went to the teachers, the teachers said nothing. To the head of the school. Nothing. It was the blind students telling the Deaf students and the Deaf students finally telling John and Herbert that permitted the knowledge weeks later. Jail. Martin was in jail. It took months of nagging, of saving and planning and persuading before Herbert and John raised the money to pay an interpreter to take them to the police station and find Martin's location. They went to the jail. Even then no one would tell them, or make clear what had caused this. They persevered to see Martin and, sure that they would be allowed to talk, had taken only a guide.

The guards had stopped them and there was no talking, nothing but the glass wall.

"A window?"

He shrugged.

"And a telephone?"

He nodded. Even now, so long after, he felt the pain and sorrow of it. He tried to shake the awful feeling away, the bitterness of that memory.

She seemed not to notice. She said, "Would you like me to find out?"

"It was years ago."

"Would you like it?"

"Yes." But he did not believe she would.

They finished the dinner. He had not been so full or so sleepy since he was a child. "Let's walk home," she said.

"All right." Sudden decisions. How wonderful spontaneity was.

It was miles home. He had not walked so long since Martin or been so happy. Stopping at a light, she said, turning to him and spelling a little tiredly, "This is good for me; careful. I never obey red lights." At another, she said, "Could you find the way back to the restaurant?"

He said, "All we've done is to go four blocks west and two blocks south so far."

They began to walk again and she was spelling while she walked, "that's wonderful," and she walked him into a fire hydrant. He fell over it, bruising his leg.

At his building's door she kissed him on the cheek and said goodbye, leaving him so tired and completed he had to stop twice on the stairs because he was smiling. Exhausted. The tension and the joy, the anguish and the fun collected in his knees. They were trembling under him. He got to his door belly-vibrating with laughter. He couldn't get ready for Sunday. He couldn't even read or do poetry. He could not get entirely undressed. Too much exhaustion, too much fun. He took off his sweater and shoes and pants and lay in his shirt and underwear on the bed.

He lay on his back, trying to keep the day, to go over all the changes of air, to remember the moose, the bear, the buffalo, the tiger, and the doglike wolf, to resavor the hot food, clove and cinnamon, to seal in his experience Leda's impatient, feathery touch, her soft, layered clothing, and under the soap and rose scent, the aromas of her body.

FIVE

He did not see her for a week. Sam said she was there but that she had some kind of acting work. She drove the van and then left quickly in order to get to the other job. Each day John had included an extra corn muffin or piece of fudge in his lunch, hoping to share it with her. Each day he ended by giving it to Bernard or someone, or to the people in the van. He had read about an actress once or twice, but the stories never really said what they did and John had not asked Leda many questions because he had been afraid of seeming stupid.

On Friday, Mr. Sherline came again. John was excited about the new poetry, ideas he had had, poems about *Moby Dick*, about *Crime and Punishment*, and one about *Captain Blood*. He was surprised when Mr. Sherline's interpreter said that Handicards had no use for those poems. He was so surprised that he asked the interpreter to ask again. No. It was

91

sure. There was something Mr. Sherline did want: a series of poems about religion, particularly about Jesus or Mary or God. Prayer poems would be good also.

John was amazed. He knew a great deal about religion, having often been to church. Many of his Deaf and Deaf-blind group were very religious; they had been taught in religious schools. Even now it was the churches that had the get-togethers for the Deaf-blind, and church people would pick them up for services. The Braille libraries had lots of prayer books and religious works. Years ago, Martin had said, such books were all there were in Braille. The interpreter was now telling what the new poems should be — inspirational, she said, talking about religion or about praying or about church on Sunday or about how a Deaf-blind man would pray — what he would say. The best thing would be to get a book of inspirational poems and read them and get ideas from them — not copying, of course, but being inspired. They had been happy with John's poetry in the past, she said, and two of his friendship and Christmas poems were selling especially well — so well they had been made into plaques and ceramic trivets. Trivet? She explained *trivet*. Mr. Sherline and the interpreter left after that, and John stood in Mr. Bisoglio's office, feeling a little nervous and foot-to-foot, shifting weight the way the Sighted did when they were restless but could not go.

All week he had been thinking about Leda. All week he had been remembering, cherishing, polishing to a shine their day together and had been reminded that his routine at work, though satisfying and his own, was also boring and bound by habit. He was the only Deaf-blind person he knew who lived alone, and one of the few who had a job. It was wonderful, a triumph. It was also lonely and boring. He thought of the Sign for *habit*, the Sign for *mind*, and then the Sign for *slave*. His work was routine and very dull and more and more he was feeling foot-to-foot, and his poetry was tired, its future insecure. His life was mind-slaved, and instead of paying attention to his daily jobs, he was thinking about her, her quick touch, her funny jauntiness, the excitement of her moments and her days. He began to imagine being with Leda aboard the *Pequod*, or reading together, she in flat copy and he in Braille.

Then, suddenly, there was an idea. It was as though two ideas, carried in his hands, had hit a wall and broken into one another and become mingled. He had wanted to write about *Moby Dick*, and Mr. Sherline had wanted prayers instead. He and Leda reading

— his big Braille book and her little paper-back. Suddenly, he thought about a big Braille book; Braille books are always bigger. The biggest book in the universe would be God's, and it would be a Braille book. God would read Braille not because he is blind but because He creates by touch. This idea was new. It was the new idea Mr. Sherline wanted and it was an idea John wanted also. John had written many poems about being Deaf-blind, but they were all, in some way, apologies. This poem was different. He was excited about working on it as soon as he got home.

John made his shopping plans with Sam, who remarked on a certain inattention in his manner. "You're standing there with your word in the air, stuck like someone trying to find out which way the wind is blowing. It's a beautiful sight."

"I have things on my mind."

"Can I let you out at the apartment this afternoon or will the cops call at three in the morning to tell me you're downtown wandering around in your pajamas?"

"I sleep naked."

"So much the worse."

"After our shopping let's go to a new place."

"Sure, which?"

"Indian."

"The only one I know is way over near the museum."

"Let's go there."

"Nothing doing. There's a Chinese place closer; we can try that. What's gotten into you?"

"My life needs to be more interesting."

"Join the club."

"I need to stop thinking about . . . "

"What?"

John wanted to say, about why she hasn't talked to me, why she hasn't come to see me, but he only said, "Things get on my mind."

Sam hit him lightly on the shoulder. "Proves you've got one."

When John got home, he sat down immediately at his typewriter and began to think about God's Braille. In the first verse he wanted to show the way God made everything by touch, touching it into life: mountains and seas. Then he wanted to describe about how God reads His Braille every day, Braille of the sun, moon, stars, flowers — everything. In the last verse he wanted to say that when God's fingers read his face, he wanted God to read his smile and look of love. That last idea was a new wisdom he had learned from Leda about faces, that people's faces in some way show what they feel. He had read of this in books, but the writers had never described

95

exactly how it was done. While they were waiting in the restaurant, Leda had "acted" for him the way people's faces looked when they were angry, scared, loving, questioning, sad, or amazed. She let his fingers find the small differences in her forehead and the ridges over her eyes that demonstrated the various emotions — such small differences. . . .

The rhyming was very difficult. Again and again he had to shift words to receive the rhyme, checking carefully in the dictionary to be sure that the words did rhyme. Then the rhythm had to be changed here and there, and some of the lines went over past the beat into the next line and he wondered if that was all right to do.

He worked until he was completely tired. It was nine o'clock. He felt restless and unconnected. It was too late for a snack, too early for bed, and the work lay done-not-done on his machine to be read again. He felt he had burst something, gone over some border in the work and touched experience, as Martin had said once. He thought if he could send *something* to Martin in prison, although it would have to be made into flat copy for the Sighted, it would be this, though Martin was not all that keen on poetry. "Don't give a shit whether I like it or not," Martin had said, his stubby fingers quick in John's hand, singular and special as his now-loved aura, "it's that *you* do."

That "God's Braille" did not apologize for Deaf-blindness but showed it as experience was a border John had not known was there. This was the border he had gone over, the edge he had found and passed. It awed him; it frightened him, too.

The next day he became aware of Leda, close, as he worked. There was her scent and then her hand. "Hi."

"Hi."

Then they were both talking together. "I missed you; I've been working."

"I missed you, too; I've been writing a poem."

"I had a good time when we went out — "

"Dinner was good when we went out."

"All the talk . . . "

"All the talk."

"Want to do it again . . . "

"Let's do it again, to go . . . " She stopped and then he did and then they couldn't begin until she said, "You talk."

Then he said, "I want to see you — so much to say."

"Me too."

"When? Saturday? Sunday?"

"I rehearse; evenings, too. Maybe your apartment after? On my way."

"Oh, yes. Good. Sam said you are in a play."

"One commercial and one play."

"Juliet?"

"Hardly. Have to go."

"When will you come?"

"Tonight about nine-thirty or ten?"

He didn't want to tell her he went to bed at ten. It would have to fit somehow — maybe he could rest beforehand, and his timer could buzz him awake. The whole air around her so vibrated with excitement and outside life that he thought whatever sacrifice he might make would be worth it. Instead of going out in the night, thrilling at the smells of it — frost-touch, dew-touch, the rising of mists that breathed a way he had never breathed them, she would be coming through the night to him bearing on her face and in her hair the scents of its promise and its peril.

He spent the rest of the day planning the visit and wishing the time would pass quickly.

It amazed John that the problems of time's expanding and contracting, which had so bewildered his childhood, could, under all kinds of conditions, still torment him now. The forced patience of waiting was a thing with which he was very familiar. Interpreters and volunteers were often late; the promised starting time of everything waited and waited for the participants to greet one another and settle into chairs; even church was not on time. That was Their way, the Sighted-Hearing way, to torment the waiting ones with lateness, to burn the energy of the Deaf-blind in the furnace of waiting. Sometimes it made him face-hot with stifled resentment.

This time-expansion was different — pull was a huge all-day pull like the days after Martin had gone.

He served his time, hour by hour, working and trying not to dream. At last it was time to go home. At the van Sam did not say anything about Leda's coming, which made John think he might not know. The thought delighted John for a reason he could not explain to himself.

Dinner. Dishes. After they were done he put out coffee cups and fudge for when she came, and then he sat down to read and wait. His book was an American history book, which told about the Revolution and then about slavery and the Civil War. He had thought to read this and then from eight to nine take a nap, resting on the floor with his timer to wake him. He had not begun to set it when he realized that he would never be able to sleep or even rest; he was too excited. Nervous waiting roughened the dinner inside him; it turned under his heart and he could feel it washing right, then left, as his tense muscles fought it.

And at last she came, holding the night air in her hair and among the folds of her clothing; an excited tiredness was in her hand and the air around her; her spelling fumbled with exhaustion. "Too slow," she said, "this damn talk is too slow."

"Leave out the vowels," he said, "I'll understand."

"Takes too long to figure out."

"Drink coffee; it will help."

"Had so much I'm seeing things."

"You think I should have some, then?"

She did not get the joke, by which he knew how very tired she was.

She told him something about the work she was doing. First there was a commercial for automobiles run by a car dealer, in which she was playing four parts: a rich and spoiled sex queen, a practical businesswoman, a busy young mother, and an old lady in a lace collar and flowered hat; in each of these she praised a different car. The play was a comedy, "very slight," she said. He did not know what that meant but he was ashamed to ask.

How did she do it all? "You make me amazed."

"*You* could do that."

"Not me."

100

"Yes; here's how. You have to imagine your-self being those people. If you were a busy young mother, how would your Sign look?" He tried to think about it and felt a mind-wall-shadow. "Remember your mother's gestures," she said. Then, "There, you're doing it."

Wall had a door. John remembered the hands on him, and before he was Deaf, the sounds his mother made, half words lost in clucking noises, her hands busy patting his clothes into order, wiping his nose, washing his face, touching; love and practicality in the same instant but so busy that the touches were a quick brush by and gone, sometimes leaving the job half done. He Signed to Leda that way, half words and then patting her, arrang-ing her clothes, brushing — he remembered his mother always brushing, the quick, down-ward-handing she did. "See — it's right. Now be old." John remembered Pastor Reiber, the trembling. The touching of that man was as vague as his mother's but less purposeful, and there was a demand in the touch — the pastor always poked you to get attention, as though standing right in front of him, hand out to his Sign, was not enough. "You're a real ham," she said.

"I've been told that before. Sam says it."

She Signed *laughter* but then raised his hand for her breath-puff laughter and as naturally kissed it. He felt himself shudder with delight. He went face-hot. She was still laughing. He could tell because he was still holding her hand. "Don't be afraid," she said, "loosen up."

He told her about his poem "God's Braille."

"I would like to see it."

"I'll show you one of my other poems." He went to the poetry box. There was the copy he had ready for Mr. Sherline. It was the top one. He went to the small portable Sighted typewriter he used for his letters to his mother in Aureole and for Mr. Sherline. He said in her direction, "I will copy a poem out for you." It was good that he could do this. He had been eager to show her all his ways, skills he had learned hard and long. He wanted to show her he was worthy of her amazing energy, of the courage of wind-tangle in her hair, night wind, night-danger. "I'll make some cocoa," he said in her direction, "and while you drink, I will copy one of my poems for you."

He went in to heat the milk. He measured and mixed the cocoa and sugar as Mrs. Pfansteihl had taught him in school. Leda had come to stand beside him. "I never saw anyone make this from scratch. . . ." She had taken his hand away from his work and was spelling into it. This annoyed him but he did not dare to say so.

"Scratch."

"From the beginning."

He leaned over a little as though to search for his salt-box for the half-pinch of salt his cocoa needed. Actually he was wondering if she still had the night-smell on her hair. "Put your little finger in the milk," he said, "if it is ready, I'll get the cups back, I put out."

She said "John" by a hand on his shoulder, like the name itself, and then another "John," by making the letter *J* on the down-ribs of his hand with her still night-cool fingers: "You are best, most considerate host. I feel like a queen."

"Queens don't drink cocoa; they drink bubble wine."

"Never the less," she said, spelling it in three pieces.

While she served, he copied a simple cat poem he had written:

> *Midnight, my cat, has wide green eyes;*
> *Midnight, my cat, is still and wise;*
> *And when she comes to drink her milk,*
> *Her purring sound is soft as silk.*

She put the cup at his hand. Someone had told her —

"Someone has told you how — "

"How — "

"How to do this."

"I asked Sam how. He showed me."

"You did that for me?"

"Well, yes, but not only. I didn't want to blow it — do it wrong."

He put the poem in her hand, then waited. "Can you read it?"

"Yes," said the other hand, "but — "

"But?"

"It's . . . as though you can see and hear."

"Yes, I'm proud of that."

"But your cat's name is Fourbuds, not Midnight. You told me why, and I liked that name." He resisted his fourth finger with his thumb and caused the snap-gesture by which Fourbuds came. The cat, blind-man wise, came to his lowered hand. "Can you hear sound of your fingers snapping?"

"No, but I can hear some kinds of vibration as air-change."

"Why not talk about that in your poems?"

"Who would want to know about that?"

"Me, for one." She took the cat from him and said into his hand, "I would like you to write about Fourbuds." She spelled the name harder into his hand than she needed to. "About how you perceive her."

"Perceive?"

"Get," she said, "know, recognize."

That would take some new kind of language, he thought, a kind of language he had no knowledge of. She couldn't mean what she had said; it must be something else. There were no words for what he experienced in his ordinary, nonpoetic life.

For a while they did not talk but sat quietly, close to each other. Her air cooled slightly; by this and the rate of her breathing, which he felt along her body, he could tell that she was asleep. Sitting next to her on the couch, John, too, began to doze. It was very pleasant and satisfying to be half awake with someone very near.

They were touching. Through the faint motions of her sleeve, he could feel the ordered, constant rise and fall of her breathing, counting the rhythm of her body. He wondered what her heartbeat was like. It was not right to touch there; he had been told many times, even hit twice by people for it, although the explanations they gave were strange, and even now he did not fully understand the relationship between all these things that Corson and others called lust. His books and reading only confused him more. Sam talked about getting girls. Did he mean that grapple the boys and girls got into in the furnace room of the Blind building at school? That was all push and shove, hands, faces, cocks and asses, need and anger. He thought he would rather rub and pull himself than do that anymore. There had been girls, one a deaf girl who was going blind and had come to the school when he was a special student. She had been retarded also, and all the boys were with her at one time or another because she seemed to want it all the time.

No touching, they said at school. Touching for talk: good. Touching beyond talk: bad. It led to disease and insanity. In insanity a person loses his sense of direction. John could imagine nothing more terrible. He had a desire now to touch Leda gently, to learn all her body, head to toe, to feel her living-places, all the heartbeat-pulse-places, all the pulses of her body, carefully, in the warmth of her, in the rose-apple-woman smell of her.

As they half lay on the couch, Fourbuds landed on John's chest and folded herself down in her fold-bone-pile, her heart trembling in the fur even as going folded, she went sleeping. Each animal had a different heartbeat. He knew that from experience as well as from books. And she — next to him, Leda, some part animal, had her rhythms and all her body processes, special, separate, perfect. How amazing that was, the separateness he had always thought of as loneliness. Body-move and the air trembled beside him.

It was her waking.

"Oh, asleep."

"Yes, me too, almost, but Fourbuds wanted my chest and woke me up."

"Pardon me, please — "

"For what?"

"For sleeping."

"I liked it that you felt so quiet here."

She took his hand in a natural, easy motion and put it to her throat and let him feel her laughter. "What?"

"I want to feel your laugh with the palm of my hand, like holding it."

"Can't. It's gone."

He knew she was playing with him, joking. Suddenly, not joking, he said, "What do I look like?"

"I think you are handsome."

"I don't know what that means."

"It means that the features in your face go together in a kind of harmony. Your hair is black and your eyes are green — Do you know those colors?"

"No, although I have read about them."

"Your face is long, your nose is narrow, almost sharp, but goes with your face. Your mouth is shaped nicely; it's gentle . . . this is making me embarrassed . . . in repose, something dreamlike comes over your face but your smile can light a room . . . your body . . .

I can't do anymore. Besides, I have to go now. It's late."

"I want to see you again, more."

"Yes."

"I want to — "

"Yes, me too."

She took his head, a hand on each ear, and held it and then tilted his head to the right and back very slightly and kissed him.

Her mouth was open a little. He escaped into it and held her. He was trembling uncontrollably but not against the floor or the air, the way thunder trembles, he was holding her, trembling against her. She had let go of his ears. He closed his arms around her to keep her. His heart was throwing itself like a child, punished, against the bars of his ribs. His member grew to shame him. She pulled away gently.

"I'm sorry," he said. "I can't help — "

"It will happen. We will. I have to go now."

"Good night."

"Good night." She kissed him again, closed lips on his cheeks one and then the other, his eyes, one and then the other, his ears, one and then the other. "Sleep well."

"I will not sleep well. I will not sleep at all."

And he didn't until dawn-smell, moist and cool from the east.

SIX

"Your windows are disgusting. I came to wash them," and she burdened him with the bucket. It was a Saturday, a week since they had last seen each other.

"I don't use windows. . . ." He put the bucket down.

"If *I'm* going to visit — besides looks funny, like apartment's abandoned." She came in warm-joyful. "Two sponges. Can only stay until two. Rehearsals."

"The play — "

"Closes next week. I got a callback on another audition. Oh, yes, *Martin* . . . "

Were they all like that, sighted women? Callback, audition, windows, sponges, *Martin?* "Martin — " John was having trouble breathing. She was suddenly not at his side any longer. He didn't know where she was. He wanted to vibrate words. The only problem with talking was that you never knew if they heard you and you never knew how loud or soft it was, except that vibrating loudly — she was back suddenly. "Please — " he cried.

He tried to be still, to feel the merest throat-motor against his hand, so he held it there. "Please . . ." She took his hand slowly. He felt fearful because the slow way she moved was like a ceremony, and she spelled into it: "Sorry. Thoughtless of me . . . should have waited, the things I found out about Martin."

"Now. I want it now — "

"Please forgive me and wait."

"Now. Please, now."

"Martin is still in prison," her slow spelling said. "He got twenty years, out in ten — parole if he is considered for it."

"I don't understand that."

"I'll explain later. He was convicted for drug dealing. When he took you and your friend all over town, he was making drug deals."

John felt suddenly parted from the body that had held out the hand that had read the words. His hand dropped. Then, because he needed Leda with him, he reached out for it again and held it so she couldn't leave. "More," he said. "Tell me."

"He was caught. That year the law was changed because people are very frightened of drugs. John, let's rest. This is going to hurt — "

"More. Give me all of it." John was wondering what could hurt more than had been given to him already. He had been standing. She pulled him a little roughly to the couch-bed and sat down. She was sitting beside him. He wanted to be standing — communication is easier standing front to front, but she thought she was doing him good.

"They gave him maximum sentence *because* of you and your friend, because they said Martin used the two of you and the school — helpless people, for a cover — " John put his hands up to his mouth to stop any cry that might come out. It wasn't true, what she said, what the court said. He sat for a moment hung in his pain. Then he began to cry. He was sitting on the couch-bed crying. She pulled him to the floor. He let her, not knowing how to stop her. He was sitting on the floor and then she sat back to back against him and let him cry out the unfairness, feeling her back against his own while he wept away his pain. That was a wonderful thing. He was private but not alone. If he did not love her he never would have cried, embarrassing himself, but behind him, away from his weeping face, she was there, present. He could feel the give and take of her breathing, but she was letting him weep. It was a singular thing, perfect tact, Deaf-blind tact.

When he was calmer she got up and went face to face, taking his hand, and said, "Do you want to go there, to see him?"

"Yes, please, yes."

"And I'll make them let me in as interpreter."

"Please, yes."

"So now let's wash the windows. I brought two rags and sponges and some newspaper."

He surprised her. Washing windows had been one of his jobs at school, but in the middle of it he was carried off in another wind of weeping. "Sorry — " Wet hand in his, "didn't know how much this meant to you — how close you were. Ashamed of my crassness."

"What is that?"

"Being proud of how tough I am. Been through a lot. I forget . . . I watch murders on TV. Tough. I forgot."

"You don't suffer, then, when your friends are in jail?"

"Oh, yes, but don't admit it."

"Is that crassness?"

"Yes. Wash windows."

As they were finishing she pulled at him. He followed. He had been standing at the late-warm side of the wall. She brought him into the kitchen. "What is happening?" she asked.

"Sun? It's always sunny here at this time."

"You see it, then?"

"No — I feel the warmth all up here, here."

"But *here,* where you are now — what is in front of you?"

"What?"

"A shadow; it's a big shadow."

"Oh, no, that's not what shadow is. Shadow is what a wall makes or trees or lots of people standing near."

"You don't see any difference between here and here?"

"The second place is cooler."

"Did you really play toreador with a train?"

"Yes, when it was passing. Using *shadow.*"

"So as to — "

"So as to not come near, to not touch."

"That's not shadow, John, it's something else. We'll have to find out what it really is, the thing you call shadow. I think it's something like vibration from something looming. I'll call it 'loom.' "

"I'll call it 'shadow.' "

"The windows are beautiful."

"The house is warmer."

"Our activity."

"No, the air."

"I have to leave soon."

"I want you to stay and enjoy the windows."

"Work. Next Monday or Tuesday I'll come with calendar and arrange for prison visit."

113

"You mean it, then; you promise it?"

"Yes."

He felt her shadow move; her hand slipped away. He wanted to assure himself that he would see her again, but Sam's ghost and Martin's ghost stood by and prevented it. Both of them had said again and again that Hearing never liked to be cornered, blocked by demands. His wish overrode their wisdom.

"When will I see you?"

"Monday or Tuesday. Next week — not this Monday or Tuesday, the one after that."

"I'll have my poem ready then."

When Sam came later to take John shopping, he said the room was a revelation. "It's hotter anyway," John said.

"Stop complaining. All they do is bitch." John was secretly pleased. Leda had not told Sam, not gotten praise from him for volunteer work. Leda had done this secretly, as friends would.

John spent Sunday afternoon writing other poems and he worked very hard, finishing "God's Braille." The second verse, which was about God touching everything every day, reading it, needed two more lines because John realized as he wrote that the touch was the heartbeat, tide, breath, in all living things. He began to think about the motion of moon and sun, things he had not experienced but

114

learned about. Their motion was a progression. He had read that word now and then and had had to look it up. He had asked Sam about it because it seemed to be a wonderful word, a Deaf-blind word. When he had told that to Sam, Sam had asked why. "It's the way things happen. You Sighted say 'in front' and 'behind.' We know things as *then,* and then and then. That's progression." Sam said he didn't understand, but John had smiled to himself because he knew there was a word for the way *he* experienced things.

That idea required two extra lines, which made his poem uneven. He went back over the first verse and saw he could rhyme his two lines with lines in that verse. His last verse was word-smooth but rhymed *love* with *above.* For this poem he wanted something new and special, something that would be a little of the surprise and delight he had had when he got the idea.

He found he had been working for two hours, looking in his dictionary and his rhyming book, changing, moving rhymes, arranging and rearranging the words without letting the ideas slip away. He was exhausted and triumphant, a sea swimmer. He got up stiffly and went to the kitchen to warm his dinner stew. He took the timer and set it for five minutes, holding it in his hand to buzz him aware. Then he went back to the big room with it and lay down on the floor. He woke to the buzzer exhausted from its long warning and his stew burned to the pot. "Deaf-blind people," Sam said the next day when John told him, "suffer more for their carelessness."

"Unfair."

"Yup."

John's life had changed. Always before, the work days had been the exciting part of his week — encounters on the job, changes in the work, and then home to read and write his poetry. Church was once a month, social hour after. Sometimes he and Luke got together. Sometimes Swede would pick him up and take him to visit. Eleanor gave Christmas parties and a picnic on July Fourth; Madonna's birthday was a landmark in the year; the church gave Christmas parties and Thanksgiving dinner. Now, suddenly, the simple possibility of Leda's presence at lunchtime or on weekends made the rest of his life sink away into wall-shadow, there, but not important as anything more than a mobility guide toward the noons or weekends where she might wait. His hope now moved toward Monday or Tuesday noon next week. He was suddenly busy with possibilities and mind-busy with stories, hope-stories about Leda. They would go to new places and she would make meaning in what had always been missing in the description of motivation, the awful always *why* in what people did. He now understood Sam's talk about choices and Martin's about intention. He felt competent and wise and he knew when he was ready with "God's Braille" that Mr. Sherline would be surprised. He would make two copies — one for Mr. Sherline and one for Leda. He had to be very careful typing because sometimes he made bad mistakes that Sam said were funny. On Thursday night he did his copies and also copied another poem, one about spring and new beginnings. On Friday morning, Leda came, touch before smell this time, as he worked.

"Extra visit," she said, "this one doesn't count."

"Where's your fragrance?" (She had taught him this word; she didn't like *smell*.)

"I got self-conscious."

"Put it back. You bring the garden in."

"You made me feel like a — like a woman waiting for the fleet."

"What's that?"

"Never mind."

"Wear your fragrance again. You still wear slave clothes."

"Have a heart."

"It's here," and he put her hand on his chest.

She spread her fingers wide. "I feel it in there." She was learning, he noticed, using the other hand to spell to him and there were one or two Signs in the forms that did not move so that he could understand them without his eyes.

The knowledge of her practicing for him moved him and made him shy. She had been practicing hard, learning. For whom if not for him? "When did you learn that Sign?"

"Alma taught it to me. You should give her another chance. She has never been educated but she's picking things up. She's not as dumb as you think."

"Nobody could be."

"That's cruel. You should not be cruel."

"I know. Arthur told us that — he said the Deaf-blind were special to God so they should never be cruel or angry."

"And you understood that?"

"No, I didn't."

"Good. I was saying something else — something about Alma personally."

"Can you come on Sunday? I want to take you to church. It's the service they have when there's a meeting for the Deaf and Deaf-blind after services."

"I'd like to come but I'm not religious."

"Me too. We can talk the whole time and no one will know. I will spell instead of speaking. There are advantages of not making noise talking."

"When will I pick you up?"

"Ten-thirty?"

"Fine."

That afternoon John waited down in the office for Mr. Sherline to come. He had a flat copy of his two poems ready. He was suddenly nervous in a way he had not been since the first time he had met his employer. He tried to calm himself by walking slowly back and forth, but his concentration was spoiled and he bumped into things and that must have made a sound because people came and with impatient hands began to tell him and then took him to a chair.

Mr. Sherline's secretary-interpreter took the two poems. "Only two this time?"

"Yes."

"We were just going — "

"It won't take long. I want to know if these are what you said last week."

John waited. The sun warmed then heated the left side of his head because it was in its springtime place and almost noon. Sam said sun came through a window, which was an idea John had never fully understood. Sun-warm, yes, but sun? How? What were the properties of light? He had spoken of this often, "sunshine through my window," but it was an idea; he had never really understood it. He felt a great urge to pee. He changed feet and waited. Then the secretary took his hand. "These are fine," she said, "very good. This poem, 'God's Braille,' will be one hundred dollars and the other one will be seventy-five. You have never made one hundred dollars on a poem before."

John took the check and thanked Mr. Sherline and after he had gone, gave the check to Mr. Bisoglio. The agency banked for him. He went back upstairs and was in the bathroom before he realized that his two poems gave him a hundred and seventy-five dollars, and that his four poems had given him two hundred dollars. It was better to write easier poems and more of them. This was a problem to discuss with Sam and Leda.

Sam's comments were unsatisfying. "I'm not much for poetry, but I guess more money is better than less. There is the number six, though."

"What's the number six?"

"It's the sixth time I got smart. I worked a job that paid thirty dollars an hour. I thought: thirty dollars times forty hours times fifty-two weeks. Very nice money. I bought a car and money down on a boat. Yes, I got thirty dollars an hour, but I only worked twenty hours my best week and most weeks I didn't work at all."

"You couldn't make them give you more jobs — "

"No."

"There's a lot to this, isn't there?"

"I'd say so."

"What should I do?"

"Search me. I don't know anyone who *reads* poetry, no less writes it."

Leda came on Sunday and John could barely wait until they were on the bus before he set the problem. "That's the oldest truth in art," she said. She asked him questions about his poems: which did he like, which were a challenge to him. He told her how happy he was with "God's Braille." She said that after church she would come back and read his poems.

At church Leda was too slow and inaccurate as an interpreter to keep up with much of the service.

"I like it better Signing to you anyway. You will be Signing so no one will know we're just talking here and not listening to the preaching."

"Very hard to divide attention," she said, but they talked about things of interest. John described his friends.

121

He did not understand so much inattention in the Seeing-Hearing people he knew. Sometimes even interpreters seemed to drift off somewhere, lost. He compared it with the meeting he and his friends would soon be having where two or three hands would touch him and he would recognize this friend and that at once, and all the hands would seek all the hands in a friendly ball of communication, everyone reaching for everyone else's word.

Leda asked him about what would happen during the social hour afterward. She seemed nervous about it, about meeting his friends. "They're just people," he said. "I won't know who is here until we get together. The hardest thing about being Deaf-blind in meetings is finding one another." He felt her laughter then.

Then there was the wonderful vibration, ears, face, scalp, hands, teeth, sometimes that made him know they were playing the organ. The congregation was singing. John loved this part. He could hear very low sounds but the pleasure was now in the all-vibrating air. The vibrations thickened and thinned like tides against the bones of his face and the bones inside his clothes and in his hand bones touching the wood of the seat in front of him. Unfortunately, from the pleasant bone-feel of the music the nasty buzz of his tinnitus rose, insistent as a bee up the nose.

As though Leda was reading his mind or his face, she spelled into his hand, "Were you born Deaf and blind?"

"No," he spelled in her direction, "I was born blind. I got Deaf when I was about nine."

"How did you get Deaf?"

"My father sometimes hated my being blind. Sometimes he was getting drunk, and then pity and hate together. He sometimes hit me. Once he did it and I fell and then I woke up in a strange bed. Hospital. When I got up I had no direction and no sound. Then I was in bed for a while and then I got direction back but no sound after that."

It seemed she moved away a little at his telling. The air lay cool between them. He reached out and found her. She seemed to flinch away.

"What — "

"Leave me alone for a moment."

"What — "

"Thinking. Want to be alone." He sat next to her. Nothing touched. Then she said, "Sorry," into his hand.

"What was it?"

"What you said upset me. When I get upset I need to be by myself."

"What upset you?"

"More than I can say."

The service was over. He could feel the floor, and through the carpet, pleasant but not luxurious, the movement around him. He slid slowly to the end of the long bench and then back along the walkway through which they had come, feeling delicately with one hand for anyone ahead. She came with him when he was at the beginning of the church.

"Where to now?"

"Stairs — here — *careful.*"

They went down. In the hall downstairs he was suddenly in the identifying knot of friends, all hands and personal smells, identities in the glad mill.

"Welcome to my world," he said, "feel — "

Everyone was stamping for attention and there was the occasional vibration of unmonitored joy.

"They didn't stamp upstairs. . . ."

"Not in the Hearing world — bad manners in the Hearing world. Come on." He pulled her along.

It was a fine day and almost everyone was there: Harvey, his slap of identification, sting-ing-glad, impatient; Madonna, two of every gesture, as though not sure he could feel her hand or her identity; Swede, who was only Deaf and could see; Eleanor and Rebecca, new to the group, Deaf-blind; and Luke, his friend Luke. The woman from the workshop, Alma, was also there. Now that he didn't have to take responsibility for her, he felt free to be polite, even though half her words were crude home-Signs, incomprehensible, and the words she could spell were dull and showed her thoughts to be slow and ordinary. John joked about Sam and then brought Leda's hand to Alma. He also invited Luke to meet Leda and stood by while they exchanged talk about the church and the pleasant day, or so Luke said later. By then the group had sorted itself out in its habitual places and postures, some walking early from group to group and person to person, others waiting until the early walkers stopped. By habit they stayed or went until everyone had mingled, flowed, come and gone to chat, and the ones who wanted longer talk, the friends, separated themselves. Leda was full of the wonder of it. "It's like a dance, like someone choreographed it."

"We need this or we would spend all day finding one another, which is hard enough."

"It's impressive — I never thought about such things."

"Let's stop and talk to Luke."

Three-way conversations were difficult. Leda, still slow and halting, was talking to Luke and the time was passing, time that

John wanted to use. It took all his patience to keep from grabbing Luke's hand for talk. He was surprised when, having gotten Luke back after ten minutes, Luke talked only a little. "I want to go where Alma is. I want to get to her before she is hidden by too many others."

"*Why?*"

"She's cute. Shy."

"She's *retarded.*"

"So what? She's not too retarded to be fun to talk to."

"She can't read Braille. She has no language, no Signs, not even spelling."

"She's learning. I'm teaching her."

John felt, surprisingly, hurt. He had had pleasant fantasies of Luke being impressed with Leda, of the three of them talking, a kind of three-man mad-chat, as he used to do in his school days. He felt childishly jealous, with a stab of the same bitter, misused feeling he had had in school. Luke left them. "I wanted him longer," he said.

"It's clumsy with three." She was trying to make up for her slowness. "I am learning that Deaf-blind culture is intimate; one thing at a time; it's as far as hands or a cane can reach, immediate as touch. That makes it private, tribal."

He didn't understand what she meant so he said nothing but, "Now we will go and meet

Swede and Madonna again. They are friends. Remember, you met them before."

"*You* met them before in that mill of people."

"But you took their hands. They will remember you."

"By that little touch."

"One look," John said, "or so Sam tells me, is all Sighted need when a woman is as pretty as you are."

"Did Sam tell you I was pretty?"

" 'Strong looking,' he said. Don't you remember when we met?"

"That's not a compliment. It means he thinks I can open beer cans with my nose or my forehead's so jutting that nothing below it gets wet in the rain."

"Sounds interesting to me. He likes your hair, too."

"The color is OK, but it's kinky."

"Are you black?"

"No."

"They are the ones with that hair."

"I thought you'd know I was white."

"How?"

"That someone would tell you."

"Sometimes they do. If they are not prejudiced, they don't."

"Liberal pieties." She spelled the words.

"What?"

"Forget it."

They went to Swede and Madonna. John liked Swede, who read a lot and, being Seeing, had all kinds of experiences — TV, movies. He was one of the few Deaf who liked Deaf-blind people and socialized with them, bearing the awful slowness of Deaf-blind communication. They often shared books and opinions about books. John told Swede about "God's Braille." Swede asked him to recite the poem. As well as he could from his memory, John Signed and spelled the poem. When he was done, Swede took his hand and held it for a long time. Then he said, in his combination of Signs and spelling, elegant and sophisticated, "It's wonderful and beautiful. You are truly a poet." John felt the happiness flying inside him.

"I never would have seen them as lovers," Leda said later. "He's so short and old — about fifty — and she's no more than twenty-five and so much bigger and heavier than he is."

"When you can't see and you can't hear — those things matter less. Let's go to the Indian restaurant and I will tell you the school story."

"Years ago the Deaf and Blind state schools were combined to save money. The Hearing and Sighted worlds are different, so within the schools there had to be separations. When

I went to school there was a division between Deaf and blind, between girls and boys, between three age groups, and between black people and white. This meant that in the lower school there had to be eight separate rooms for each class dormitory and for school rooms. When Mr. Lavater came as new principal — "

"How did you learn this?"

"From a friend in the Deaf Division. Mr. Lavater saw this system and decided to combine the black and white students, which would double the time each teacher had, but cut in half the house parents they needed. The dormitories and classrooms were combined, groups of Deaf kids and blind kids from the middle and upper schools began to walk downtown to the ice cream parlors, caning together if they were blind and Signing together if they were Deaf. The town people were angry."

"Where was the school?"

"In Florida."

"Go on."

"The town people sent important representatives to the school to tell Mr. Lavater that he must stop the walks right away and redivide the schools. Mr. Lavater told them that he did not want trouble in the community, that it was necessary to have peace for mobility training and toleration between his students and the outside. He told them he did not understand these racial differences, and so the members of the community must come to all divisions in the school. First they must explain the principles of separation to the Deaf students so they would understand them well. Then they must teach all four divisions of blind students how to identify black and white people immediately so as to learn to separate themselves. Since the representatives could not do these things, they went away and the school stayed combined."

"I thought you went to school *here.*"

"I did, later."

"Why did you change?"

"They never tell you why, only what. Things happen and people never take the time for why."

They were unspeaking a long time. Then Leda said, "Your school story was nice, but are you telling me that Deaf-blind have no racism?"

"I'm telling you that Mr. Lavater had no racism and that Freddie Taplin didn't have any Deafism."

"What's that?"

"The Deaf don't think much of the hard-of-hearing because they don't have Signing skills. Deaf and blind people are really scared of us Deaf-blind. The blind don't think much of the almost blind because they don't have Braille skills and mobility skills. At school the groups never mingled. We liked Freddie because he would spell to us and talk to us and never used Signs we couldn't touch. He was one of the few students who crossed all the lines."

They were at the Indian restaurant, on his urging, but the day, somehow, was not going as he had hoped. Something was tightening her fingers instead of loosening them; something was stirring her air, making her move a lot in what he had learned were nervous ways, head shakes, sudden changes of hand or arm, rockings, tappings. He knew he shouldn't say anything. They hate being told that their feelings show in ways other than words. They hate it that sometimes their words say yes and their air says no. But she said she was his friend. "Is it true — that you are my friend?"

"Yes — "

The word, meant to be forceful, was only tight in his hand. "Then tell me what's wrong."

"I guess it's too much — I liked meeting your friends but it's a whole new world — I'm strained. It's exhausting — the new language — interpreting."

"You don't seem tired, only nervous." She

sat beside him; her hand said nothing.

And suddenly he knew that he, too, had been nervous, was nervous now, that his own air must be tight, that his teeth were clamping when there was no food between them to be eaten, and it was what Corson had called the Animal and what Arthur had called Blind Lust. "It's blind lust," he said, "or in my case, Deaf-blind lust."

"What can I say? . . . " Her fingers had gone blind, stumbling in his hand.

He felt the old hurt. "What would you say if I could hear and see?"

"That would be different. I'd say let's eat and then go home and make love."

John's vitals collapsed and slid inside him. He suddenly couldn't breathe fast enough.

"What is it — you've gone white."

"Nothing," he said, "it was power of your word, that's all."

They both sat still, side by side, not touching. At last John said, "Why am I different?"

"Because with you — " her hand paused, picked, and paused again. "I've had lots of sex. I used to do it as easily as you take a bath. I was married once. After divorce, felt ugly, clumsy. Went on a binge of sex to prove I wasn't ugly. Only proved I was. Sex is easy with me. Have the feeling it isn't with you."

"No," he said. "How did you decide this?"

"When you told me about your father — about what he did to you."

"I don't understand."

"I can't explain."

He wanted to rage, to cry, to shout. He only said, "If They swim, and I can swim, I want to swim. If They dance and I can dance, I want to dance. If They have sex and I can have sex, I want to have sex, too."

"I'm sorry . . . "

The food came. They ate it halfheartedly and then went to his apartment. They did not kiss at the door. She did not come in and he did not show her his poem "God's Braille," and they did not begin what he had long ago begun in a week of dreams.

SEVEN

Now the days, which had been work days and poem days, wealth of detail, cooking of stew, making of fudge, corn muffins, and school cake, Independent Living, pride he had as the only Deaf-blind person he knew who did this, all of it went stiff and lonely. The pride seemed empty. He lay in bed and thought achingly of her and of her scent and her hands and of the clothes she wore, dishcloth skirts and dishtowel blouses, and her strong, large wrists. She was nothing like the women in the books. A body-motion nerviness was in her, hair flying even when he touched it, it was flying up from her head as though she had just landed on earth. It all cried to him: alive, alive! Texture went boring and taste went flat.

In the middle of the week, at work, Carol came with a message for John. It was a letter written by Eleanor's companion. Eleanor's birthday was next Friday. John and Luke and two of Eleanor's friends from school were

134

invited to share the evening at her home. Since John and Luke lived in opposite directions, would it be possible for her to pick them up downtown? She gave the time and suggested the corner. John gave Carol a strong yes. She told him she would call and accept for him. That evening he asked Sam if there were a way for him to drop John at that corner on Friday. "I have a date that night," Sam said. "If you wouldn't mind being early and waiting for a while, I could swing by at six and pick you up."

"Night stuff," John said. It was exciting.

On Friday, he told Bernard about the party. He had to do this coming in because the place where John was now working was inaccessible to Bernard's wheelchair. Since Bernard couldn't use the manual alphabet, John spoke in his direction and received the slap on the knee Bernard used for assent. It was impossible to have anything from Bernard beyond *yes* (slap) and *no* (punch) and a good fellowship greeting. Bernard's mind was hidden in John's darknesses.

As soon as he got home on Friday afternoon, John dressed carefully and went down to wait for Sam. Halcyon was over and the air was hollow with cold and a sudden, stinging wind. There was rain in it, here and there. He had his coat on and a muffler around his ears although he hated heavy clothing, which limited movement and seemed to affect his directional sense. He went out to wait in the touch-deadening cold. The rain had increased.

Except in the worst weather, John didn't wear gloves. He preferred cold hands to touch-muteness. In ten minutes his hands were stiff and his ability to feel, gone. Sam was late. John would have waited in the little lobby of the apartment building, but most people said they didn't like the extra work of getting him from there, and his presence seemed to bother people coming and going through the small area. He stood outside and rocked and weight-shifted to keep from shivering. To take up his mind he recited some of his poetry, his hands moving sympathetically in his pockets until there was Sam and a quick walk to the car.

He thawed out and dried a little as they rode. The pauses and stops were many because of the hour; rush hour it was called. In it, people did the opposite of rushing. John was used to such contradictions. It was half an hour before they had covered the necessary distance. The problems of driving automobiles and the realities of traffic were beyond his perceptions and so seemed artificial to him, unreal. He kept still, dreading the second wait in the cold and rain, the wait for Eleanor's companion.

They stopped there. Sam helped him out. "Can't stay. Double parked. Luke is here already. Bar right there on corner. Go in. Have a couple of beers and keep warm. We gave this plenty of time, for once. You're early. Don't come out until seven." The words were very hard to read in the wet. Sam took him to Luke, showed them where the bar entrance was, and then was gone.

It was warm inside the bar, a beery, smoky smell; noise — John could feel the noise to be music, a changing sizzle in the floor like hot fat with egg in it, or a heavy rain with beats. At the lower end, like a growl deep in the throat and at the very highest, like a needle in the eye, was a sort of movement of the tone and this he knew to be Hearing. It was strange and wonderful to have these feelings of vibration in a dry, warm place and over all the body, not just the touch of a finger against the side of the frying pan. Unfortunately, the smoke thickened the air and made direction difficult, but together Luke and John caned carefully, circuiting until they hit the bulk of the bar and found stools. They folded their canes and put them away.

Luke took out his Deaf-blind card and asked John what he wanted. It was too cold for beer. Thanks to Sam, John knew how to drink, and he spelled into Luke's hand, "a shot of bourbon and a cup of coffee. We'll still have to wait outside." His hand was stiff with cold and so was Luke's. Luke must be writing. Sitting very close, John could just feel the cloth of his coat as his arm moved.

Slowly, John got warmer. He took off his coat and put it over one knee, keeping the other in contact with Luke who had moved his stool closer to him. "Did you write?"

"Yes."

John took out his money clip and got a pre-folded five out. Whatever came back, if it was paper, would be ones and he could fold those properly in his clip. But for the smoke-thick air he was feeling pleased with himself and refreshed. They had another half hour to wait and they wouldn't have to do it in the bone-biting cold, unable to communicate while daggers of rain sliced at their faces. The drinks. Luke alerted John and he felt for his drink over the edge of the bar, wood-finished and smooth as warm glass. He and Sam had gone into some research on the subject of what to do with a shot. In one gulp or sipped? Or should the drinker pour it into the coffee? John didn't want to be staggering or disoriented at Eleanor's, especially since the place was unfamiliar to him. One was all he should have. He raised the shot carefully, set it against his lip, took it all at once. It was like sucking the end of a live electric wire. The warm fingers began in him, throat and head. He breathed, coughed once, and reached for the coffee. Luke, by this time, had also taken off his coat. They drank. Luke said he had coffee, too. He thought it was good, maybe they would have one more of each before they left. A kind of loose-fingered fun was in them now. He and Luke began to talk, sitting very close so they could get each other's laughter. They bantered. It was Rahner's word, talk for the fun of talking. John wanted to tell Luke the joke about the midget and the housepainter that Sam had told him. He began it but because of the drink, or an incomplete understanding of the beginning, it got a little loosened in his mind and came away with pieces left behind.

"Wait, I'm telling it wrong." He wasn't drunk at all, just letting himself be easy, relaxing the stern concentration of every waking moment, position, location, direction . . .

He was suddenly, violently grabbed from behind. He struggled for balance. Something. What? The fall took all his attention, that he not fall on his hands — there was no time for a question. Vibrations close to his head, a slamming blow to his back. He was tangled in something. Another blow to his head, explosion of pain in his head and face. Nothing more.

Awake. Where? Smells not his own place, pain. His head, and the whole box of it alive with tinnitus. Taste of what? He stank with a rank sweat and he was ice cold. He tried to reach out with his hands. Something was keeping them. Terror broke like the wind of doors slamming against his face. The doors beat inside him, opened, then closed like car doors slamming on his hands. He cried out to whom? To what? Hands came restraining him, tying what had restrained him still tighter. He was hand mute. He cried out again. He cried out: "What happened?" vibrating as loud as he could. Warm, cold, naked somewhere, stretched long, probed by fingers. Hands tied, feet tied. "What is this?" No answer. Sweat burned his eyes. He cried. Tears and snot ran away onto the place where he lay. Calling for help. No help. No location. No direction or position. Yes, he knew position. Flat and held was position, and therefore he thought, he was not insane. Only that. Not insane. Naked and being held. "I am not insane," he said, hoping to turn *them* sane, to make them respond to him if anyone was there to respond. Nothing. Loosened. Sat up. Something put on him. He gave up and stopped fighting and let them do to him and felt himself begin to die. A needle was put into his vein, injecting him with despair. He tried to talk to them. Nothing responded. He went cold into a sleep.

In a reeking sweat he woke again and tried to keep the invisible forces calm by asking for water in an unvibrated voice. Nothing. He tried to get up but was tied down. He lay beached and beaten. Then a long time later a hand, one hand, was released and it was she. It was Leda. He wished, dry-mouthed, filthy, and stinking as he was, that he could die of shame, die and be no longer conscious of anything at all. The hand was talking to him slowly, gently, even though in her flickering, cat-heartbeat, nervy way, her ineffably familiar and dear way. "You got beat up. Hospital. You are all right. Couldn't communicate. No one. You were screaming, fighting. Got them scared."

"Why? Why?"

"You are yelling again. They will put you out again if you yell."

"Why did this happen?" he said as quietly as he could.

"Some of the story. Not all."

"Please, some water."

"Yes. I tell them you are quiet. They will take the restraints off and the catheter out of you." She was formally interpreting. Someone else or other people were there.

"Yes," he said, quietly. "I am quiet. I am quiet." The tube was pulled from his penis. He closed his lips against the pain of it. He lay utterly still. The cloth around his other wrist was removed. He lay passive as a corpse, afraid to provoke them. When it was done Leda sat him up, "Where are they?"

"It's all right; I can talk. They can't see what I spell to you. Why don't you spell slowly to me, too. That way we are private." He relaxed.

"You and Luke were in a bar. It was a very macho bar."

"What is macho?"

"Tough guy."

"We didn't fight."

"I know. The men who came in didn't see your canes or Signs. Saw your backs, close, holding hands, bodies touching. Thought you were lovers."

"What?" He wanted to be sure, perfectly to understand what it was. She spelled HOMO-SEXUAL very slowly. Her flutter, her dear, familiar beloved flutter fell on his hands as a bird would spell, Signing with its feet. A bird, or any animal, even a little mouse or the lightest baby of any animal leaves its mark, the mark of its feet upon snow, so light is snow and so delicate: told to him by Swede. He sat up in the buttonless dress and thought of being covered over, monogrammed by mice and birds but buried in his awful shame.

Water again. She was giving him a pleated paper cup, school cup, delicate. He took it and drank. The water was tooth-crack cold. She hit his hand with the cup and he nodded, realizing even in his wretchedness that she was picking up Deaf-blind habits. The cup again. This time he held it to warm a moment. A warm washcloth. He used it, passing over an aching bump on the side of his head. "How long?" he asked.

"It's Sunday, Sunday afternoon."

"I'm not homosexual."

"I know."

"Where is Luke? Is he all right?"

She nodded, fist going up and down inside his hand, "So you remember."

"Just now, when I used the cloth. We were just talking."

"I know," and to his great surprise, she sat down beside him and took him in her arms, spelling. "They've gone now. We're alone." Then she lay him down and lay down beside him, trembling all over with sobbing.

The dress he wore let him feel her body move in the sobs, warm mouth-breath each time she let it out against his chest.

"Don't," he said to her. "If they find you

crying they will tie you up and put tubes and needles in you." It only made her cry more. They drowsed after that. He moved away from the death he had begun.

When he woke up again she had his clothes, the nice suit he had put on countless years ago to go to Eleanor's party, and after he was dressed she told him the suit would have to go to the cleaners and the shirt, too, because of the blood. She told him how Luke's brother had been called and had come and taken Luke home. John's card had had only the workshop number and his mother's home in Aureole. "When Luke told his brother about you, he called around. He didn't get me until this morning."

"Is he all right?"

"Yes, they left. The hospital people saw your head bump and thought you had a bad concussion — that you were fighting because of that."

John wondered if Luke had struggled, had been tied up and hurt. "And they call ours a silent world," he said. She didn't answer.

They were standing, the Deaf-blind way, face to face, at comfortable half-arm's length, so that she could spell easily into his hand.

"I am not homosexual," he said, "they are fags."

"Bad word."

"School word, *fag*. It's where I learned. Degenerate. Rahner told us, diseased, insane. They thought I was *that*."

"No . . . wait. . . ." She was confused, stuttering with impatience. "We have to sort all this out — important. But not now. None of it is like that. What you learned in school was a mistake, a stupid mistake — " and her hands stopped and hung in front of her and then said, "They gave you shit. They gave you stupid ideas." He saw that somehow he had offended her. He turned away. She pulled him back. "Not your fault."

"I want to go home. Please — "

"We have to wait for the social worker."

The social worker was a good Signer — Signed English. "Sorry I didn't get here earlier. I was away Friday and Saturday." He had wanted to know what had happened, but if he demonstrated any stupidity or wrongness they might keep him here. So much always depended on what other people thought. He stood quietly, waiting. "Do you have any questions?"

"No," he said.

There was a pause, then the social worker said, "Your friend asked about payment. Do you have Medicaid?"

"I have OASDI." There was another pause. He reached out, wondering if they had gone.

The social worker was talking with Leda, per-haps about him. They did not make a move to interpret. "Is there an interpreter?" John asked.

The social worker said, "I'm interpreting."

"But you are not interpreting this."

"If you want someone else you'll have to pay for the service."

And wait, too, he thought. They were talk-ing again. He waited, now wanting no more than to be home, to take the rags of his week-end shirt and stuff them in his mouth as he lay on his own bed, gagged and vibrating into his own pillow until the anguish died down. "Let me go home," he said. "Call a cab and let me go."

"Wait." The worker had turned back to him. "The hospital is sorry. The mistake we made was unintentional. No one knew you were Deaf *and* blind, and when you came in you were fighting and struggling and you had to be held down and given medication to calm you so you could be examined."

He knew she wouldn't let him go until she had done all this. The school people were the same and so was Bisoglio. They all had to tell their side of it and get him to think his side of it wasn't right. He stood still and stupid. He wanted desperately to talk to Luke, to learn if Luke had been hurt. He hoped not. He hoped that Leda and the social worker were right and it had all been a mistake. The social worker was not talking to him again. Tinnitus was still rushing in his ears. "Let me go home, now," he said. "Send me a letter about all this and Carol will interpret it for me, or Sam."

The social worker said, "Someone else has come. It is a man from administration services, Mr. Thompson. I will interpret for him."

She launched into the explanation. They were sorry, very sorry that he had been inconvenienced in his treatment, but it had not been cruel because he had struggled and they had had to restrain him. There was a bump on his head and people with head injuries often have to be restrained because they are unaware of their surroundings and might hurt themselves. In all, there was no sense thinking about lawsuits and court judgments, dreams of big money from the hospital. The hospital could prove that its treatment had been based on sound principles and a high standard of care. He had not, after all, been hurt. Something more. Leda was holding his hand, the one that was not receiving. He felt a tug on it and began to move. Another hand stopped him. Paper to sign. Leda said to wait.

John said, "If I don't sign it they will make me stay," and signed it. She took him home in a cab.

Over the next week, he learned a little more. Eleanor's companion had arrived, right after John and Luke had been taken away, and had been told they were drunk and fighting. She went to the hospital and was told the same thing. On Monday Leda made calls to Luke's brother, Fred, and on Thursday he brought Luke down to see John during the lunch hour. The truth, according to Fred, was that the bartender was at the far end of the bar when the trouble had broken out. He had thought they were blind but could hear. The attackers had made many comments against gays before they attacked Luke and John. He thought they would hear the comments, too, and leave. The attackers were two very tough guys, who, of course, did not know that the friends were Deaf or blind, and did not know it was possible to be both and be out in the world. They thought they were gays who were choosing not to react to the suggestions and then threats. Everyone was very sorry.

One of Luke's teeth had been knocked loose and he had gone through the same experience at the hospital but not for so long. His card had given Fred's number and the hospital called Fred at three o'clock Saturday morning. Fred came and released Luke on Saturday at about noon. Luke had wanted to go and see John but they had told him John had been badly hurt and was not able to have visitors. Luke had begged his brother to take him back on Sunday, but by then Leda had called them, and Fred, disgusted with the whole thing, had told Luke to forget it. He had dropped Luke here on his way to an appointment and would pick him up at about three, on his way back. "I had to see you. I had to see you were OK. I get angry when I think . . . "

"So it's better not to think and not to get angry. If we get angry they'll lock us up somewhere and there won't be weekends of fun like we just had."

"Did they put something up your — "

"Yes. Stops all that asking for the pot, doesn't it?"

"Homosexual."

"Yes. They must walk around in armor like knights, fags."

"No, not fags. Another thing. Leda told me fags are a different thing."

They sat companionably, shoulders touching. John shared his sandwich with Luke and they ate and then John went back to work.

EIGHT

Two weeks went by. The streets began to heat. Rain fell warm, and sometimes he breathed fine rain like second air. Fourbuds left fur in his hands. He stopped wearing his sweaters except at night. He asked Sam to take him running now that he had enough money to afford more of Sam's time. Leda was doing a commercial, she said, and the money paid for her to go to acting class. John saw that she had been ashamed of him. He did not think of the anguish he had undergone but again and again of her finding him. He imagined himself in her estimation, lying stinking, weeping, tied to the bed. He knew he did not understand women at all, but he understood how she could be disgusted with his humiliation. Sam himself, hearing and seeing, declared he could make no sense of women either, but John knew that his confusion was more than Sam's. Luke, whom he saw at church, said that Leda did not see him

150

because she was too busy being Sighted and Hearing. It was better with one of their own, nice Deaf-blind women who would understand how things were. "Those others — they say we can't see how pretty they are. They resent that. And we're not rich and they resent that, too." Since Luke's afternoon at the workshop, he and John had not mentioned their experience in the bar or the hospital. John listened to Luke talk about Sighted women and believed him, and nearly vibrated with despair.

And no poetry. None. Perhaps he had written everything that was in him. It was more than his tiredness with cats and friendship, sunset and mother, God's love. Religious poetry was what Mr. Sherline wanted now, God's love, but not God's carelessness. They never talked about that in church, either. Luckily there was his work to go to, and his reading — it was Dickens, now, and a routine that set confusion away at the outer air of hand-reach, there as a shadow but no more — seen as Sam had said the mountains were, present but not lived in. But when John had no work to do, no excuse of activity or need, he was haunted by Leda. Then she was there and there and there — a smell, a thirst, a yearning, a feeling of shame. She had seen him dizzy and begging and weeping like a baby.

And dreams: He and Sam. The beach. He had been to the beach when he had gone to the Deaf school far away. At the beach there is no shadow anywhere. It is singular in that. The thump vibration of the ocean was missing in the dream but there was wet sand. He had, in that dream, a sense of terrible loss and anguish, not for reason, wild as new grief. Nothing more in that dream.

He had dreams, above all, about fire, the old, quintessential horror, when no senses work and no call is heard, when location-direction is lost in the new environment of smoke. He had dreams about the hospital, but as he had been, waking up, no guidance by sun-warm or shadow or memory. That dream was a sweat-waking fear-strangle. His belly was so hard with fear he lay and winced with the pain of it. He had a dream of someone, a stranger, spelling competently into his hand, one time only: "You are going to end up in an institution for the Deaf-blind insane." No more than that and waking full of bitterness and confusion.

He could not understand his grief and sense of loss or the sudden emptiness in his mind. Sam said, "Perk up. Saturday we go running. Milo is taking you to the picnic. You and I have to plan our trip to Aureole. See your family. Word's out that Alma and Luke are serious, and I've found out about some new people downtown who have Telebraille. They play checkers and socialize on it. If you got one, you could have telephone conversations transcribed into Braille." Why did John not spin his hands with joy at this news? Sam was trying to encourage him. The average Deaf-blind person couldn't afford the machine, not to mention the phone bills for this electronic miracle. "Why don't you put off the trip until fall, or even next year, and get yourself a Tele-braille and widen your social life?" The thought, which would have been exhilarating a month ago, left John dubious and tired.

And then she came back, smell before touch, a shadow at his neck, her air, her hand. "What?" He made a Sign she knew, a wagged finger.

"Good news," she said, as though she hadn't ever been gone. "I have a theater job." He nodded in no particular direction. "It means I'll be busy for three weekends. After that we take a weekend — go down to prison. See Martin. They have visiting hours Saturday and Sunday. I called there. Talked to assistant warden. He says to write to Martin, see if he wants us. Otherwise waste of time. *He* has the choice."

Her words astounded him. "I thought you forgot — "

"No; I told you we would do it."

"I thought you were . . . that you had . . . since I was . . . " He stopped, wretched and wordless.

She said, "I didn't understand and I don't understand yet. I keep forgetting that being Deaf and blind means that you can't initiate . . . that you can't call me up when you get confused and worried. I should have told Sam to tell you — "

"No — I want our talk to be for us alone. I could have written you a letter but . . . I didn't know where to begin." Ways she had seen him, humiliation of being bound like a madman, sweats and stenches and the tears like a kid — either she had forgotten or it did not matter to her. It was a danger or a mystery. Going into it was too frightening. He shivered away from trying to feel into it. She was greeting him as though she had never seen him begging for water.

She told him about being in the play, which meant she only had time to drive the van in the mornings and afternoons.

"It's all right," John said. "I will write to Martin."

"I have to go now — they're waiting rehearsal for me." She gave him a quick hug and she was away.

He tried to be as dry-minded, as work-

154

world as school had trained him to be, fitting rules together as though they were parts on a table in the assembly room. He knew he wanted to touch and be with Leda, to have her hand in his, to learn whatever part of her life, her mind, her body, her day, and her night she would show to him. He knew this was impossible and also unwise. Corson had said, "Stay away from normal women; they only pity you." Corson said many things that gave pain, but other guide-interpreters had said similar things in smoother edges. John sighed. It was difficult to keep a clear mind with all this, yet when he sat down to eat his lunch he realized that his bad mood was gone. He felt interested and hopeful again.

On Friday Mr. Sherline came, even though John had told Sam to call him and tell him there were no poems. It was about the two he had written. Mr. Sherline had come to get John's signature on a contract for a poster and a plaque — which he had talked about when he had first read "God's Braille." Sam was translating in the stiff, automatic way he used when he was being professional, word for word, which was sometimes ridiculous. Their sentences never ended, and they asked questions they answered themselves and used strange expressions that meant nothing, or not what they seemed. When it was over John said, "You translated, not interpreted. What was it about?"

"It looks like you're going to be famous in your way. There's money in this. I would get a lawyer if I were you, or an agent." The thought made John nervous. His hand came up and hit Sam's hand away involuntarily. "Wait — Sherline's probably OK — he's paying you a percentage . . . part of what he will make from all that stuff, but you should have someone make sure that it's enough and that he gives the right accounting of everything he does. They must be some poems."

John said he would think about what Sam had said. He wished Mr. Sherline had paid him a big amount for "God's Braille" and "Another Way" and not parts of parts. It worried him. "Can we talk to Mr. Bisoglio?"

"I guess so. Listen. This is not bad news. It's going to mean a Telebraille and your visit home and more interpreters and a party for your friends if you want one. I'm only saying you should get someone to help on the business end. Who's your caseworker?"

"It was Mr. Bonifay but he's gone — it's a woman — written down at home."

"Are you reporting your income from your poetry?"

He had not been. He did not answer.

"Do you want me to call for an appointment? Your worker should know about this."

In the evening John finished his dishes and settled himself to read, but the events of the day were so disturbing that he couldn't follow his fingers with his mind. He liked his poetry. He liked thinking about it and writing it. He had been very happy in a new way when Swede had taken his hand and said those words into it: "It's wonderful and beautiful. You are truly a poet." He knew there was a difference between "God's Braille" and his other poems. Something was moving in him, changing. He had been frightened of what Leda said about writing the words of his own experiences, but she had spoken the idea and now it reached him whenever he thought about his poetry. She wanted a poem about Fourbuds, about *his* cat, not Midnight, the poetic cat of his cards. John got up and walked the room for a while. If it was to be a poem of his own experience, the dictionary and rhyme book could not help him, yet he was still a prisoner of words. He still had to translate skin-feeling into a word, smell and touch into how it was, what it was like.

What it was like . . . He had done this before, "like the sea," "like the sky." He knew nothing about the sky; he had no way of knowing except being told, but he had read about the sky so often, heard about it so much; Sighted people were so taken with it. . . . An idea came, unattached to any other, unrhymed:

> *Fourbuds, unfolded,*
> *Fourbuds is swimming my leg.*

He went on, smiling. "Southsleeping, she is hot-side, cool-side, and she swims me cool and left." He went on, trying to remember his experience rather than an interpreter's words.

Ah, he thought, "like spiders." When it was done it wasn't like a poem at all, but it was like Fourbuds, his real cat. Working on it took him all evening and all the next morning and evening. He had tried to think away everything he had been told about cats, their eyes, their sounds, their looks. It was difficult to start over, from nothing, to tell only what he himself knew.

> *Sometimes she plays cool-nose-hot-teeth.*
> *Her teeth game says consent is not*
>   *surrender.*
> *The teeth are dots of pain but she is*
>   *playing.*
> *The pain is no pain more than her biting*
>   *decides.*

It took a lot of thinking to come to the idea

about Fourbuds's teeth. He thought of what Arthur had said to him once about cats; including that idea would not be fitting in a poem, but since this poem was not a real poem anyway, he thought he might include what he and Arthur had talked about so long before.

> *Arthur says cats do not love.*
> *What is the game with teeth, almost*
> *   hurting?*
> *Consent but not surrender is a love I could*
> *   carry*
> *Like a banner on my shoulder.*

It was true that he had learned an important word, *consent*, from Arthur, a tutor-interpreter he had had briefly. Long ago Arthur had gotten married and told him the vows and explained the words in them. This work pleased John even though it was not a poem and had no rhymes. It might be what Leda was trying to tell him. In some deep way it was what he wanted. He thought he had had such good results from "God's Braille" that he would show this one to Mr. Sherline, even though Mr. Sherline had said he didn't want another cat poem.

Leda came early to where he was working. "Your fame is all over this place. According to

Sam, your poem is going to be on every flat surface in the country."

"Not every."

There was a pause and then she said, "I'm sorry; I was funning, and it came out patronizing."

"But understand why it can't be on every flat surface," he said. "All those dots on a mirror would make people think they had chicken pox."

She let him feel her laughing and then said, "How can you know about that, what people see in mirrors?"

"I don't really; I had it explained to me. It was a joke the Deaf school kids told about the Blind school kids. I have something for you. It's downstairs, in my coat."

"OK. I'll walk with you."

At the top of the stairs he asked her about her play. He wanted to keep her with him as long as he could.

"It's not good, but I am."

"That's lucky."

"Not really. Audiences and critics will lose me in the bad reviews." He grinned. She was always giving him things to learn and think about.

They began the stairs. She tapped him a quick, glancing blow on the shoulder. He continued down and turned when he got to the bottom and hit her back, lightly at the level of his breastbone, but his blow was high and landed on the side of her neck. She punched his arm. He bent a little and got a good slap on her behind. Then she was in close and they were softly pummeling each other. He felt the stairs door-draft. Someone had come. They both stopped. He was heart-laughing and breathless. Another wind went by as the stairs door closed. Someone had passed. "You were yelling," she said.

"Was not."

"Was too."

"Was not."

And she hit him again with her left fist as she spelled every letter with her right. "This time shut up or someone will get wrong idea."

"What?"

"What we've been doing. Headlines: WORK-SHOP EMPLOYEE BEATS UP DEAF-BLIND CLIENT IN STAIRWELL.

"Did not beat me up."

"Did too."

"Did not."

"OK: DEAF-BLIND MANIAC RAVISHES BEAU-TIFUL ACTRESS IN STAIRWELL.

"How do they start?"

"Rapists?"

"Lovers."

"Two different things — they are two different things."

"Show me."

He was holding her other hand as they spelled to each other. He had begun punching her very lightly with the other hand on her left arm and shoulder. Soon they were grappling. He was spelling nonsense at her open hand and then he grabbed her and held her and began to tremble with her so that they were in danger of falling. He tried to kiss her but missed her mouth because her head was turned and down. She raised it, turned, and they did kiss.

It was the second time they had kissed. For a moment, John remembered the stuff in school, the grapple and grope. This had none of the school feeling, done-to. He had been done-to by the gang from the Deaf school, a boy's dirty sock stuffed in his mouth to keep him from crying out. Some of the same stirring was in this but without the anger or the shame. Low in his body, his low belly and all those parts that urge, the urges were felt stronger now than he had ever felt them except in dreams. This time was different. It was the same urge but another experience of it. John did not want this to be over as he had the other times.

She said, "Not the place; not the time,"

softly into his hand. She had taken his arm from around her. His whole body ached for her and he hated being pulled away. He resisted it briefly but he knew, too, what she would do. She read his mind and said, "We seem to want to be together in all the wrong places."

He said, "Why don't you go with Sighted-Hearing men, men who could take you out the way Sighted-Hearing do?"

She said very lightly, "Don't ask that question. Who knows why people choose the people they do?"

"But — "

"It's time to go."

"We were coming down so I could give you my poem."

"Let's go, then."

They were on the ground floor. He found the door and pushed it open and went competently to the coat rack for the daypack he always carried and used as pockets for his necessary things. He had been carrying the poem in the pack in hopes that he would encounter her. There it was. He had done well to put it in an envelope. He felt about for her and then she was there. "Here. Do you have time to read it now?"

"Yes, but I want to give it time it should have — to be serious." He did not want to let her go. Gently, she took his hand away. "When you get the letter from Martin we will go to the prison. I will call and make plans with the warden. None of that phone-through-a-wall stuff."

John had wanted to visit Martin for years, had yearned to be with him, yet suddenly the best parts of the trip he planned would be the parts not concerned with Martin at all. The part of the trip he now wanted was the part going up and coming back, parts once insignificant and even boring. How strange life is, he said to himself, Signing it, and was suddenly embarrassed because someone might be around, and for some strange reason, people ridiculed the talk a person did to himself. At home he often talked to himself, Signing fully when he did not need his hands for work. Signs meant more to him than the words he could not hear, and could no longer remember the sounds of. He had been so taken with his thoughts that he had momentarily forgotten he was in public. People often came past in this place. "Shit," he Signed to the no one there, "look your look. I am riding away with Leda all day long."

NINE

The bus trip to the prison took four hours. Leda had told him to bring a book so he could read for some of the time. "I will want to rest. It's exhausting, talking a foreign language for so long." He had been disappointed and surprised, but he nodded to her. "We'll still have plenty of time."

They went through the difficult routine of travel. John caned well but without knowing where he was going, he needed Leda's guidance. He tried for independence as much as he could, going to the bathroom while she bought the tickets. He had given her five of the prefilled money envelopes, which he made up at the bank.

"This is too much — " He explained that he wanted to pay for their trip. "Yes, but it's still too much." Had he gone alone, he would have found out distance and cost and direction before.

The first part of the trip they both slept.

John was tired because he had been awake almost all night trying to figure out ways of acting if any problems came up. With Sam or Arthur or any of his other interpreter-guides, he had not been so shy or self-conscious about mistakes. With Leda, he wanted only to be gifted and gracious, moving easily in any direction. He had told her he could get to the downtown bus terminal and wait for her there. It had been she who insisted on coming to pick him up. He was, he knew, too taken with trying to impress her, which caused a strain despite the excitement he felt. Once on the bus he was glad to sink away for a while into sleep. When he woke up she was still sleeping. He lay back against the seat again and daydreamed.

They were traveling south by the map, the pull he called wind-going in his mind. He felt the direction as not due south. He liked the aesthetics of direction, the order of the round world, lines meeting on a grid at last, like the training grids at school. But in divergencies from true north or south, there was pleasant discord, like the tang of wine or the skin of a peach, not rough, not smooth, but both-and-neither. Excitement had given him belly-clutch, just mildly, and he had had too much coffee, so his skin felt cold.

She was waking up beside him, stretching,

turning. "Hello," he said and wrote it in letters on her cheek.

She smiled. "I didn't know how tired I was." She was spelling the words into his hand more easily, more Signs for complete ideas, skipping more vowels.

"You are getting very slick."

"Oh, yes."

John began to talk about his poetry, his hope for a union between his poems and the ones he had given Mr. Sherline.

"I liked 'God's Braille,' " she said, "but not as much as I could."

"Why not?" He was hurt.

"Because it's not blind enough and not Deaf enough."

It seemed, although he wasn't sure, that she wanted what she had spoken about before, his own experience, his own seven senses, and nothing he had heard about from the outside.

"Why should *I* write about France?" she had said. "I've never been there."

"Do you have my poem about Fourbuds?"

"Yes, I like it," she said, "it's in my purse." She moved, and by that he knew she was getting it. There was a long still time. "When did you write this?"

"A few days ago. I thought about what you said." He took the paper.

"I like this," she said. "I like it a lot. It's

real. It's what *you* feel, *you* know." (She threw the *you* into his hand like the old number-guess they used to do at school, violent and fresh. The sheets from his mother's washline had slapped him in the face like that when he hung them long ago.) Her fingers were slim, lithe, and cool, and as she gained skill in her finger-spelling that fresh snap was emerging.

"Is it true that cats get hot on the sun-side when they sleep?"

"Of course. Didn't you know?"

"I never felt one. I like this poem better than 'God's Braille.' 'God's Braille' tells things you have never experienced, and it's too . . . too grateful."

"Shouldn't we be grateful?"

"*We* should, but why should you?"

He was dumbfounded. She went on. "*You were beaten deaf.* You were made to perform tricks for Corson, that dangerous sadist. Three weeks ago you were . . . abused. How can you smile and thank God for *that?*"

He tried to frame the words. "When my dad . . . when people . . . " He did not have the words.

"How can you write a thing like 'God's Braille,' all flowers and mountains and sun-shine?"

"Don't Seeing and Hearing people have rape and cruelty? Don't they know about it?"

168

"Why are you denying it — it's that blindness of yours — forgive me — it's that . . . " Her fingers stuttered as she tried to find a word she could use.

He sat amazed in her attack. It was like something she had said to him before, a way she had acted at the church. Then she had decided she did not want to kiss and be close. He was mystified. He had no idea what she wished of him.

"Why don't you write a poem about what your father did?"

"No!" He must have spoken too loud, because she held him quickly and put her finger to his lips. "Too loud!"

"Too bad," he Signed in the air, the Deaf Sign, and then said, he thought quietly, "Too bad. You object to loud words and want me to put worse, worse ugliness into the world with poems about beatings."

"I want you to tell the truth."

"And 'God's Braille is the truth."

"I want *your* truth."

"My truth is that we are visiting my friend who helped me for two years, who made me laugh and taught me all kinds of things and who gave me mobility and confidence and competence. Two years. Even Corson was more good to us than bad, although he didn't mean to be. He made us strong. My father

169

was drunk and sad about me and beat me, but he never wanted to make me Deaf."

"Shit," she said violently into his hand and sat in sulk posture, belly-anger-guarding for the rest of the way to the city where the prison was.

The prison. They had to get on another bus, and because of its absolute sundown westerliness John thought that the town must have come first and the prison after. He asked many questions about the geography. When she kept saying she didn't know and, at last, "Why is it important?" he said, gently, because he loved her, "Because two of my senses are involved. I have seven, just like you."

"What are they?"

"Location, direction, smell, touch, taste, duration, and rhythm."

Where they went in was at the end of a walk from where they had alighted. Gravel, fairly large pieces, and a hot-dry stone-dust smell coming up at him. There were others traveling with them. He could feel them around him. He moved comfortably among them, a slow walk, caning in a narrow arc and close in, feeling neighbored. Leda was beside him. She was learning not to be so nervous, to walk behind his cane so that it would not trip her. She was trying to recover her good feeling but was having a hard time doing it. Her movements were a little rigid and jerky.

The search. Luckily this was almost summer so they were wearing light clothes. He was patted up and down. Pockets emptied. Dogs came and smelled them. Then they were led into another building. Leda told him they had come through a kind of wire corridor. Other people: smells, then presence through his feet, but he couldn't tell how many. She interpreted — rules. They waited. Did he want to use the restroom? No. He catalogued the air of the place, its direction and smell, to be remembered. Then up stairs. East. They waited. Then corridor — loom both sides. Wind-coming-ward through a door. They waited. Airblow, and suddenly Martin, smell before touch, those cigars, awful-Martin-wonderful and John was howling with eagerness, holding Martin and pounding both his arms at once and Martin's stubby fingers spelling that wonderful Martin-self, "What kept you?"

"Your stink is wonderful!"

"The word is *fragrance.*"

"The word is *stink.* Stench. I looked it up special."

"Who's the chick?"

"Leda."

"The hair on her! Good bod, too. Solid.

You been in it yet?"

"No."

"Want to?"

"Yes."

They stood the Deaf way, talking. It was more comfortable for enthusiastic Signing, hands out. John asked about the life in prison. Martin said it was better than he had expected and also worse. It was like Deaf-blind school. "Nibbled to death by hamsters." He spoke of hours, time clocks, searches, passes, checking in and out, no privacy, no ideas, no decisions. "You were in Deaf-blind school. It's like that."

"And no one has hurt you — guards, others?"

"That stuff is mostly among the younger cons. I have nothing anybody wants."

John found himself crying again. Martin hit him in the chest. "Ask your damn question. Don't keep it in."

"I heard about what they did to you — because you were with us, with Herb and me, working at the school."

"The judge said it was the most craven act he had ever heard of, using a school for the handicapped as a cover for dope dealing. You know the word *craven?*"

"No."

"It means cowardly."

"Did you take us all over town *to* make

dope deals, or did you take us all over town *and* make dope deals?"

"The first two times, *to*; the rest, *and*. There were drugs at the school before I got there. I mostly dealt away from the school and I didn't feel any guilt about that. You and Herb *were* a perfect cover. When people see you regularly, you get in a category and they stop noticing you. I dealt all over town. People knew my route and came to me. Later I had three different routes and I made buys at prearranged places." John felt Leda beside him. "She's going for coffee," Martin said. "We have two hours if we want."

"You're out of practice; your spelling and Signs are rusty."

"Spelling is rusty; Sign is improving. There are two Deaf here."

"Really?"

"One of them is from dear old D and B."

"Do I know him?"

"Before your time."

They came close to the subject of imprisonment again and John perceived the hesitation he had felt before, a knowledge that Martin did not want to talk about it. He had come all this way — "Please . . . "

"OK. Ask another one."

"What made you change from *to* make, to *and* make?"

Martin's answer sounded relieved. "You did, you and Herb. You were so — hyped, wired, so *alive*. I couldn't talk fast enough, walk far enough, show you quick enough. I had had lots of experiences in my life and none of them got me ready for you coconuts."

Coconuts. It was a half-spelled, half-Signed word, one they had made up after some joke or song of Martin's. The memory bit into John. "You coconuts are more nut than any-one can swallow," Martin used to say. Once an instructor had stopped John on the way out of school and, not understanding he was a special student, had scolded him for being up after curfew. When John protested, the instructor had spelled with insolent rapidity, "And who do you think you are?" and John had answered, "I'm one of the coconuts," and he had been proud and happy.

"How long in here?" he said to Martin now.

"Five years more."

"And that's because of us, Herb and me, because we're Deaf-blind."

"Wait — "

"We can go to them, to the police, and we can go to the judge, too, and tell him that we weren't kids but grown-ups and that it wasn't a trick you had been using to hide in. We can't hide anything . . . Sighted-Hearing know what people think."

"It wouldn't help," Martin said, "save your strength."

"But it's not fair — it's not what happened. We'll — "

"Hey!" and Martin gave a downward slap, the familiar, impatient, joking, memory-biting Sign that was Martin's Sign more than his name-sign. The fat fingers hit down and paused an instant in the palm in a way that said "get this." "It's no good. It would wear you out and it wouldn't help me. They did what they did. I was selling dope and buying dope and I was in the dope business. It's an illegal business. Don't get confused. I got caught. I'm in the slammer."

"But — "

"Hey, coconut; do coconuts have ears?"

Old joke. It made John weep. He stood as he was and rested his face in his hands and let the tears down past his eyes and nose and the push-breath-pull-breath of full weeping. In a minute Martin's hands were on him. "They think I'm beating you to death. Stop yelling."

"What?"

"The guards are here. They see us through a mirror, but the ones who can't see have come because you are yelling."

"I want to yell."

"Then go to the can and beat your head against the wall."

175

This was a memory, too, and it stung John and made the tears stop in a kind of anger. It had been his way of rage when he was a boy, getting in some small space — closet or cubicle — and flailing away at close walls, enemies within reach. When Martin came he had laughed at it once or twice, calling it a show and saying he would sell tickets and make lots of money getting people to come and watch. John had stopped doing it. "It hurts," he said, "all this."

"I know."

"Where do you put it, you wonderful Hearies, the pain?"

"In our hats."

John breathed out and in hard several times to clear his nose and throat. Smell was gone. He felt the uncomfortable swelling after tears and sighed.

"They call it a silent world, deafness," Martin said. "I should only be so lucky," and he hit John a light blow on the arm and then said, "So tell me about your life now."

John used the comfortable talk he had adapted with Martin, a combination of talking, spelling, and Signing. He told Martin about "God's Braille" and about his fear of its complications, about Leda saying that his poetry was too Hearing and Seeing and so false in some way, about his job becoming

176

suddenly silly and boring to him, about Leda and the pull of his yearning for her. "I want — "

"What?"

And wretchedly, "I don't know." He told Martin of her accomplishments, acting and the plays and commercials and rehearsing she did, of her driving the van, so many talents and so busy that she went by like wind, like the winds of doors opening and closing, there and gone.

Martin accepted John's words, giving taps of assent or encouragement. The thick fingers had lost some of the quickness, but John felt so good with them and with the smell of Martin and with his big shadow bulking reassuringly real in front of him that he did not notice the loss of fluency until later.

After a while the door opened. John felt its draft. Who was it? Was Leda back, or was it the jailers ready to take Martin away? "Who?"

"How did you know?"

"Air-puff, vibration."

"I forget what hot stuff you are, you and Herb."

"But who is it?"

"It's Tucker, a friend of mine, a guard."

John began to weep again. "I don't want them to beat you. All the things they say — "

"That's shit, John. Prison is no worse than

any other place where other people have control over your life."

"Is it time?"

"Yes, it's time."

"Martin, why did you sell bad dope?"

"The dope I sold was *good*. I sold it for money. I made a lot of money. I had bimbos and the bimbos wanted things, jewelry and cars and making love in fancy hotels, which we did."

"I didn't know that. You didn't tell me. I thought people told their friends things."

"I liked you guys, both of you. If there's anything else that bothers you, why sweat it?"

Martin had had to explain "why sweat it" years ago. No one had used it to John since, so it remained Martin's absolutely and, with his hands, a kind of theme: Martin, my friend. John wanted to tear down the thousand passages through which he had come today, to feel solid things breaking apart all around him as he caused the breaking, to be at the center of a vibration the size of every building, total and complete. He had known these rages before. Sometimes he had lived them, flinging himself floors-walls-furniture until someone caught him up or until he was too exhausted to move. More recently he had learned control; to wait the rage away. Nothing lasts forever. Quote someone. He had forgotten who.

So he stood completely still for a long time. Leda came. Martin said goodbye. John could not move. Someone, not Leda, tried to take his arm to turn him into the goodbye-and-going posture, but his lower body would not turn. Leda took his hand, and he followed, unconscious of location or direction. At the bus he stood unmoving a long time, the unvibrated thunder ringing in his head.

TEN

"You scared the shit out of me!"

"I don't smell any."

"Don't get funny. What were you doing?"

"You are funny. First you want me to get angry and hate my father, life, everything. Then when I *am* angry you don't want that. School words, work words: don't be angry. Everyone wants me to come away and not be angry. You want me angry, but when I am, you are scared. Explain."

"I can't."

They were on the bus back. Martin had said five more years. John Signed half to himself, "five more years." Then to her, "Good they let me see him this time."

"Much as I'd like to take the credit, they allow it. It was just the jail where they wouldn't. What was wrong was all that yelling. There were other people there, visitors, and you blew up like a rocket."

"Are you angry?"

"We are arguing."

"I don't understand."

"I'm sorry. You scream and it upsets me. Your face has a frozen look and it seems to say: stay away. And your body — you made me afraid back there after I went through all that mess. I had to convince them to let you stay." They sat for a long while. Then she said, "Stop sulking."

"Five more years," John said. He was tired, drained, heavy with unspoken resentment.

Her hand showed the slight impatience of the argument. "What else did he say? I was there only part of the time and missed a lot." She, too, was exhausted; he felt it in every gesture of speech and in the muscles of her hands; even her breath scent had the slight acetic tang of it.

He told her. What he couldn't tell her was that it was not what Martin said but the fact of him, his touch, smell, shadow, body-memory, that was important. He tried to go back in his mind and remember the words exactly. He was a poet, concerned with words; why couldn't he remember? Finally he said, "Martin told me it would not help, me going to the judge to make his sentence less. He did what they said, dope-selling, and getting rich. He said he had bimbos who liked nice things. He called me a coconut."

"Are you a coconut?"

"Yes, it was a special name, once."

"Have you eaten coconut?"

"Yes; sweet; chewy; it means sweet."

"Nothing of the sort. I'll show you. It's round and hard on the outside and hairy and when you shake it, it sloshes inside. That's the coconut he meant; the unsweetened stuff — and hard-headed."

"You like teaching."

"I like the real world."

"My anger is part of that."

They were still, a little afraid to argue if they spoke. Time went by and suddenly there was in John the idea for a poem, a poem to Martin and Leda, a poem, some part defense, some part introduction, to what she called his world. He didn't have a Braille notetaker with him. He thought that when he got home he might go and work on it. They were still quiet, but the air had relaxed between them.

Leda said, "Are you sleepy? You can put these seats back a little and doze."

"No, I am thinking of a poem."

"About your afternoon in the prison?"

"Prison is not a good topic for a poem." He wondered how she could be so ignorant of what poetry was. She had said she read a lot. He loved her, she had changed his life, his hopes, his smallest act and wish, but he was confused by her. She seemed to keep wanting him to be different and to feel differently about everything than he did. Frustrating. That was her word. "You are frustrating," he said. "Being with you is like combing knotted hair."

To his complete amazement she clapped his hands in hers, laughing. "Don't you see — that's *your* image, *your* metaphor, yours — Deaf-blind."

"But it is not poetic — it could never be in a poem."

"Why not?"

Amazing. She was full of surprises.

They came home late, John stumbling with exhaustion and the dislocation of broken routine. So much joy and so much pain. In addition, it was tiring now to try to step back into usual life. He realized he was also disappointed in his expectations of Leda. Desire had come and gone a dozen times, all bundletied with anger, sorrow, and despair in the wrong-foot-caning-in-corners day. Around his ankles Fourbuds tied herself in sliding catcoils. He went, tripping on her, to get water and check her food. Leda was still there, resting on the couch-bed. When he came back from the kitchen he sat down beside her. She was there, curled up, asleep. He began to touch her, stroking the long hair, which was warm at the scalp, cool at the middle, roughened at the ends. It was evening-cool, and the warmth of her head pleased him. He moved his fingers into her hair, combing it gently with his hands.

Then she was awake. He did not know how he realized it — some movement, probably a change in breathing.

"I dreamed I was blind," she said.

"Funny, I dream I can see."

"We didn't put the lights on."

"Do you need them?"

"No."

He was stroking with one hand, waiting with the other for her talk.

"I suddenly understood why we don't get together, you and I, why we have had so much trouble making love although we both want it."

"Why?"

"Because these invitations, questions and answers, are all visual for Sighted people. We do it all with our eyes and eyebrows."

"Now no one has light."

"Yes, and it's better for this."

He had thought he was tired, but he found he was not tired now. He went to the window and opened it. A warm, humid breeze, city breathing out, came against his face. He went back to the couch-bed and sat down. She had gotten up from where she lay. He took his hand and put it on the warm spot she had left. She took his hand and showed him, bringing his hand up to her throat and down, that she had taken off the top of her clothes. She spelled into his hand, "Should I undress you?"

"Why?"

"Considered sexy."

"I will undress myself. Your way is too much like Sighted people doing things for blind people."

"You mean you feel passive?"

"Word?"

"An object, a thing, the person done-to, not the person doing."

"Yes!" He hit her hand a joy-bounce in affirmation, and while he unbuttoned his shirt with one hand the other rehearsed the word *passive*, learning it.

"Suppose," she said, spelling on his bare back, "you undress me." That was not passive at all. Her hooks and buttons and zippers were not hard to learn; she helped him, leaning her body away or toward as made the taking easier and then it was all right for her to do a button, a hook, a zipper for him.

They moved to each other, flesh to flesh. Lying close and in what he knew was darkness for her, he thought, She is blind and real.

She sees with her fingers, familiar. He read the warm and cool of her body. In none of the love poems that he knew was this most wonderful thing — cool breasts, warm thighs. Cool shoulders, warm belly, a soft down on her back above her division and wiry hair at the front where she opened. While he was exploring her, she was exploring him so that moving on her, his hands trembled. When they went into each other, he broke too soon. When he began to move away, she said on his arm, "Can you wait until I go?" He went back in. She was soon in a kind of convulsion. It was the kind of shuddering his school friend Bobby Romano had, so that he was frightened and collapsed inside her.

"What!"

"Are you sick?"

"I am . . . I was having an orgasm."

"Word?"

"I was doing what you did."

"But you were shaking all over."

"That's what happens to me."

It awed him. "I can do that to you?"

"You can if you stay long enough. There is something you can do now."

"What?"

She showed him.

Morning. Exciting to wake up beside her, to feel her movements and experience her

waking in the very narrow bed, the turn, the
slow arm. He had set his alarm without
remembering he had done it, so before morning they had been awakened and made love
again and he had been slower and had understood her shuddering, even though he
couldn't stop remembering Bobby Romano
who had also lain under him where they had
fallen together in the school-outside-play-
place, fluttering his hands, trembling all his
body along in what at first had seemed to John
like laughter.

She was up then, quickly and altogether
and spelled a quick *rr* for restroom before
being gone. He went in to put on the coffee.
Nothing had been done. Yesterday's dishes
were still in the sink. The coffee cup was not
ready; the pot not in its place. Where was it?
John had a feeling of dislocation that was
almost anger and one that in a small way
threatened the competence he prized. Fourbuds moved in her disapproval at the backs of
his legs. He bent down. She had water. He
sighed, vibrating slightly, a low buzz in his
throat that Hearing didn't find offensive and
that he could feel. He filled Fourbuds's food
dish. He found the coffeepot and, after a
search, the coffee. He felt a weakness in his
concentration. His mind was with her and not
where he was. It made his fingers slow and

clumsy so he put the coffee in the saucer, not the cup, and didn't find it until his fingers brushed the table and felt the grains there. He had to start over and the open upper-cupboard door kicked him in the head in the familiar place. Start again.

He had put on his robe, which he now did every morning since he had heard about the blind man in Detroit who was arrested because he liked to go naked and forgot to pull his window drapes; he washed his hands in the sink before starting. Something strange — something — She had crept up on him from the back and was blowing her breath down his back as he stood clearing the counter to begin again. There was her scent and the warmth of her face surrounding the cool of her blown breath. Down and down. He turned quickly and caught her. "Doing what?"

"Playing."

"We have to be serious now; it's time to go to work."

"Let me fix breakfast while you get showered and dressed."

He let her because it was easier than demanding his own way. She was quicker than he and they were late in their preparation. As he showered, he remembered that the Sunday cooking had not been done — no lunch made. Part of him was a little frightened, being set adrift from habit, which like location and direction, gave his life borders and a form. Part of him was as excited as he had been when he went toboggan-riding one day at school. He had loved the speed, the unbraked downhill rush, moving in a new way under a new set of laws. They had, with Corson, learned vital things: rhythm by duration, which is speed. Before Corson, speed was something John had had no way of perceiving other than as he had experienced it to himself. Corson had put their heads on railroad tracks and let them hear rhythm and feel duration. Leda had been horrified by what Corson had done, and only then had John learned to judge him as sadistic. Some of the "games" had been cruel, but by the time the games had been stopped and Corson gone, Herb and John were smart. They had learned enough world-wit to make them warm and triumphant inside.

"Are you still hungry?" she asked him after breakfast.

"Yes, you know that."

"How can I tell if you are happy?"

"I'll tell you."

"You show very little on your face, and when you're talking your voice has no expression. It's somehow — it bothers me sometimes."

"When I vibrate . . . "

"Oh, yes, then I know you are very angry or very happy."

He felt her stirring near him. "What's happening?"

"You nearly upset the milk."

"You should let me set the table. Then I know where it all is, but I knew anyway. *Nearly* has no meaning to a blind man. You do or you don't. The wall is there or it is not there."

"And *almost?*"

"Fiction."

"But in your reading — what do you imagine when you read those words?"

"A different world."

He left at the usual time and waited for Sam and the van. She had left earlier, taking a cab to where the van was. She was afraid of being late. It was dangerous, she said, to let people know they had slept together. Too personal. Mr. Bisoglio wouldn't like it either and it might cost her the job. John, too, was puzzled by his feelings. He had at first been gratified by Leda's secrecy, the private world they had together, but lately he had wanted to brag a little, to show her to people. His Deaf-blind friends had not responded to her as he had hoped. She seemed anxious about the Hearing; there was a careful quality, a hesitance about her talk of them. He thought about this as he stood waiting outside the building. Then he realized that she was nervous, and he tried to reason why. At school, gossip and rumor of all kinds went around the Deaf division and the Blind division. Sometimes the Deaf-blind students learned about the rumors, too. When John had been hurt by the boys, he had been afraid they would tell and that he would be changed from a boy into a something that everyone used. A fear about bad things. Could there be reason to fear people learning about good things? He might ask Sam or Swede about it later.

He didn't see her for three days, and during those three days his waiting senses made him dream her into being. Was that a rose-smell moving toward him, faintly, to become stronger as she approached? Was that her hand brushing the back of his neck? Was there a hum on the wood? A warmth left in the air near his face that was her face?

His concentration suffered. He became inattentive to his location and banged his shins and his elbows. He dropped things. He scalded himself on the arm at his oven. On Thursday she came to lunch and ate with him and he told her what was happening to him.

She said, "I wish I could call you on the

phone, just for a minute, to let you know I'm thinking about you. I've got a job demonstrating cosmetics for a new company downtown. Six weeks."

"But — " and his hand was over hers and his word left his mouth with nothing more.

She said, "I'll still be doing the van in the A.M. and we can have Saturday nights."

"Church next Sunday?"

"Maybe." Hearing's "maybe." "Maybe one more time. There's not much for me there."

"I have a poem for you. It's at home."

"Show it to me. I'll be over on Sunday and we can go out during the day. I can't come this Saturday night, but I'll be there for breakfast Sunday morning."

On Sunday he got up at five to cook and do his Sunday work. She came and her rose smell, too, and the smell of her hair and face and body, exciting-familiar. They embraced happily. Then he gave her breakfast and they ate and afterward he showed her his poem. It was a love poem he had made for her.

> My love is like the ocean
> It has a rhythm, tides.
> It pulls me warmly, eagerly.
> It abides.
> My love has given me wings
> To fly above that sea

And hover, waiting, hoping
For you to be.

He had typed it on his Sighted machine hoping he had made no mistakes. He gave it to her. She put her hand on his while she read it, spelling so that they were reading it together. He was moved by that sensitivity. She seemed to know by magic what was gracious in his world. She read it to the end.

"Do you like it?"

"I think it is nice," she said, "but it is not your poem. It is a Sighted person's poem."

He was hurt. "Where does it say I'm Sighted?"

"*Ocean* is a Sighted word. *Tides, sea.* The poem depends on your knowing what you can't know."

"But I've been to the ocean."

"*Your* experience." She hit the *your* hard. "Your ocean is not *ocean. Water,* maybe. *Sand,* maybe — "

"I'd have to invent a whole new language — "

"You could do it in English."

"I thought the poem would make you happy." He was ashamed, confused, a little angry, too. All his life, teachers and tutors and house parents at school had said, "This is the way Sighted do it. This is the way Hearing act!" The highest compliment anyone could have was to be told, if he was blind, "He acts like a Sighted," or if Deaf, "People don't even know he's deaf," and if Deaf-blind, "It's just as though he sees and hears." His own parents pitied and hated his Deaf-blindness. "Do you want me laughed at?" he said toward the place where she was. He had taken away his hand in surprise. For all he now knew she was gone. Then he felt her air, the slight rise in warmth at his face and the shadow of her, close. His face was already hot with shame; it was harder to read her presence.

"You don't understand yet, do you?" she said. "I want you to be *you*, to speak from your own experience."

"You also want me to be angry and not angry in your idea of it."

"I suppose that's true — I'm guilty of that, but it's only human, normal to be — "

Now he felt anger pulling him like ocean, experienced though not seen. "No more humans and no more normals! I have been human and normal all my life — not Sighted and not Hearing but be angry, be peaceful, everyone's human and everyone's normal. You want from me, just like the others, something you fill, like in a cup, which is me — "

He was vibrating, he knew. That meant he must be shouting. He stopped. The air was alive with his anger. His first real understanding of the word *room* when he was only blind had come from the quality of sound bouncing around him. He had long since forgotten what sound was like except for his tinnitus, but air-bounce was part of his sense of touch, vibration, a kind of internal touch he felt and knew was sound. Leda said that might even be what he called "shadow." He felt it go on, satisfyingly, and then perceived difference. "There's a window open."

"Yes. The neighbors think I'm raping you. How do you know, though; there's no draft."

"Air bounce is different; three sides not a fourth."

"Good god, man, that's what I've been telling you. No one but you, but one of you, knows any of that. Tell us. Take us to your world. You have to live in ours all day. At night in our dreams, take us through the door."

"Too hard; too tiring — "

"So you're not so wonderful; you're only lazy. Alma's less lazy than you."

They fell into each other's arms.

This time they did not talk. He perceived she didn't like talk, or rather that she liked, when she made love, to be Deaf-blind, to sample vibration, location, position, touch, smell, taste, rhythm, and duration in just the way he did. There is a place where the Deaf-blind and the Sighted-Hearing are wise in the same way. He had begun to learn what it pleased her to do and have done and she had told him that these things were special to her. Later, they spelled a little, small things, chat. She was learning to compress meaning into a few words of drowsy talk.

By noon they were walking to the park and Leda was telling him that "God's Braille" was important and that it was necessary to guard the money that was going to come. He would have to find a way of keeping it, of using it properly. Did his caseworker know about the money? John had never told his caseworker, though Sam had spoken of it also. The Rehabilitation people had gotten him his workshop job, but he felt his poetry was his own to sell or not to sell. He had no regular job in it. "God's Braille" seemed to be different, though, more complicated. Sam had said that, too.

"My acting class," Leda said, "next Sunday evening, a party, sort of. Maybe ten, twelve people at my place. Can you come?"

"Interpreter?"

"That would be best, really, if you can afford it."

"I'll try to get Sam."

On Monday he asked Sam if he would be free.

"I'd like to come," Sam said. There was a hesitation about his fingers. Was it tiredness or anger of some kind, a drawing back? "I have something to tell you."

"I know."

"Damn grapevine again?"

"No — your difference — body posture, something . . ."

"I have to leave this job," Sam said. "I'm going back to school."

The world lurched leftward, the way it did when a day went bad. "Why?"

"You know I've been in school part-time. Part-time the van. Part-time you and others, interpreting. There's not enough money — interpreting doesn't pay enough. No future in this. I like it and I like you but can't afford it. I want to say goodbye nicely so Sunday will be on me, OK?"

John nodded, feeling finger-numb.

"New man, though, Melvin. Religious. He'll like taking you to church on Sunday."

"Oh, no!"

"Wait — not heavy on the Thou Shalt Not. Also, not a 'come to Jesus' guy; at least I don't think so."

"Sometimes they use us . . ."

"I know. I think Melvin is OK."

"Would you — occasionally — extra money —"

"I don't know; depends what school is like. I may be able to — I don't know — I've been here two years."

"I know."

"See you Sunday."

The workshop. John started for his place, caning easily because he was familiar and only caned at all because people with wheelchairs or other people were sometimes in the hall, and now and then there would be a cleaning cart or a coffee cart to avoid. He was just starting up the stairs when he felt Mr. Bisoglio's hand. He turned. Mr. Bisoglio's clumsy spelling told him that his caseworker was in the office waiting for him.

The interview was short. Mrs. Farrell Signed impatiently and she was angry. She said he was a liar and had cheated and that he had been getting money for years, two years, and not telling the agency. Surely he knew that outside income must be reported. He told her that people knew about the money — Sam knew, Mr. Bisoglio knew, and he had told one of the workers last year.

"But you said the amount you were getting stayed the same."

"So — "

"So it was cheating. How much money have you made over the year from your part-time work?"

"It wasn't work, it was poetry, but I had about a thousand dollars."

"We'll have to fix that so the money comes off every month until your debt is paid. You know you are committing fraud, don't you?"

"I think I am not supposed to make more than two thousand more dollars or then I will be thrown off."

"Whoever told you that was wrong. Every extra dollar must be reported."

"So it doesn't matter what I make, and 'God's Braille' is no different?"

"If you earn over a certain percentage of your grant, you must have it deducted. That includes food stamps and medical care." The message seemed to be warning.

When Leda came on Sunday he told her what had happened. "Did you tell Sam?"

"Sam is leaving."

"The one man. You need an advocate."

"You — ?"

"I'm working the wrong hours. I don't know the law, either. You probably need a lawyer for 'God's Braille.' "

"That takes money."

"I know."

Then he thought of Mr. Bisoglio and Mr. Sherline. They knew what he needed to know. He decided he would make an appointment to talk to both of them when Mr. Sherline came again about the poetry. The decision gave him some peace.

Over the confusion about the welfare money — and Mrs. Farrell kept telling him not to call it welfare but SSI administered by welfare, a distinction he did not understand — lay the sorrow about Sam. The new man, Melvin, would bring his own reality. Would it be like Corson's or Rahner's, or any one of the dozen interpreters he had had over the years? It was so important, and no one else thought so, or understood.

ELEVEN

The party was to start at seven. At five Leda came for him and they went to her place. John enjoyed going to people's places although he rarely got to do it. A person's home-place is all his arrangements for living. John's apartment was one big oblong that opened to the wind north-south and from which the small squares, kitchen and bathroom, opened to morning sun and afternoon sun. His bed was athwart the sun arc because he liked it that way wherever he lived. Doors and windows for air were all on the morning sun side, and that meant, unless the curtains were pulled, he had morning warmth as he worked on that side, going up his body until late morning when the directional warmth stopped all at once.

Before the party began at her place, Leda took him wall-walking. In that way, he could become familiar with things before the presence of many people made that impossible.

The inside smelled of cooking meat and tomato sauce (not tomatoes), and of old plaster, painted wood, radiators, clay — he associated that part of the smell with school. This was square after square, some large, some small, and on an off-sunup-sundown axis by about fifteen degrees, a pleasant disarrangement, like the sweet-sour of fruit in the chicken dish they had eaten at the restaurant, like the rough-smooth of a cat's fur. "This is an old house," he said, "and has steam heat and old bathrooms and maybe a bathtub that's deep and long and has bird feet on the bottom and is off the floor. It has wallpaper on the walls and the ceilings are high. It has an upstairs that is convenient, big warm beds, and wood floors with booby-trap rugs to slide on. You have only the furniture you need, which makes it pleasant and restful for people."

It was a bit of a game to play; perceptions and deductions obvious enough. In the city's west side, the older houses are farmhouses from the days before the city spread out to meet them. Told to him by Sam. John's knowledge: these were off the due sunup-sundown axis because the city had been laid out on straight lines. John scarcely knew Denver, but he and Sam had been to a few people's houses and had walked in certain special neighborhoods. Sam was fixing his old car so they had visited two or three specialists once, and some junkyards. John had gotten a lot from such city walking, thanks to Sam and to Martin. He thought of Sam again, the awful, familiar pain of need and loss. Tonight he would be saying goodbye to Sam's generous fun, his bold, happy version of the world, the extra perceptions he gave, most of all — He tore Sam out of his mind, though the fingers clutched at the edge of it, holding on. Familiar pain. Here it comes again. He began to tell Leda about old houses. A house off the axis has probably come from an older, less-regimented time. The age of the house was further proved by the special radiator smell that he could catch even when the radiators weren't being used, a special, not unpleasant dust-rust-smell; and the high ceilings changed the vibrations of the air, which was cooler on his legs and feet; warm air rises. Old houses are draftier. Leda was amazed. They had gone forward-walling, coming in from the door, and after doing all the downstairs, following the right-hand wall all around to the place of beginning, she gave him a seat in the corner, presiding, she said, as they waited for the guests. She gave him a drink and said she didn't want his help with the buffet. So he sat, smiling, his "seeing" look — lips pulled up a little in what he had been told was a friendly expression. It had become habit with him when he was with Sighted to hold that face. Sometimes his jaw and cheek went stiff with holding.

People began to come to him. A woman, Merle, nervous, with a cool, damp, thin hand although she was large. She didn't want him to touch her face, although she said it was all right. Where was Sam? Leda interpreted her. Bennet waited patiently to John's touch and knew a little fingerspelling. His hand was light-boned and healthy. "Where did you learn fingerspelling?"

"Boy Scouts years ago; I never thought I'd get to use it."

Doris — ah, the hair, a thick fall of very fine hair. "Blond?" he asked.

"Yes, how did you know?"

Leda was still interpreting, and he smiled more and told them it was practice and felt their laughter and their interest. Tricks, really. Lee, at a touch, "Oh, you're black, I think," and she drew away. "How — " He had only touched her cheek, brushing. "Very smooth skin, even older women who are black, this smoothness, and you wrinkle later and not in the same places." Scent with her, of heavy, melony fruit. Marlene, a woman of tiny, nervous little pulses and twitches. Tiny

204

hands, tiny fingers, a small woman, cool. Soap and the smell of her nervousness. She was bleeding her period: a metallic tang on her breath and in her hand-smell. Sam had told him that that smell was probably metabolic — ketones, he called it. John was still pulling his own face for pleasantness. Ted: a firm, confident hand, a regular face, crisp, thick hair. The smell was warm oil — baby oil. Now John did want to smile, but his face was sore from smiling. Louise: a big hand like a man's. No perfume. A body-smell of liquor and soap and something from a body cave, exciting, not pleasant but provocative, and all the hair of him rose in reaction. He touched her face; ordinary, a wide forehead, rough hair, dyed maybe. He wanted to wrestle with her and then make love. It was the smell of her, a smell of sex-ready, because there were lines in her face that made him know she was older. Hugh: a soft hand, delicate. Hands were often cold-sweat, but this one was warm and pleasant. Oh, a beard. The beard was thick but the head hair was thin. Glasses. Smell of what he ate: spicy food. An undersmell of bad teeth, subtle, though, so not dentures. Leda again. Her familiarity was a relief. Groups were tiring for John. "Have a canapé." He didn't want to hold a plate, so he used the napkin. A pleasant, salty taste —

fried, warm, wettish. Oh, cheese, *fried*. Strange. He had something else, too. Hot dog, very small, like eating fried fingers. He got up and went in search of more of the cheese things. He moved slowly through the group, saying politely as he passed, smell by touch, by shadow, "Excuse me, Bennet; excuse me, Lee; excuse me, Ted." He was moving toward the kitchen, trying for a line almost true to the house's long axis because that was without furniture and would lead to the kitchen. He was there in twelve doublesteps, touching Hugh, who was at the opening. He had met this pattern often with the Sighted. They liked to group at doorways. He wondered why, since it stopped the go-in and come-out and was inconvenient for everyone. "Excuse me, Hugh," he said and went past, and there, as he expected, was Leda. "May I have some more of that cheese thing?"

"They're all talking about you," she said. "You stopped everyone dead."

"Is my fly open?"

"How do you know who everyone is? How did you find your way straight here? They think it's a trick; they think you can see."

It was a trick, in a way. He had learned long ago how the Sighted are amazed when blind people remember. They talked about intensification of the remaining senses to a supernatural level. It wasn't true, of course. It was only an indication of how serious he had to be about the messages of smell and touch. He had played this game before, mystifying the Sighted with what was obvious and what they did not want to accept: that their bones were different and their smells personal and identifying, that their habits were not entirely being controlled: sweats, cold-spots, twitches, tremors, odors, like the steam and the water of cooking that escaped the pot lid and that both Corson and Arthur had spoken of as metaphors for various things. They had both told him that such steam, held in too long, can blow metal apart. He had also learned long ago that the Sighted did not like knowing about their odors and tremors, so he said, "Direction is easy, thanks to you. You showed me the place before, and room to room, so I learned it. Now I'm here to eat some of that cheese thing."

Afterward there wasn't much else. Now and then Leda came and interpreted some little of what was being said — theater talk, actors' talk, a new play. Now and then Bennet was at his hand for talk, hesitating and difficult. Did he like the city? Did he work? John used his voice, trained carefully, not to vibrate. It was hard to know whether or not he was speaking hard enough to be understood in the noise of others or whether the way he was speaking was understood. The friendly smile was beginning to cramp his cheeks. Bennet left and then came back later and asked him about his reading. John spent most of the time listening to his own body going about its work. The spice of the corn-dog-thing was heating his face and the fat of its frying made his innards work harder at the work of digestion. There was also the marijuana smell of the cigarettes they smoked. Leda did not use tobacco, but she often smoked grass, and he smelled it as penetratingly as any burned substance.

Above all, John wanted to be dignified, yet friendly, to Leda's friends, because it was important to her. He did not know the world they walked in — he had read plays in Braille but had no idea of what a play was like. He had read four of Shakespeare's plays, and *Cyrano de Bergerac, Medea, Death of a Salesman*, and *Waiting for Godot*, but he thought of them in terms of touch and Sign; he had dreamed of Willy Loman Sign-muttering to himself — he did not think of a stage or actors. These people used words specially, had a special language that was foreign to him. Leda was too hurried to explain it.

Her presence was a water he drank, an air he breathed. While he sat and smiled away the long evening, he began to compose an ocean poem for her — it was not like anything he had made before, being in some ways a defense of his previous poem about the ocean:

At the ocean, the state school's Deaf-blind
    picnic.
Beside me George, and except for George
No shadow in any direction.
Without such shadow, ten winds from a
    kiss to a push
Ride the day.
Heat from the east. June morning:
I have learned, my darling,
To call its name The Sun.
A smell like apples and old iodine.
George says people write poems about that
    smell.
We walk barefoot in sand
That's like hot salt hard and soft together.
"The seaside is a privileged place,"
    George says.
The sand goes hard, remembers it was
    stone
And down by slow degrees until I feel
The heart of the monster beating slow
In my feet, and in the air its trembling
    breath
Like fear of dying.
A heave of water is its pulsing blood;

The pulse pushes, pushes: George is
gone. I clutch the air
And the water eases. I think it has for-
given me, but it begins to pull me
Forward toward its heart. The long pause
was a pulse I did not measure.
The push, the pull, like a Sighted guide in
traffic
Not human now, stronger than wind.
Strong as love. Again, Again.
Ten winds. No shadow.

He was saying the poem over, mind-spelling it, when Bennet was there. "Bad news," Bennet said into his hand, now moist with the ice-busy drink he was holding like a blind man's alms box.

"What?"

"Sam. Can't come. Broke down," and then Bennet's booze-breathing shadow was gone.

Breakdown. Mental? Physical? Automobile? Now Sam, his friend, would be gone — no one would know where; the way his dad had gone, and Warlock, his dog long ago in Aureole, and Margie, the cleaning girl. people were not like buildings. Buildings, once you knew where they were, made trusted shadows. Again and again. People never said where they were going or how or why. John always had the feeling they were hiding somewhere, all of them out of his range, that if only he could tell in which direction they had gone, he could follow and find them. He dreamed often of what he called his door dream.

A wall. In the wall a door and no clue to where, not even direction. Find the door. It is a through place to where the others are — all the people he has met and known: school friends, tutors he has liked, his father and dog and Margie and his brother Irwin. He can feel their touches and scent them all around him. An immense excitement overwhelms him and he wakes with it, sometimes sure there is a way to this that he still knows.

He was yearning for the door, missing Sam, when he began to feel air-stir around him. The party must be ending. At last. They came to him to shake hands and say goodbye, which he did. Bennet apologized for being such a slow speller. John said that was all right. "All going home?"

"No," Leda said, "they are taking the evening to a late club. A friend is appearing."

"Do you want to go?"

"I want to stay with you, here."

"Let me help clean up."

So he stayed, getting up and going all around the room, helping. John was glad for the opportunity to move although he felt Leda's nervousness at his moving; she

211

doubted his nonseeing senses and almost could not endure him among her cups and plates. "You think I will turn my cane into a duel sword and go slashing here and there?"

"These drinking glasses are hardly crystal, I guess."

"I will treat them as crystal. I will be a gentle-breeze-fingers to pick them up. Magic carpet service."

Later she said, "You amazed everyone — identifying them, calling them by name. You never told me how."

"Smell, mostly, and touch."

"You mean perfume?"

"Not only, not even mostly."

"What smell?"

"Body smells, breath smells, touches, tremors, sweats, dryness — "

"Unpleasant . . . "

"No, human. You praised it . . . "

"I praise the *idea* of it. It seems — it feels like a betrayal."

"I will smell myself on your breath after we make love."

"Impossible. Imaginary."

"True. And one of those women had sex before the party."

"Who? Never mind; don't tell me. It's not nice."

People had said this to him before, but not

212

as boldly because he himself had never been so bold. He couldn't understand why his senses of them, which made life possible for him, would seem the betrayal it did for them.

"Let's see how good your memory is," she said. "Put the chairs back." He did.

He delighted her; he could feel it. He helped with the dishes and cleaning up and ran the sweeper. He liked doing it. It taught him her house even better, although he had stepped in two ashtrays people had left on the floor.

"How did you get such a wonderful house?"

"My grandmother left it to me when she died. I was married then."

He had forgotten she was — had been — married. He had rightly guessed how competent she was, how exciting and vivid was her life. "Married — " he said. She changed her position. They were half-lying on the floor facing each other, each leaning on an elbow, one hand free for talk.

"I was in acting school, after college. I wanted to go to New York but I had no money."

"You were here, in Denver?"

"Yes. I had work here and there, dinner theater and things. It was at a production of *Venus Observed* that I met Steve Milan."

"What was he like?" John didn't really want

to know. The unknown Steve was Sighted and Hearing and competent and wise.

"He was unlike the other men I'd had. For one thing, he was my age. He was untired, unjaded. He came from a big, wide-open, loving Chicano family. We were lovers and then we got married."

"Were you unhappy?"

"Not for the first year. What I didn't know was that he was trying to get rid of the barrio in himself, the speech, the family. What he didn't know was that his big family and his belonging were what I needed. We had married in . . . in a passionate misunderstanding."

"So you divorced . . . "

"Not right away; we stuck it out for three years. Before it ended Steve had started drinking heavily and Ed, my dad, came through and stayed with us and turned Steve on to drugs. The house — which you asked about, this house — broke us up in the end. My grandmother had left it to me. It made Steve think of roots and settling and debts and repairs, a life like his parents'. To me it was the only stable part of my past. I would stay with my grandma while my parents went commune-shopping, love-swapping, or pill-popping."

He laughed. "I'm sorry, it rhymes."

"I know," she said, "I wrote it in a school poem once without any idea of how bitter it sounded. They were scandalized."

"You loved your grandma."

"Yes, I did. She died the first year we were married and left me the house. She thought she was doing us a favor. She did *me* a favor. I love it and I want to keep it."

"Do you see your parents a lot?"

"I can't. I don't know where Ed is now, and Leatrice, my mom, went into Jehovah's Witnesses in Phoenix. Whenever I see her she tries to make me join."

"Your life has been so . . . " He couldn't find the words to describe its combination of excitement and dislocation.

"My parents were sixties people . . . "

"Sixty years old?"

"Nineteen sixties — it was a time, they said, of great *illumination.*" She spelled *illumination* carefully into his hand. "Lit up," he said.

"Yes, and after such brilliant fireworks, on July fifth, the fields are full of Deaf-blind people wandering around crying for water."

"Deaf-blind?"

"Not literally, like you. I think your vision and hearing are better than Ed and Leatrice's."

What she said made John unhappy but he

215

could not tell why.

"But I have no money to run the house. I don't want to sell it because it's all the stability I have."

"I like it, too — its age and smells."

"I don't like the neighbors, though, or they don't like me. Granny always seemed to get along OK with them. Let's go upstairs."

TWELVE

The next week Leda did not want to go to church with John. He went with Melvin, his new guide-interpreter. She said she would come over later in the afternoon. He was lucky enough to bump into Luke outside, striking cane on cane, and after they had identified each other and told Melvin they could go on themselves, they remembered such meetings at school and dueled a bit with their canes, having fun, fencing lightly up the church steps one by one, the counted number, until they were at the top and before the door. Such play had been discouraged all through school where dignity was a prime virtue and one blind man was said to represent all blind men. The worst punishments were for things done in public, play like this. "What if people were around you?" the teachers said, but everyone knew that the canes warned them away. It was spring now, a time for less heavy clothing and fun and opening up.

217

"Listen," John said, "Leda says that what we call shadow is not shadow. Something we feel, maybe, but she says you can't feel real shadows."

"What is it?"

"Something else. 'Looming,' she says, but not shadow."

"You are with her a lot."

"Yes. I'm in love with her." It was the first time John had said the words to someone else. He was proud of what he said.

"Silly man."

"No — she's not like most of them. She's different." Luke didn't know Leda's fun, her humor, her liveliness, how she would love their dueling up church steps, their need for risk and freedom and laughter.

"It's a pity," Luke said.

"No, not pity."

"Those people — you can't depend."

"Depend. You know the Sign for that? It's fingers of both hands pushing down. I don't want to push down anymore. I want to go up, to be new a little."

"Senior citizens' dance tonight. Here. Minister says us, too. Balloons. For the music. A real band. Floor-beat, air-beat to dance to. And there's a woman who will teach everyone the new step. Why not you?"

"I'll ask Leda. You and who? Maybe

Melvin can take you."

"Alma."

"Dumb."

"Maybe, but I think only ignorant. Very nice, though, kind and generous. We may get married."

"Dumb. All your life with a dummy?"

"All *your* life with a Hearie?" Luke did a blistering imitation. His agile fingers went stubby and hesitant. His arm bobbed. "No time. Too busy. Too busy seeing; too busy hearing. Why don't you hurry up? Why don't you get the idea of our funny jokes? I'm tired of interpreting. My fingers are tired; my leg hurts so I can't interpret. My nose is running."

John had to vibrate. "All true, but not Leda."

Luke had begun to lead John clumsily and with humiliating pushes, intrusive and bossy, from place to place. "Come on, Deafie, come on, Blindie. There's no time for you to find your way yourself. We have to hurry up or we'll miss the destruction of the world. No time for you to learn the rooms you will be in, the streets of your mobility. *Independence* and *mobility* are words — we just don't have the time for yours!"

Again John felt the humor and vibrated, letting Luke know he got the joke. "It's time to go in and stop playing."

"I think the service has started." They had had no sense of people near them. It was what had permitted them to play, and when John touched his watch he realized that this was probably true. The service was already in progress.

Luke had been funning about Hearies, but some of his ideas had hurt. John could not wake up in the morning without yearning for Leda; he could not eat or read without thinking about her. His steps to the van, his steps at work, were shared with her in his spirit. Every action and day's event was shared with her, mind-spoken.

The poetry she wanted was beginning to stir in him. He was beginning to see what she meant, or to think he saw, and the poetry, unrhymable because of the change in it, was slowly moving into his fingers and thoughts. Now he sat in church with Melvin as interpreter. He let Melvin's hands play in his, but he was not reading Melvin's signs or spelling. He was beginning the idea for a poem.

When the service came to an end, he and Luke went down to the Deaf-blind social hour. Alma was there and Eleanor and her companion. Eleanor had not spoken to him since the night of her party. With her delicate, exquisite Sign and spelling she told him how sorry she was about the confusion. She still did not know he had been humiliated, restrained, thought insane; only that there had been a fight and he had been taken to the hospital. He did not tell her more. Could he and Luke come again, perhaps next week, to make up for the dinner that had been missed? This time they would not be waiting outside but would be taken in cabs. John accepted gratefully. "Do you miss Sam?" Eleanor asked gently. John could only give a mute nod of his head. "They're not like friends," she said. "Friends stay longer. How is Melvin?"

"All right, but no sense of fun. His feet stick to the ground." John's hand was hit by Swede. "I'll be ready," he told Eleanor. "What day?" They made their plan.

John said, "I have a new poem." Because Swede was deaf only, his presence among the Deaf-blind people was special, and sometimes John knew he got impatient with their blindness, and sometimes laughed at them with his Deaf friends. Sometimes John wondered why Swede liked him as a friend.

Swede spelled into his hand quickly and competently. "Can you tell me now?"

John Signed the poem. It was the one he had composed during the church service; it had only six lines. He missed some parts and limped on others, but he felt approval in

221

Swede's hand. Madonna came touching him. Swede had been spelling to her as John spoke the words. "Good," she said. Again he thought not of Swede or Madonna but of Leda. Alma came to his hand then, and Swede and Madonna disappeared.

John knew all the Deaf-blind people who got out and went places — some more, some less, but his real friends were people who had not been born Deaf-blind. Luke had been Deaf-blinded when he was four. Swede could see, and Madonna had been deaf first and then had gone blind when she was nineteen. John's friends were people like himself who had had language, and having lost their hearing, hadn't lost their understanding of English, or who were Deaf but had had sight and lost it, and whose sight had given them understanding of the words and world of Sighted people. The people who had been born Deaf and blind, except for Eleanor, were different in many ways. They did not read Braille much because they did not understand the words or the ideas the words made in the mind. Their spelling was quick but had no Hearing metaphor to it; their speech, Sam said, was usually incomprehensible. Some of them were retarded. Some, like Alma, had not had any education and used only crude home-Sign for their daily needs. Others were locked up in a world the ways to which seemed closed even to him. Worlds on worlds. He knew Madonna hated being Deaf and blind. Before she met Swede she had been bitter to everyone. People forgot when they talked about the couple they made, how it was when they were first meeting and how they had been before they met, because Swede had been in the Deaf world, Signing, competent, and he had felt very superior to Deaf-blind people.

"How are you going home?" It was Swede, back again.

"Melvin came with me . . . "

"Tell him never mind. I'll take you. Save time."

"I have to learn this city, now, to walk places. You can't learn by riding. Sam is gone. We rode too much, got spoiled. Now I need someone to teach me walking this city. I need a Braille map and some time to go on adventures." Not since Martin, he realized, had he been city-wakened. Now there was need. He wanted to go to Leda's house, to meet her at her play or downtown where she worked, to have dinner again at the restaurant. He knew he could make mistakes. Muggers and criminals like to pick on blind and Deaf-blind people, but there was worse trouble in staying home. It was easy, pleasant, safe, dead. He needed wider worlds, wider dreams, and there were reasons now to venture out as there had not been since Martin's exuberant spelling and big Sign: "Are you going to sit on your big fat ass all day!" and the jabbed "You!" sliding off John's shirt button. How he had come to love Martin's words: "Dumb? He can't find his ass with maps and bloodhounds." "Sick? I was on my ass!" John remembered answering a question from one of his teachers, saying, "bet my ass." A half-hour harangue followed. If John had not been a special student, he would have been punished. They gave licks at the school.

Alma was touching him now. She held a bad feeling in her posture; hesitancy and the drawing back that John associated with sorrow or secrets or anger. "Where is Luke?" John asked. "Is he with you?"

"You no want Luke Luke-me," she said, "you think too dumb me."

"I guess so."

"Me, yes, dumb. Day, night, year-year." She beat the year-years against his hand to show the continuing of them. "People come, take me school. Show. Luke teach. Luke say, 'Smart me, good me.' Luke say learn yes. Luke say, take yes. Learn Braille. Learn thing. Learn me spell, talk."

The spelling and Signs were so crude John

could barely understand. He realized that Luke wanted him to be part of helping Alma, to teach her. He knew the months, probably the years, of time it would take to teach her Sign and reading Braille, to teach her ideas and expressions. Life with Leda was just beginning to open for him. He had his own learning to do, his own ideas to express. He felt a rise of bitterness. What did Luke expect him to do — give up everything he was hoping to do to go in on a project that seemed to him to be useless? What if Alma did learn some Sign, some spelling? Her ability had been frozen in her. By the time she was fifty she might learn as much as a ten-year-old knew. But she had a job, which few enough Deaf-blind people had, which even Luke did not have. Luke was suddenly there and had found his hand.

"Come with us, talk to her."

John stood still, annoyed and unwilling. Luke went on. "She never went to school. Her parents keep her inside, no school, no going anywhere, no experience. Years of that. State people say she's retarded. I don't think so. She needs people like you, bright people, readers, people who talk good. No one ever talks to her at home, no Braille, no nothing. Home-Signs, ten of them. That's all she had."

"I want to talk with Alma," John said, "but

not now. Leda is coming. We are going to her house." John began to tell Luke about Leda's house, about how old it was. When he was finished, Luke said, "It's *their* world you want, but they'll never let you in it. It's their intelligence you want, their experience, but all you'll get is their restlessness and their uncaring."

"You think our people care more?"

Luke didn't answer. Then he said, "I guess I love Alma; she's been through so much and she's not bitter or angry; she's like sweet water or a home-smell you keep wanting to go back to."

John thought about Leda, that she wanted him to be bitter and angry and he didn't answer Luke. He had said to Leda, leaving the jail after visiting with Martin, that good religious people had told him he should practice love and forgiveness. She had said people didn't think so much of those things anymore — that they were more honest now, less hypocritical. It puzzled him. The most puzzling thing was not the hurry of the Sighted-Hearing world, its busyness, even its lack of caring — it was the restless shifting of its beliefs. Sometimes this bothered him terribly. When his social worker talked, things seemed to be one way. Pastor, another; that reality a world away from the social worker's. Leda's world was still another. Be bitter. Do not be bitter.

Above it all drifted the promise in her air, rose-smell and the oil of her body, tang-hunger and the ozone-thunderstorm smell of excitement. World-throb — it was like the vibration of the drums of parades, the time they had made the cannon go off on the July Fourth picnic at the state school.

"Do you remember the joke when people at the Deaf school fainted because of the cannon? We were so close, too close, being deaf, and vibration threw us on our ass and people thought we were faking and really heard it all?" But John realized that Luke's attention had left him and he was Signing into a hand that was not receiving.

Luke was receiving someone else. "Oh? What?"

"Nothing."

"Here's Madonna — " He Signed Madonna's Sign-name, one *M* on the lower part of John's hand because she was so short. Then Madonna began to talk to John. She was a quick Signer, her fingers bird-nervous in his hand. "Where's the girlfriend?"

"Home, busy."

"She has hard time with all us Deafies."

"I guess so."

"They have their own world, Hearies. They make their own ideas."

"I guess so."

"My brothers, my sisters, they hear and see."

"Yes."

"I don't understand what they do and what they want to do."

"If you could go into that world — "

"You mean see and hear?"

"I mean understand people who do . . . "

Her hand went hesitant. "I would like to see again, but I don't know about hearing. If I could see *and* hear, I would be someone different."

"If you could *understand* — "

"I can't think their way — I can't — it makes me tired. They're so busy understanding one another they can't understand anything else." Her hurried Sign hurried on and on. "When I was girl I went to handicap camp. What's that? With ramps. Four steps, big bathroom for wheelchair kids. I don't need ramps, big bathroom. I was in that camp three years, no Deaf kids to be with. But they teach me how to swim and dive there, and now when I want to go, my brothers say it's not safe. Same with skiing, skating. Roger Kovach skis all the time and he has a special person helping him. NOT SAFE! NOT SAFE! Everyone says."

"Insurance," John said. "Sam told me about it. They're afraid our families will give them a lawsuit."

"Lawsuit. That is some suit. I think it has straightjacket sleeves on it. One reason it's hard to be in their world is all the smiling you have to do. It hurts my face."

"Why do we do it then? Act included?"

She nodded, her fist in his hand, her *yes* Sign emphatic. "You're a poet, I hear, so do a poem."

He gave her the poem he had made at church, spelling it quickly into her hand.

Now and then she trembled with approving mirth. "Good. That was good, but it's not poetry. It doesn't go pulsing or make the end-business like poetry."

"It's a new kind," he said.

"It doesn't pulse."

"It pulses different."

"I like it a lot," Madonna said, "but are you sure it's poetry?"

The next day was work. He had stayed up late with Leda, making love and eating, and she told him more about the emotions of people in the theater. She had once said that actors in the theater must be ready with feelings, must know and identify feelings because they must, she said, have them available for the work.

"Can you save up anger and use it later, like money?" he said.

"You can feel it and remember it and so you

229

can call it up again."

"Amazing."

"It means that theater people are volatile and labile in their emotions."

"Labile?"

"Easy glum, easy glow," she said.

"I haven't seen that in you."

"Just wait."

"It's an interesting word — where did you learn it?"

"It's a long story."

"Tell it."

"Ed and Leatrice joined this commune. It was in Boulder. I was thirteen then, and dumb, like they say, as a barrel of hair. The leader was a man named Eugene. He was a big, bearded man, about fifty, and he had been a professor of philosophy before he dropped out. I was attracted to him. He got me reading. When the commune broke up a year later, Ed and Leatrice left and *they* split up and I went to live with Eugene and be his pupil. I learned all my special words from him."

"Did you make love with him?"

"Why not — I loved his world, he opened me up. He encouraged me in my acting. If I had not met him, I wouldn't be an actor now."

John started to speak but realized that if he

had not met Martin, he would not be a poet now, either. "Why did you leave him?"

"He had a lot of liberated ideas about natural food and natural sex. He thought sex should be as easy as eating and drinking. He shared me with a lot of his friends and I didn't like some of them and I was getting too much VD. I kind of collapsed. Grandma took me in." John sat absolutely still, stunned. "It's hard to describe it right," she said, "because it's not a conventional thing. . . ."

On Friday, Mr. Sherline came. "God's Braille," he told John again, was a big success and there was going to be money coming from it. There were special ways of getting the money that could make it be given to John little by little so as not to come off his aid grant. The poem itself would be appearing on trivets and wall plaques and posters and cards. They had had a photographer take special pictures at the school for the blind and at the Special Olympics and they had settled on a picture of a lovely child, no more than two years old, who was delicately touching a daisy. Because of the way the picture was taken, the viewer could not tell if the child was Sighted or blind. John had nodded without much comprehension. He did not understand how a picture could be taken that made something hard to see. He thought you either saw or you didn't see a thing.

"Was it dark?" he asked.

"No," the interpreter's quick hand said, "it was a bright summer day."

John nodded but did not understand.

"There may be more publicity . . . photos, interview."

John nodded his head to show he understood. Then he said, "I have more poems now, different."

"If they're anything like 'God's Braille,' they will be a great success."

John took his three new poems from his day pack and told Mr. Sherline what they were: a poem about Deaf-blindness, the Deaf-blind picnic love poem, and another love poem, a new, different version of "God's Braille."

"Another 'God's Braille' —where is it?"

He had written it for Leda but thought she would like to have it to read herself on one of the Handicards.

I think God
Signs to His Deaf-blind —
One sense especially I will give:
A sense made sense to all your body over
From the wind-lift of your hair
To the floor-side of your foot?

It is not in a node, a bump, a hole.
My Braille is feeling and your body reads
Because the joy of it is much too much
To hold in hands alone.

There was a stillness in the room. Their air was still; they were not moving, not laughing, not going away. He tried to smell their air. Pleasure? Disapproval? Ah, Mr. Sherline was talking. He could feel — Sam had asked him once how — the disapproval was communicated, and then Melvin took up.

"*Feeling* is not a good subject for poetry. *Feelings* are. Do you understand? It's good to show people how deeply a Deaf-blind person can feel *emotion,* but it is not good to talk about the skin's ability to feel all over his body. That is vulgar."

"Vulgar?"

"Too . . . sensual. People . . . want to think about love and caring when they read our cards or posters. That's why 'God's Braille' is so good. This Braille poem is . . . embarrassing."

"But sensual means about the senses . . . "

"Yes."

"That's how we know reality."

The interpreter's hand paused, stumbled, paused again. "A poem *about* loving, not a love poem. A poem *about* feelings, not a poem that describes how the sense of feeling is used. Don't you see the difference?"

For a minute John waited, wanting to say "Leda says . . . " Something warned him to be still.

Has fire form, wind none?
If a heartbeat can be felt
Why not a shadow?

THIRTEEN

They moved in together — that is, John moved into Leda's house. The caseworker expressed great disapproval. From a convenient, familiar placement, she said, John was moving halfway across town into an older, less safe neighborhood. John did not tell her it was for love, that Leda and he were lovers and that he could help Leda by paying rent to her instead of to people he didn't know.

"I can use the same van to get to the workshop," he said. "In fact, it's much closer, Melvin told me." He stopped for a moment, distracted by the idea of Melvin, who was precise and very careful, but had no powers of description and none of Sam's sense of fun. Had John not had Leda now, he would be dying of the dryness of "adequacy." Leda. To be staying with Leda . . . He had said to the caseworker, "The Sighted and Hearing move. I'm just being like them," and he felt the tremor of irritation in her hand.

He was surprised when he got to the house and Leda told him they were not to have one bedroom together. She said she wanted independence to come back from rehearsals late at night and maybe to sleep late some days. John knew the problem of independence well; in school his teachers talked about it all the time. He had had the idea of night-sleeping with Leda, and her idea disappointed him. "We'll have plenty of time to make love," she said, "in your room or mine, an ease-up on money for both of us and . . . "

"What?"

"Someone to be here when we come home after a bad day."

He had stood in the warmth of late afternoon on the worn carpet, facing the windward wall, held in wonder. All his recent years he had been content enough with the time-filling work of his separate day. He had ordered the time with things to do, all the jobs, competence, and independence his teachers praised. He had accepted loneliness leaking through his middle-moments like water through his fingers. Not now. Not anymore.

He learned the house well. With a long stick he went the walls and ceilings of each room, with his hands the doors and door sills, on hands and knees the radiators and stairs, the furniture and rugs, the aspect and direction of each hall and closet, enjoying the pleasurable off-line orientation of the house as Sighted called their direction east-northeast. It was a house of cubbies and tricks, of halls and doors, of closets big as rooms and rooms as small as closets, of pantries, and with a front and back stairs, front and back porch, and an attic where heat lay waiting as in ovens.

He spent all his first week learning the house, and once his possessions were set in his room, he began the long and tedious process of making marks of various kinds on kitchen things with tapes or strings or with his Braille marker as he had learned to do in school. Leda's kitchen was huge, a room and a half — two rooms, really, with pantries and big closets, but her utensil drawers were a hopeless tangle of gadgets and tools and her pots and pans and cooking things were jumbled here and there in haphazard disorder, lids and bottoms one on top of another. He cut himself twice trying to learn the contents of a single drawer. "Do you use all this?"

"Well, no, but — "

"Don't you have *always* use, *sometimes* use, and *seldom* use?"

"No."

"I can't risk my hands. If my order is bad, I'll take too long to find anything. Didn't they teach you . . . ?"

"No; certainly not."

"They taught *us.* "

"Superior, aren't you?"

"If my hands are cut, I'm ruined."

"Disorder is declaration for me," she said, "political statement. If it *really* bothers you . . . I understand . . . "

So he got her to submit to order; all the knives running one way, his lid racks, his understanding of function and frequency of use. He could see she hated it; that she had some odd pride in her kitchen chaos. The bathroom was another combat area until she took another bathroom for herself and gave him the one with the wonderful bathtub, backward facing and cool-floored in what were hundreds of tiny, icy, six-sided tiles. White, she said, and hard to clean.

Because she had been angry about his need for order, he was careful to help her with all the cleaning. He went into it happily, scrubbing the kitchen walls, which were also tiled, and the floors, glad for the exercise, working, she said, like a maniac. Of that he perceived she was glad. "Don't get too tired to make love." He didn't.

Learning the neighborhood was harder, and a disappointment to John. The people where he had lived before had been older people, mostly, retired, and had been patient and friendly. He knew the people on either side of his apartment and he made cookies for them at Christmas. He could always get help for his walking in the rain or on an icy day, always a back pat or a word spelled or traced into his hand, if they saw him outside. Leda, he learned, had not done well with her neighbors; she scarcely knew any of them and said they were no help in any case. Busy and healthy and Sighted and Hearing as she was, she had not missed having help near her. There were always her actor-friends, she said, to come if something was needed. This difference made it clumsy to go around for introductions. He sensed that she preferred him not to meet the neighbors, although she approved of his street-learning. Around and around he went, a two-block, a four-block, then a six-block radius, learning the gates, the doors, the walls, the garbage cans, the back alleys, and the bad dogs. He worked out bus lines and their timetables. He felt ambitious again, as he had with Martin, to learn the city, to be going and coming independently. The days sprouted a dozen new plans and ideas. He had new experiences of everything, mobility, poems, ideas about life.

He had been thinking over what Mr. Sherline had said about feelings and feeling. He had been looking forward to writing a poem about moving, about Fourbuds and himself learning the new house together, about the way he was learning the neighborhood, out and back, out and back. Mr. Sherline had said his poetry should make the Sighted and Hearing grateful for those senses. Thinking about what that meant, long buried memories came back to him, announcing in their strange way: we are part of this present thought. What was it, that memory of Mrs. Devlin and the young guy who volunteered a couple of times? That they were using him for something, using his gratitude to praise themselves for the ability to feel it? The ideas were difficult and the words for them elusive as memory-smell. . . . Was that what Mr. Sherline wanted, praise for the readers who could pity a Deaf-blind man? He had defended a poem by beginning, "Leda says," then changing it to, "Some people say these poems are closer to the Deaf-blind experience" — in this, he was quoting Leda word for word — before he felt the hand that used Mr. Sherline's words go impatient. "Your friends don't write cards. Your job is not to state the Deaf-blind experience; it's to show people that Deaf-blind are just like the Sighted and Hearing; no different. We all need love."

Surely that was true, but if all experience was the same, why did they want a Deaf-blind poet to state it? "Did you read 'A Plea to the Owner of the Gate'? That poem is not like the others; it doesn't speak against Hearing or Sighted people the way some of the others do. Let me show it to you." He felt their hesitance in the interpreter's hand, but he took the page out of his folder, feeling for its title, Brailled at the top:

A Plea to the Owner of the Gate

Two blocks north: cool left-side mornings
*   and the warm right rising*
There is, to the corner's turning and my left
*   hand out to meet it,*
An iron fence of special splendor
That walks the block with me.
Each post is a sword or spire rising from a
*   flower,*
Each horizontal link a twisted bar.
I think they might be weapons placed and
*   ready for their soldiers*
Or the spires of a Lilliput for which I'm
*   Gulliver.*
In the center of the fence there is a bolted
*   gate.*
What does it introduce, a dungeon or a
*   park?*
Who works the heavy hinges long as my
*   first finger?*

Outward in the morning I am happy at the
  meeting.
Homeward in the evening — here's pil-
  grimage's end and welcome home.
I have found this romance in the center
  of the rough-walled city,
And I become afraid of city's hunger
  for the changing thing,
That the owner of this fence, and gate,
  who does not know me
Might carry it away and leave me friend-
  less and without a fantasy
In my geography.

The interpreting fingers said, "It's not for a card. No one could send it to anyone at Christmas."

"That's true."

"It has no *inspiration*. The idea of a gate is OK, but it's the experience you have in common with other people, not your difference, that you should be expressing. A gate can lead to God. Try that. We all want to go there."

"Heaven?"

"Right."

At home he tried to write a poem that would be acceptable to Mr. Sherline, but something had happened to his confidence and the words were harder than ever to fit to thoughts. He wrote two poems about gates

242

leading to God, but they were not what Mr. Sherline wanted, he knew, poems that showed blind and Deaf people seeing the gate, hearing the call because the sight and sound came through their souls. He wrote:

> *My soul has eyes to see your loving face*
> *My soul has ears to hear your words of*
> *hope . . .*

but he couldn't finish and sat at his typewriter until Leda set off his buzzer and the vibration told him she was home. She would be unpleasantly surprised because he had promised to make supper and nothing had been started. He went downstairs to meet her.

When she was annoyed her fingers stuttered and she went so quick she couldn't catch up with herself. "You are hot under the collar," he said. It was an expression he liked because he understood it well. "If you wait, I will make what I planned for us — cheese fondue. Mrs. Pfansteihl taught us in case we were Catholic."

"What?"

"In case we were Catholic and had to eat Lent."

"Mrs. Pfansteihl looms large."

"No, she was skinny, but very tall. She was like Corson, only good."

"How long will it take?"

"Half an hour."

"I'm dying of starvation."

John went into the kitchen.

When he had first come they had tried cooking together, thinking of a companionable moving past one another, each at his job, a kind of love-making that ended not in bed but at the table. Not talk-eat, which was impossible for him and the thing she said was his real handicap, but passing touches, the talk-no-talk that Hearing called chatting. The table was a joy for him now; she said she had gotten used to his blindman's table manners, fingers here and there and missed bits and bits dropped. The cooking did not succeed. She got nervous, afraid of his dropping things and burning things, of his use of knives and puncturing tools, of nearly this and almost that at the edges of tables and stoves. He was upset because he couldn't tell what she was doing, so the knife he reached for had been moved from where he had set it down, the pot handle he had set due one way to tell him its degree of cooking and to be come at easily, shifted to what she vaguely called "the side." He was amazed that it didn't seem to matter to her which direction it had been set. It had taken two weeks of trying and then they gave up and alternated their cooking even though the kitchen was so big he kept getting lost in it. It was almost as big as the one at school.

In the kitchen was a table that stood in the middle of the room. Leda had been surprised when John suggested they put it on a true sun axis, the one thing that would orient him in the whole downstairs since the house itself stood so . . . he spelled . . . indirectly. He had looked a long time for a word that would express the sense of what he felt. She had protested. Turning the table in such a way would seem "off" and furthermore would present its corners to bite them whenever they tried to walk to or from the stove. Sometimes when he was cooking a big meal on Saturday or Sunday, he moved the table anyway. It was pleasant to feel the natural directions as he ate. In the same way he arranged his bedroom to reflect directional truth. This made his bed be what Leda called free-standing. But it was not free, it was tied in with the streets of the city and the world, appealing to some innate directional sense he had and could not clearly express.

There was no time for elaborate arrange-ments, now. The dinner was late and Leda was angry. Potatoes and meat took too long; he would do well to make the fondue. He would toast good bread in the oven under the broiler and cut up the two cheeses. He got a saucepan out of the bottom cabinet of the backward wall and put it on the stove to wait. Grate the cheese. He went to the refrigerator, competent and easy. Dinner would soon be ready.

The butters and cheeses went top left — where? His hand hit an unfamiliar array of glass bottles and something covered with — he went up one shelf. Milk, soda, beer, tall cans. The mayonnaise he had marked with its circle top left. He went down two shelves. Part of what he found was in its familiar configuration, as he and Leda had marked and planned it. There was more he had not planned or known about — a pan of something. The covered bowls of yesterday's canned fruit, which should have been one shelf up on the right. He sighed with impatience and defeat. He would have to remove everything and replace it until he understood. He had not yet found the cheeses. He began.

Time was passing. He was half done when Leda came and hit his back so that he turned from the refrigerator. "What's all this mess?"

"Where is the butter and the cheeses?"

"I had to move them to fit the cake in. Now it's too late to eat. I'll have to grab something on the way."

"*I have to know.*"

"I know, I know. I'm sorry."

She was gone to rehearsal all evening. Later, she came home with all of them in the play, on a high. They were excited with their evening and the play. He had learned the phrases of their elation. He knew all of Leda's current friends well by now, smell, hand, height, emotional range, but the miracle of this knowledge was past and they greeted him quickly, without much more than a happy hello, the women hugging him, the men shaking hands; no more. John, having said his greetings, went to his room. He now knew that they disapproved of his being Leda's lover; he was not sure why. He did sense this in a combination of overenthusiasm in their greetings and hesitation in their postures, a conflict of emotions regarding him. This conflict baffled him so that he had no way of reacting to it. Teachers in school had been very definite about the immorality of having sex without marriage. Sam and some of the other interpreters had talked jokingly about making love — their opinions were not the same as school opinions at all. Was this opinion or something deeper? He had no way of finding out. It was difficult to think about all this. He sensed that the disapproval, never stated but always felt, in Leda's friends might be because of this. He had begun to disappear whenever her friends came. The dream about being a part of the exciting life they had, of learning the meaning of their actions and words, had begun to draw away fainter and fainter on his air.

They argued the next morning: "Why did you buy a cake for Lucy? I know her. I could bake a cake for her."

"Snap decision; on the way home, saw it, thought I would get it. As it was, I couldn't even eat before rehearsal."

"That was because you changed the refrigerator."

"John, I have a right to these decisions."

"I think you didn't tell me to bake a cake because you didn't want me to be with your friends for more than greeting."

"I came up and asked you — "

"But you didn't want me."

"You're too sensitive."

"I have to understand you my way. Your friends don't like it that I am here." The unfairness feeling invaded him. It was a chill in his hands and a leadenness in his feet. He would stumble and be thick-handed as though injustice was an icy day against which no warming of the outer world availed — paralysis . . .

"It wasn't a party. It was for the rehearsal group and the director of our show. Wives, husbands, lovers do not come. It was for Lucy after rehearsal. You came and said hello. That was right; you live here. Beyond that you did not belong. No one except the people from the play belonged and maybe that was why I decided to pick up a cake on my way home instead of asking you to bake one."

"If you had not changed the refrigerator . . . "

"I am *sorry* about that, but I do need freedom to come and go."

"I don't want you to feel bad when you come and go — " John felt that the argument was almost over and then she said, "Bennet spells to you — you don't have to feel slighted," and like someone walking, John moved past the cake and the party into another alley, another street, where the footing was even less sure. "Bennet is the worst of all. I feel anger in his hand and I don't know why. He doesn't like me or Deaf-blind people."

"Don't be silly; if he didn't like Deaf people he wouldn't have learned to Sign."

"That's not true." John felt heat rising in him, an anger that burned through him, cutting off all thought and feeling. The anger was so sudden and frightening that he stood trembling with it, afraid of violence. He had begun a vibration that gave him a greater sense of release the harder it got. Soon he was vibrating at the limit of his power to vibrate. He wanted to be locked in the closet again, where there were four close walls to beat and kick, but his fear was now as great as his anger so he stood pounding on his own body and vibrating to the walls until he felt all the air around him flowing to his power to make it his, until he was exhausted. Of course, by that time she was gone. After it was all over, he had wanted the answering touch they had begun to use, not assent but presence. Of course nothing came. He felt so tired he could hardly drag himself up the back stairs to his room.

Later, she made little of it, or said she did — their first fight. He felt that something had changed. She said no, but her fingers were unsure and would not give him wit. She patted him; he patted her; comfort-did-not-comfort and would not tell him why. He spent the day sick with anxiety, waiting for her to come home and use the vibrating door buzzer they had installed. He tried to break her silence by coming again to the closeness they had had. She pulled away. She seemed annoyed.

"Can't you give me a little room?"

"You have your own room."

"Time, time, then. We've had a fight. Leave me alone, now."

It was a mystery to him and she would not tell him. What were their separate rhythms, their tides? Why wouldn't they speak of their tides and how they came and went, Hearing people? He had trusted her. It wasn't fair.

Afterward the fight went softer-scented. Their air came slowly back to easy-breathing. She had forgiven him. When he thought about it his feelings were confused. At church he said a few hints to Luke and Madonna.

"It's just a fight," Madonna said. "Swede and I fight all the time, but Hearing are impatient and Sighted-Hearing even more."

Luke was uncomfortable, shifting his weight and direction and stuttering his warm bear-paw hand. "They don't understand us. They pity us and they put us aside and they don't even know they're doing it."

Alma said, after Luke told her, "You want go in their world. They don't want in ours," and John was astonished because it came from Alma and it was true.

As for himself, he did not know why he had raged, why his rages came sudden and violent over him, through him, and the world knew none of it, or else knew all of it and did not care. The angers are best hidden. Trust is best kept for walls and doors, the tangible world. But his insides were hollow and quaked with his angers. She had seen them now and hated them, yet she had wanted, or said she wanted, his expression of everything; the good and the

251

bad. It was philosophy with her. He was learning the difference between stated faith and daily experience.

For the last month, Leda had been urging John to get an interpreter and go to the office of a tax adviser. Money from "God's Braille" and "Prayer at Night" was coming in. "You need to take care of it now, to save it," she said.

"By the time I pay an interpreter and a tax expert, I won't be as rich as I am now," and they argued again. In this, John consented. It was part of her world, the law, and she said he would be silly not to listen to her.

"Take everything you have," she said, "all the receipts and tax material that you have, all the royalty checks — "

"Can't you come with me?"

"Ask the interpreter to write everything down."

The session was long and a great strain. John had been accustomed to sending his simple work statements home to his brother Irwin in Aureole and letting him work on the taxes. He had always assumed that the poetry money was his own. The tax money man soon set him right. John sat in the welter of numbers and words and thought with exhausted wonder that this was never what he had imagined the Hearing world to be, Leda's world that he had embraced so eagerly. They had walked many places in the city, and now, since he had moved, they never walked anywhere. Money, a positive good, was now a source of terrible worry and the state's hatred and vengeance. There were bad and dangerous forms of it, which the government eyed angrily. More work for Irwin, more dependence on him. Suddenly, the money and income from "God's Braille" and his other poems were now sources of fear. Mr. Sherline had rejected many of his poems lately, but John could tell that reading them interested him in a way they had not done before. This was a new source of mystery, a new area of ground. . . . What was the thing he had been told by Sam about the Vietnam War? . . . Land mines, yes. "Land mines," he said, "this thing is full of land mines." The interpreter continued. John had the interpreter's hand. She was a woman and her hand was cool and pleasant, but he didn't really understand and drifted away.

He was thinking about Mr. Sherline. Mr. Sherline gave him books in Braille to show him what poetry should be, how it should say the things people wanted to have on their cards and posters. He had ideas from it, but not what Mr. Sherline had thought of. Why not, he had written in a letter accompanying his recent work, compile a book of the poems that were not appropriate for greeting cards or trivets or posters but were about being Deaf-blind. They could be illustrated, too. He had not gotten Mr. Sherline's response. He suddenly realized he had been thinking of this letter instead of what the interpreter was saying.

"You have been committing fraud by not declaring your past income. You will have to live on the money coming in and go off your grant until it is spent."

"Does that include my medical . . . "

"Everything."

"Can I refuse the money?"

"No."

The interpreter's fingers were beginning to scratch and irritate his hand; the messages had been so quick and complicated, long, elaborate words. He felt exhausted, overwhelmed. He raised his hand. "Time to stop —"

The hands of the interpreter were still, then slower, "There should be regular meetings . . . careful attention to tax problems . . . you're going to have to fill out an estimate . . . a percentage of your income. . . ." The summing up began, almost as complex as the original explanation. "Save your material . . . special account . . . " John was exhausted by the complexity of their world.

It was raining when they left, a cool spring rain, but a heavy one. John hated rain because it produced deceptive smells and made some of the walks slippery, and when the rain was heavy its vibration deadened the touch of fingers and the signals of the cane. He and the interpreter came from the office into the downpour.

"Can you give me a ride home?"

There was a pause and then her wet hands answered, "I'm not local here; I'm from California."

"Are you leaving for there now?"

"No, I meant something else. I meant I'm a professional. We're trying to establish interpreting as a profession. You wouldn't expect your doctor or lawyer to provide transportation."

"I'm not asking you to provide transportation, I'm asking for a ride. Is it out of your way?"

"Even if it wasn't, that's not the point. The point is professionalism. Professionalism and insurance." She left him.

It took him an hour to walk to a bus stop with which he was familiar, and he stood in the downpour hoping the bus driver would notice his white cane and help. People were always less patient in the rain. . . .

Leda was at home. "You look terrible! Why

didn't you take a cab?"

"Too long a wait in the rain. I wanted to come right away."

"What is it?"

"Tired, confused. A world I don't understand . . ."

"You have no training in it, that's all."

"It's more than that, and more than all the words . . ."

To make him feel better she said, "Let's plan our trip to Aureole."

FOURTEEN

Years ago, in the spring-smell world, there had been sound. There was then mother-voice, father-voice, family- and friend-sounds, each identifiable from a distance. He had been told that with sight the distance was even farther, that one could tell mother, father, friend, house, a thousand steps away. He had not believed this. His proofs seemed ridiculous to Irwin and Richard, who were older. "You say you can tell who it is from far away? How come you couldn't even find Cathy yesterday?"

"Stupid, she was around the corner and behind the tree."

This made no sense, since sound came from distances and moved from all locations.

John lived in the middle of his family, happy and unhappy almost minute to minute. Fed or warm or tired or drifting off to sleep he was often joyous. Loneliness or cold or pain made the dull misery that could take over his body head to toe. He could go from fear to joy in a spilled minute, from joy to fear in a half-gasp.

The occasions of joy were: when his brothers were peaceful in the time after supper or when they roughhoused with him on the scratchy rug of the living room; or when they talked him through TV, describing the actions of the story, whose gunshots or cries he was hearing; when they forgave him his blindness and took him with them; times alone with his mother, big and soft and smelling the soap-sweat-wool warm of herself. Sometimes they shelled peas together, he and his mother, he sitting on her lap, tink, tink, her peas and his into the bowl. She sang as she worked. His favorite thing was riding the sweeper, a huge pulsing animal that, his mother said, ate the dust and dirt off the rugs. Inside: safe. Outside: exciting, but not safe.

One of the occasions of fear was his passing into the outside beyond the slatted fence that marked home. He could feel his mother going cool and secret under her smooth skin. Sometimes she put him in a little harness. Most often she would take him by the hand, saying over and over, "Stay close" or "Keep close to me." But things would happen, things not his fault. There might be a moment's inattention, and then he and his mother would be separated, or his brothers from him, and there would be a doorslam panic in his throat and he would stand in a moving bustle of strangers, all direction gone, and begin to cry.

Because his father was from outside, went, stayed outside each day, he brought the Outsider's fearsome qualities home with him like the coat-air of winter. His father was a stranger, mysterious as zoos, frightening as parks where no walls guide, and like all of those things, liable to sudden changes and madnesses that blew sour winds across the world and stopped throat-breath like a strangle. This strange breath his father, Outsider, would come home breathing. It was from what he drank; years later, through his sister Catherine's hand, John talked a little, just a little, about his father. His mother said that he drank but that he was not an alcoholic because it was only wine he drank. Catherine told him that was the smell, wine. John had smelled wine in the bottle; it seemed impossible that the fruit-flower perfume he smelled could change on the breath of the mouth to that sour-meat-hot-garbage smell his father breathed. Once he had mentioned the smell and his mother had said, "When your dad comes home with that smell, Johnny, stay away from him. Go get in bed, under the covers, and make out like you're asleep."

Those times were not many. His mother would know somehow, in the way grown people know everything, and she would say, "Johnny, go in," and he would go in. Most times the wine-smell was only an unpleasant thing like a splinter while playing. His father might come and pick him up and toss him, muss his hair, joke and laugh with him and his brothers.

But now and then, he would be home slamming, breaking, roaring, weeping, and he would scream into John's ear, "Blind!" and "My little boy is blind!" and hug him to smothering. Then it was the most dangerous. In John's efforts to get away, to right himself, to protect his head or his hands, he occasionally hit something, broke, spilled, over-turned, or spoiled it. As quick as water, the sorrow in his father sometimes turned to rage, and there would be a blow or blows, or he might be thrown against something violently. He had, for these moments, learned the art of complete collapse, going boneless beneath the hitting. It hurt less and somehow satisfied his father, that impersonal and complete capitulation.

Once, he tried for silence, and was magically answered. It came during one of these times of his father's when the breathing wine-storm was on him and he had racketed through the house and beaten all the children for disrespect or inattention and Ma was howling and ran to the neighbors for the police. The kids were screaming, furniture was breaking, glass was shattering, clamor, his father roaring and then his father had found him where he lay in the closet behind a pile of his mother's clothes. "Come out of there, you little sneak!" and his father was hitting and shaking him so that his head flew back and there was an odd-sudden blowing —

. . . a bed, a bed not his own and peaceful except for the fly-buzz in his head. He lay listening to the fly-buzz, rocking himself gently back and forth until the fly-buzz sent him to sleep. When he woke, he moved his hands. They moved. Legs, body. His head was bandaged. At last he thought he would call Mama. Even as he had the wish, he felt her near, her hand, magically, on him. He tried to talk to her but nothing came out. He tried harder. At last she put her hand on his and held his hand up to his own mouth where the air was making words he could not hear and then to hers where the air was coming and the lips were shaping them; back to his again and back. This was because he was dreaming. It had to come slowly to him over a long day he could not tell from night, what had happened. He had been granted silence. It was a wish he had voiced only to himself in his father's wall-pounding, dish-breaking rage. He had received the wish; the wish had gone too deep.

Another wish had gone too deep also: his father disappeared. Years later, when he had fingerspelling and a few Signs and had taught Catherine, she told him in fragments some of what had come from that night. All he had known then were mysteries: the sudden death of sound and the sudden not-there-ness of his father, both caused by his sudden wishes being granted.

Aureole in summers. Mobility began for him with Irwin, his eldest brother, and with a stick, not a cane. There were four places, and they were the beginning of the abilities that would later give him the spirit and independence that Martin would praise and Corson would perfect in him and then try to destroy. Irwin took him to: 1. The place by the river where the boys had their secret cave and clubhouse; 2. The candy store; 3. The stone man on the grass at Prospector Park; 4. Mrs. Teagarden's house. By the time he was ten, he could go with the help of a cane from home to any of these places. After his father left, his mother went to work in the bank downtown. Irwin was given care of John, but sometimes John was left at Mrs. Teagarden's. Often he was Irwin's job.

Mrs. Teagarden was an old lady and very religious. Old, he could tell by her smell and the smell of her house; religious, because every day there he had to spend a long time on his knees with his hands clasped. When he was eleven, people came over to Mrs. Teagarden's to see him and they used Signs and fingerspelling and brought him Braille books. He had learned Braille in the Blind school he went to during the winter. How these visitors happened to come he never knew; nothing was linked by explanation in those days. Things were or were not, reasonlessly, causelessly. Sometimes Irwin would pat him, sometimes punch him. He might miss meals or be roused from sleep or left to sleep with no clue as to why. These Signing, fingerspelling, and Braille people changed often and some days, waiting in passionate eagerness, he would suffer the time, as if under blows, and they would not come.

Mrs. Teagarden learned to fingerspell into his hand but didn't want to. She would say single words like *eat* and *toilet,* things that were self-evident without the word. Irwin didn't want the touching; he would slap John's hands away. His mother was the one he began to know a little by fingerspelling — just a little, because she was busy with the house and work and the other kids, but one day one of the visitors said, "Your mom wants to send you to a school in another state . . . more training . . . "

"Am I bad?"

"No, no — you're a good boy." Then, "When school starts in the fall, you will go to a school where there are other Deaf-blind and where you will learn lots of things. It's far away, but you will be coming back for vacations and a long summer." Late that spring, the miracle happened.

Vacation. One window slid up, another window slid over, and the wind came through and puffed the curtains under his hands. At breakfast the day was hot on the back of his head as he sat at the table. Smells of pine trees and a smell like after-storm and apples blew in the streets. Feet stuck to the ground in the rain-is-over yard, and Irwin, cursed with him, pulled him along from Mrs. Teagarden's to the house and then to the place where his friends met to be together.

John never felt the beginning of when his mind first made the links between spring sun on his head and the directions, sun morning and sun afternoon and the streets of Aureole, the town where he lived. He had gone to the river and the cave and front-back of the stone man in Prospector Park, and what you could walk to from the stone man's pick hand and what you could walk to from the hand that held something, but that spring and summer a unity began to come to John, a sense he first guessed and then knew. Location-direction in Aureole. The full miracle came this way:

It was summer and Irwin had him most of the day. Irwin and his friends liked to play in the field that, when you walked toward home, passed the stone statue of the prospector. For quite a while on that special day, John did what he always did when the boys played, walked the place, waiting, his no-cane hand taking him from signal to signal: the fence, four trees, cars' fronts, then a long nothing where he had to depend on what his feet knew, grass or dirt or walk, all the long way until the gravel, turn with gravel, gravel now with the direction of the prospector's found-something hand, his direction until a bench, another bench, a third bench, and then to the prospector and beginning again or the other way. This he did now and again until he became aware in some way that the boys might no longer be in the field. He could sometimes catch clues to their presence. Sometimes they would come to him or touch him and if he wandered near where they were playing, they would shove him away. For a long time he walked with none of these assurances. Then he began to go toward the playing place, the part slightly lower, tramped on, where the boys chose up. Nothing.

They had left him. He was angry and a little frightened, but he knew the way home and knew that he could go there. He decided instead to look for Irwin and the boys. It was still good day. The streets walking away from the pick hand of the prospector were busy with truck-shake and car-shake. John knew this walk well because the boys often went for sodas and candy after the games. With his cane he felt the street and all edges; it was still familiar. He was near the school and the 7 Eleven. He went to the 7 Eleven and up the little hill and inside, aisle by aisle, and Morty, the manager there, took John's two hands and held them up to his head and shook it so as to say, "No, not here." John framed his question, "Are they at the school?" and Morty shook his head again. Not there. The school was across the street.

Standing outside with his back to the cool glass of the 7 Eleven, the miracle happened that John believed was vision. The river, to which he had never gone from here, was, he knew suddenly, ahead of him, down the hill ten, fifteen blocks, but there. *There.* The high school, as he stood now, was up the hill on his pick-axe hand and his home on a line between that and the river, the line tilting across, as though the prospector raised his pick-axe hand and carried the line across to his found-hand's foot.

Pattern is meaning. Meaning is place. Place is power. A tremendous joy surged up in him. There was no one now to whom he could tell this, that he could *see*, that he understood the joy all sighted people have, adventure, puissance. No wonder his brothers loved seeing so much, no wonder they had pushed him aside! He clutched his cane and, walking the ridge of the hill upward, went to the high school, checking its playing field by walking around it and then into it where the boys were, another group this time, playing there. He was caught by a boy and "guided" none too gently down until he said he was home so the boy would leave him.

The sun was now a little past the top of his head and concurred with his visual skill. He went around a new place on a road made of hard, cindery material, a place he had never been but he was sure because the sun was sure and because he could see. Down toward the river. Mama's bank would be on his found-hand, left. Most of the town was that way. Mountains on his pick-axe hand, right. Snow direction, wind direction even now, breathing out a little, that was the way, the way the gentle stir came. And at last, the river, and the left hand, keeping the river on the right hand, to the caves and the banks of the river. John arrived there in magnificent sufficiency at the cave mouth to the awed presence of his brother and his friends. "I can see," he said.

Of course it wasn't so, or they said it wasn't so. They "tested" him and then laughed. He could feel their laughter and the scorn in the way they shoved him. He never got Irwin to tell him why the boys had left him or where they had gone. Mama was home when they got there, although it seemed early to him. John got from her slow and angry fingers that he had been seen all over town; reports had come to the bank that he was wandering here and there alone. She had left, hurrying, trying to follow him, fearful, trembling. Irwin was then stripped of his pants and bent over John's knees and hit hard with the slipper. The house was thrown into gloom.

Why? They had all walked past the miracle, a truth so wonderful John had thought it was sight, a sense for guiding and freedom all over town, usable anywhere. No one had the time or the words to understand him. That summer, desperately and as a last hope, he began to teach Catherine. She was only five and had no real ease with letters. That fall he was sent away to a distant state school where there was a class for the Deaf-blind.

During vacations from school when he came home and over the years, John built his mother's faith in his mobility. Catherine got older and learned to fingerspell a little. She was the only one who developed skill enough to talk to John and explain things. This Aureole-vision lay in his mind so that at school, when north, south, east, and west were introduced to him, John understood immediately and was able to extend his truth to cover any town or city he could learn and across the nation and into the world.

Year after year the truth he had thought was sight was refined in him. When the sun in summer and winter changed by a few degrees, its rising place, John knew, and by that knowledge came a sense he called Place-Perfect, a sense he later learned most Deaf-blind did not have as well developed as he, and some not at all. Some of his Deaf-blind friends used this sense to some degree. None of the Sighted or Hearing thought it wonderful or exulted with him in its miracle. Poor man, they said, poor man.

FIFTEEN

It was after the July Fourth holiday that John and Leda took their weekend in Aureole. Leda said that to go by bus was too long and exhausting for the time they had. If he would spend the money, they might go by airplane. John had traveled to Denver from school in the summer by air. This was his first short flight. They left early in the morning, excited and happy with the thought of many adventures. They took a cab to the airport, a new direction from where they lived. John had studied it on his Braille map. The airport was oriented north-northeast. "Why?" John asked.

"I don't know; I guess so the sun doesn't ever shine full in the pilots' eyes when they take off or land."

"Why is that a problem?"

"Too bright. It's the brightness that blinds us."

"How can that be? I know you can't see

270

anything when there is no sun."

"Yes, but the sun itself . . . never mind; too complicated to explain. I'll never understand how you got away with writing all you did, sun, moon, stars, sun this and moon that."

"The sun shines east / The sun shines west, / But I know where / The sun shines best."

"Who? . . . "

"My dad used to sing it. I remember it from when I could still hear."

John did not like the sensation of the plane at first. It had been years since he had flown; he had forgotten how disorienting it was, how it changed his location-direction sense in such a way that he thought he would become ill and was only kept from it by their landing. He wondered about the addition of up and down to what his directional sense told him. Being raised in Aureole, he had always known the hills' up and down as a part of his experience; up and down were valuable in location and direction, like sun and wind, validators of his feeling for where he was. The airplane's up and down was very different, and it had bothered him that although their destination was about twenty degrees from sundown-west (he had gotten Leda to point for him on the map), the plane rose and flew, as the schools would say, south-southwest and then due west and then turned north and no one seemed to

271

mind. It wasn't as though there were rivers and houses and streets to go around up there in the sky.

"No," Leda said, "but there are mountains on the ground."

"And the mountains have shadow?"

"Precisely."

"But I don't *feel* anything," and so he began to be queasy as the plane dipped and heaved in the streetless air.

They landed. "We are three thousand feet higher than we were."

He didn't feel it. Irwin and Ma were to meet them as they walked with their suitcases. John had still not received a true feeling about direction; he didn't know where he was and it meant he had a tendency to pull toward the secure loom-shadow of walls instead of walking in the middle place where there was people-flow. It meant that he collided with people coming quickly from doors along the walls and this he did immediately before the sudden disappearance of all walls and the uprush of vibration signifying they were in a huge room. Leda, busy with her own luggage and direction, was not able to lead well and John crashed into a quickly walking someone and then there were Mom and Irwin, Mom stiff, Irwin angry, and John feeling the old horror, one that he thought he had lost at school: their shame and disapproval hanging in the air like the smell of dirty clothes. Standing, helped up, and unable to introduce Leda to his family — they seemed to be doing it without him, he said, "Which direction does this building face?" Ma took his hand to lead him. "Let me do this myself," he said, "if Irwin will take my bag." There was another conference. "Can we go outside so I can orient myself?"

"Cool off," Leda signed into his hand, "we're talking about whether they should leave and bring the car around."

"I wanted to introduce you . . . "

"It's all right."

It wasn't. The years of control, hard won, had slipped away. Out of the range of his power to cane and beyond the power of his carefully controlled voice, they were planning his going in ways that took no account of his ability to act for himself. Bossy Irwin; Mom, who wanted no fuss and wanted to please everyone.

"Where are Richard and Catherine?" he asked. "Will we be seeing them?"

No one answered. Then Leda said, "They've gone to get the car. They want us to wait here. This is my fault; I should have gotten someone to help us."

"At least let's go outside. It's not raining, is

it? It doesn't smell like raincoats."

"Stop shouting. Ease up."

John began quietly. "Suppose you were in a play and they wouldn't let you say your words —"

"We can stand here and talk."

"Please. I want my location back. I want to go outside. Please."

"Stubborn."

He had picked up his bag and begun caning. She led him toward the door.

Standing outside but in the loom-shadow of the building, John couldn't feel the sun. Why would they not understand? "Don't you care where you *are?*" he asked her.

"It isn't that you have to go alone," she answered. "I'll be here."

"I WANT TO KNOW MY OWN LOCATION."

"Stop yelling."

"I want to know my own location." Even as he said it he began to feel it, and when she took his hand and turned him to point to the sun of the forenoon, he was not surprised. "Where's town?"

"Ahead of us, I think."

"Where's the river?"

"On my right."

"How far is it?"

"I don't know —"

"Where's the mountain?"

She told him.

"Oh — that accounts for that turning we did when I kept bumping the wall. Why didn't you tell me we were in a curving hall?"

"I guess I didn't notice; the curve was very slight."

The curve had not been slight. If seeing is such a big issue, he thought, why don't they see?

They waited. "I thought we would smell pine trees; the summer smell here." They were smelling hot-street and car-fume. The noon air simmered out of the protecting shade of the building.

"I'm looking at the mountains," she said.

"There," he pointed, "is Pickaxe hill and over there are mine tailings."

"How did you know?"

"Orientation."

"Car's here," she said.

In the beginning John had thought it was Mom's excitement, but he realized as they rode along that Mom had forgotten most of her spelling. She moved clumsy fingers up, down, confusing *g* with *q*, *d* with *f*, *p* with *k*. She kissed John and patted his hand; it was not enough. He had yearned to be in the presence of her love, but now he felt the loss of her skill bitterly, although he patted her hand

275

back. "How is Warlock?"

Leda interpreted, "Warlock died, six, seven years ago."

"Why didn't you tell me when you wrote to me?"

"You were far away. We knew how much you loved . . . didn't want to give you pain."

"And Catherine; is she still alive?"

"Of course!" and Leda's hands at the end of the word gave a back-flick with the little finger that had become her Sign for half-laugh, the laugh that was a comment on the world, more than on the joke. Suddenly the way went wrong.

"Why are we turning?"

"We're not going to the old place. Ma has moved and we're going to Irwin's new house."

"Where? What street?"

"Cascade."

"Where on Cascade?"

"Out near the old mine dumps. Cascade used to stop edge of town. Now goes miles past. The dumps have all been leveled, all fixed, made into big subdivision. That whole side of town's been built up. You should see it now — "

John sighed. What he had wanted, fantasized above all, was to walk his miracle walk again with Leda, to go, comfortable and wise upon the gravels and walks, the park, the prospector . . .

"The statue?"

"Yes. . . ." Leda took time and then interpreted. "The statue of the prospector? That's been moved to the new mill. The park was needed for the new medical complex."

"What's the same?"

There was a long pause. Leda said, not interpreting, "They're surprised. They thought you'd be proud. The town has doubled in size. Very new, modern."

"Is there anything?"

"They're thinking."

"The river?"

"A flood wall and walkway, they say. You can't get to the river from the main part of town anymore. Victory Pass and the Victory Pass Road: same. Old high school and most of the downtown: same."

"Oh." Those places were not what he had wanted. "And the road we are on . . ."

"New business loop. It cuts off that long trip through town to get to Gold Flume and Bluebank. We take the third exit and cut out the hassle. We come out near Prospector Village."

"What?"

"The new development."

He rode for a while without remark. He

was exhausted and it was only noon. Then he told Leda, "We used to play on those hills, off the mine tailings. Each little hill had a different texture to it; hard or soft, powdery or sharp, some like rock salt and some like sugar and some, after a rain, like pudding."

"That's all gone. It was an eyesore, ugly, there by the river."

"How can you tell when something is ugly?"

Leda answered for no one. Her hands were still.

But in their description of the new streets they had at least given him what he still secretly thought of as sight: he knew how the river came and then moved, a long going, sometimes almost straight as the prospector faced long ago, then it went back to its fall, north to south down the world, as had been explained to him in school. They had been going over bridges and now they were riding smooth and fast almost toward true sunrise. "Is the river north of us?"

"North?"

John could never understand why Leda, in some things, did not have even as much sight as he did. He sighed. "Left," he said.

"Oh, yes, it's on the left." They slowed abruptly.

"What — "

"We've been cut in front of by another car."

"Rude."

"I don't think he saw us." Leda was laughing. She said to him, "I thought your brother was stiff and formal, but he just let out a couple of good ones. Two birds dropped down out of the sky, poisoned." He knew she was saying this into his hand without saying it to the others at the same time. He spelled back to her, understanding the visual picture well, grateful for the joke in it, because he was feeling exhausted, defeated, and sad.

He began to grieve into her hands. "I don't know this city anymore. I dream taking you to soft-ground river cave, to statue. I want to kiss and touch your warm sun-bare-body all your head to toe, and then body to body in the soft grass backyard my mother's old house when they were all gone out slow Sunday afternoon all long afternoon, bare body to bare body until we were so tired we fell asleep dead as Fourbuds dies in sleep."

"Put your hand down; you're making me blush."

Something in Leda's interpreting had made John know that Irwin was proud of these changes in his life and in his city. He was happy with the prospector moved from his park, the river forbidden to the town, the cave destroyed, and the place circled with new roads and bridges. Did the Sighted take their anguish without a flicker? No one seemed aware of what these changes meant to John, the death of a home place in which he had moved easily, knowing as a birthright, town and river, mine tailings, history in his hands and beneath his feet.

They moved in their group. Leda began interpreting. Catherine and her husband, Dean, and their kids would be over to Irwin's house later. Richard and his wife, Judith, also. They did not have kids. Irwin's wife, Marie, would be coming now, here. The car stopped, turned, and went the final way into the home-place. They got out. John oriented himself.

Marie. It was a big hand, warm and competent. Because of the size of the hand, John looked up and felt her shadow. Her words, "How did you know I was tall?" from Leda. "Tall and friendly," John said, "like the tree north end of Prospector Park."

"Gone now," she said, from Leda's hand, "dammit."

He looked up again. "You don't believe as Irwin does."

"I think this town has Alpine fever. It had gold fever in the 1880s, silver fever in 1910, and uranium fever in the 1950s. Now with

Gold Flume gone fashionable, we have dreams of being Gstaad-on-the-Ute."

Leda liked Marie's face. She liked Marie. He could tell. He smiled, feeling easier. "You don't agree with Irwin?"

"Not in this."

"How can you be married, then?" He felt her laughter. Leda stopped dead. Her hand hung in his.

It was for John an ultimate question; it had been nibbling at him ever since he had moved in with Leda. Could people agree on everything? If they disagreed, what did they do about it? Did one of them give in? He was about to ask this when Mom came and put her arm around him and began to guide him away. "Wait, I . . . " and Leda quickly, "She wants you to meet the grandchildren. Anyway your question was rude."

"I need to know. I want . . . "

"Not now," she said. "We were all standing here. . . . Not the time for conversation."

The kids. They were terrified of him. Corson had told him that normal people didn't want to come as close to strangers as people had to, to speak to a Deaf-blind. Normal people didn't want their bodies touched, their fingers dabbled at. It was so with Irwin's children; their hands were limp or tense in his, twisting out of his greeting-embrace. Mom

281

came and embraced him again, comforting. It annoyed him in a way he could not account for. He felt soul-scraped, too sensitive and raw. He had wanted to wait with the children until he was familiar, letting them come to him slowly, their curiosity bit by bit overwhelming their shyness; this he had often discussed with Swede. He had forgotten how little his will prevailed among these people.

All that day he tried to be close to Marie again, to ask her the question that was pressing on his mind, the question about disagreement and agreement.

"Marie — "

"Playing hostess," Leda said, "getting cool drinks and running and puffing and making me glad I'm single and have no family."

"What is this new place like?"

"Why don't we get out of here and take a walk."

Curves, streets that were like branches bending, windward to sunrise on one side and windward to sundown on the other, in a curve that was not irregular as a hill, but careful. "This is very pleasing."

"This is very fashionable," and she described the houses and the careful artiness of the landscaping. "Neighborhoods like this bring out the worst in me," she said. "So goddamn tasteful I feel like I'm strangling to death. I wish there was dog shit in the street!"

It was this above all he loved about being with her, the opinions, the feelings, the doorways into the complexity of the world. "How can someone hate beauty?" he asked her.

"This beauty is meant to be seen without people," she said. "Human presences spoil, rather than enhance it. In your old neighborhood, all those black people made the streets interesting. Their yards were pretty, but more fun with them sitting out, using them." They had stopped walking because Leda talked more easily at a standstill, but they were not facing each other in the ordinary way. He was facing straight ahead on the roadside while she was beside him. Her left hand crossed over her body and she was resting her right by using that posture. She said suddenly, "It's nice talking to you this way — beside you but not facing you when we talk."

"You said I was handsome, once, good-looking, anyway."

"You are, but your face — I can't find my words reflected in it. You don't show me you are understanding what I say. There is, besides words, a communication that goes on between people that's visual. As an actress, I know what constitutes it, I know it's in the blind part of your Deaf-blindness. You can't see me seeking for the effect of my words in your face. Your lack of expression is the hardest thing I have had to get over when we talk. Suddenly, it's all easier; it's like talking in the dark. I don't look for your signals." They started walking again.

Starting to walk and stopping to talk, they had ended at what Leda said was a cul-de-sac. She declared herself lost. John was surprised. They had done nothing but go back-to-wind and morning sunward, mostly back-to-wind, and all there was to do was retrace their steps. Once again he wondered what vision was that the Sighted were so proud of it. He led her as easily as breathing back around the road, moving into, into, then full into the wind by sundown-turning until they were at Irwin's and the sun had gone away. "Isn't it early?"

"There's a mountain a mile away and the sun went behind it." John nodded, understanding nothing.

Supper. Fried chicken . . . corn on the cob. Once again John sensed the concern of Marie, making a supper at which he, eating with his fingers, was not at a disadvantage. This was so, but it was offset by the inability to receive any talk from anyone else without elaborate wipings and dryings of his fingers. After dinner he helped with the dishes, again amazing the family as he had amazed Leda's friends, but he was becoming tired of showing this skill. He was beginning to feel that it was a useless game, that it led to no greater sharing between him and the people who seemed so impressed. They were happy when he used his hands at work, folding, stacking, drying, but those acts kept his hands from communicating, from teaching Marie to spell, for example, so that she might tell him herself, alone and uninterpreted, her words about agreement and disagreement. He didn't want Leda in that talk; it was about his relationship with Leda. He would be talking about fears and simplicities — his ignorance, weaknesses he didn't want her to know. Marie was standing next to him at the sink. Now and then he felt her air-stir and warm shadow.

"I want to talk to you," he said, "to ask some things. You can draw letters in my hand and we can talk that way."

She took his hands and put them to her head, nodding yes.

At last the dishes were done and the children were in bed and Leda told him that Irwin and Marie were sitting on the soft, big-pillow chairs John had located in his trip through the room before. Mom was on the couch on one side of him, Leda sat in front of him as interpreter.

They had talked for a long time about what

he would say. She was still rough enough in her interpreting to be unable to speak to them and spell simultaneously. He began with his own news about "God's Braille." Of course they knew about his poetry; he wrote to Mom every week and she had received his plaques and the cards he had sent through Mr. Sherline. Their letters had not told anymore than his had, the weather, their health, a vacation trip — not that Warlock had died, not that . . .

" 'God's Braille' means money and trouble," he said, "tax trouble. I thought the money was mine because it was from something I *made*, something that wasn't there before. That's not true."

Ma praised "God's Braille," and then Irwin talked about finances. In Leda's literal, word for word hand, Irwin said his accountant would help, if John sent everything to him. John asked if there was a way to use the accountant without Irwin's having to know. There was a long pause. Was Irwin thinking? Angry? After a long time John reached for Leda's hand. He took it and felt in it the light vibration of her activity. She was talking. He pulled it. She took it away, impatiently.

"What?"

"Wait a minute."

"*What?*"

"I'm speaking for you."

"Then let me know — "

"My Sign is too slow; it's too frustrating."

"What are you telling them?"

"I'm saying you need privacy, independence — "

"Then give me those things. Let me go slowly and be interpreted."

Her hands fell. "Irwin doesn't want you cheated. He wants you safe, psychologically, financially. He doesn't know, for example, who *I* am — what I'm doing here with you. An actress. I told them that. They think I was cause of the bar fight, that I was at the bar and got you into trouble. They know I'm not real interpreter. They know acting work doesn't pay well, that it's come and go. They ask if I'm looking for easy money, moving in on you because you have money coming from 'God's Braille.'" It was a long speech and Leda was tired from a day of spelling. He could feel her tiredness stuttering and slow, the Signs unwilling, stubborn as hangover. In his own shock and anger he didn't know how to answer.

"I wrote that *after* we — it's not true!"

"He has right to wonder," she said as herself, but slowly. "My friends all wonder."

John could only sit in mute shock. He had asked for these words, this honesty. He had not suspected any of what was on their minds. It was true that Swede and Madonna and Luke and Alma had expressed disapproval at his relationship with Leda, envy, he had thought, but their questions were on a different level from these, which hinted at something evil in her. This revelation was like descriptions John had read of a surgical operation in which a doctor cut into someone's body and found disease and stench there. He wanted his subject returned to, the money he was getting.

"About the money — " Leda was interpreting for Irwin. "Don't you think I take care of you? Every year I do your income tax and your finances — twice I got your SSI payments when they were late!"

"That's good," John said, "all I am telling you is that with these poems they said I will be off SSI until I spend the money I'll get. Medical, too . . . "

"And you expect me not to know? I have to know. I've always had to know all about you!"

John remembered, too. Every day in spring during his boyhood and young manhood, John would have to strip before them; first it was in front of Ma, later of Irwin, to be searched for ticks. Raise your arms; bend over. As he grew, John began to hate having to do it; Irwin hated it also. When they found a tick, Ma came. If it had any blood in it, Irwin was punished. Leda was now too tired to give the extra description of Irwin's expression as he said these words — were they strong in saving? strong in love? strong in damnation?

John said, "I guess you need to know about the money since you are helping with the tax. I will send you the amounts I make — the numbers. . . . My poetry has been a bad thing after all," he said. "I will lose all my benefits." He felt tired, uphill-going. "Leda is my friend and she doesn't want my money. Why do I have to explain this to you, when you don't explain things to me?"

"What do you want explained then?"

There was nothing for a long while. Leda had taken her hands away, waiting. John stood still, trying to add up the years but take away the confusion about it all. Things that had pulled at him years ago still caught at him. He felt numbed by old pain he could no longer even identify.

The hands that had given him Irwin's words were impatient themselves. Was it Irwin's impatience or Leda's? In the stillness, the room seemed unpleasantly alive with discontent. Whose, besides his own? "I want — " He knew he was talking a little more strongly than he should be, vibrating a little. "Why didn't you tell me about town changing, how Warlock died, why Dad left us? Is he alive now? Is he dead? Why did Ma let her spelling go and why didn't you let me talk to Marie before, before you made me meet the kids who weren't ready and who are now scared of me?"

He was vibrating too much. The bounce-back, very subtle, was there against his face. Nothing. They said nothing. Had they left the room? He waited. Perhaps they had all gone outside to sit in Irwin's yard. He was tired and angry and very sad. He got up and began to walk to his room, trying to remember in all the new instructions, where it was and how to go there. Once in the hall . . .

A hand. Catherine. He thought Catherine and her husband had left earlier in the evening. "We want to spare you any more pain," in the slow, slow letters.

"Why? I'm not different from you."

"You are. You react like a baby, throwing fits. Dad is alive; he lives in Gold Flume. We see him sometimes. He stopped drinking, eight, ten years ago. He runs real estate office now." The words were dragged and full of hesitations and mistakes.

"Why won't he come here?"

"Irwin doesn't like him. Dad is very ashamed of what he did to you."

"Was that why he went away?"

"Yes. He tried to suicide but he was drunk and it made him clumsy. He shot himself in the heart but he missed and hit some of his lung and his spleen. He is still ashamed, very, for what he did to you, making you deaf."

"I thought he was dead."

"No. He is married again, though. She works with him."

"Does he know I'm all right? Does he know about me?"

"He knows where you are."

"Can I see him?"

"Maybe you can visit him next time. They're away this week, I think."

"Will you answer my other questions?"

"No; your questions are all messed up together and you start yelling."

"I won't yell. Why is Irwin angry all the time?"

"I won't answer that. That's private. Not nice to ask about people's feelings unless *they* tell."

The talk stopped. Leda took his hand after a while: "They're discussing it. It's going too fast for me to interpret. All I can do is listen and try to save it up for later."

John was suddenly exhausted. The trip and the work of learning had tired him almost to falling. "Good night," he said. He went the room around, shaking hands with his brother-in-law and Catherine and with Richard and Richard's wife, Judith, Marie and Irwin, and he went into the hall and turned in the remembered direction to his bedroom. Door. Door. He went through the second door and found the bed and sat on it to take off his shoes. The bed heaved. He put his hand out and found the heave — a person. It was one of the children. "I'm sorry," he said. The little figure went stock still, stiff with terror. He told it not to be afraid and took his shoes, got up, and went as he had come. The door. Now sunward in direction. Another door; the bathroom. He remembered Marie had taken him the way, but only to the rooms related to his needs. He had not an idea how many more doors there were, leading to how many more embarrassments between what *was*, and what had been shown to him. Onward. Door. Door. Which to try? A hint of Memory of this afternoon, memory of four paces between bathroom door and "his" door. The second. He opened the door and went in. If this was correct there was a bed head against the right-hand wall and his . . . Aha. Suitcase. In his exhaustion he fumbled with it. Leda had told him that they were not to be together, for propriety's sake, but no one had told him where she was. Perhaps this was her suitcase and not his. In the awful expense of effort and energy involved in all this novelty, new rooms, new roads, new houses, he couldn't seem to identify . . . he opened . . . Smell. Not hers. No-smell, by which he knew the things were his. He fell on the bed, too tired for any of his night preparations, and he slept until three in the morning and then got up and went to the bathroom and did his teeth and got into his pajamas and arranged his clothes for the morning. At four he went back to bed again and slept until Irwin came at nine to get him up.

SIXTEEN

They were eating. Leda got to him. He wanted to embrace but she was embarrassed and held him away. "Who is here?" She told him. Again he was conscious of Marie's care. His place was convenient. Catherine and Dean had gone, Leda said, Richard and Judith, too. Mom was gone but would come for lunch and spend the afternoon. John wanted to talk with Marie quietly somewhere, to ask her — what? Maybe there was a way to end the pillow fight feeling of being hit from a dozen directions by something too big and too soft to have a shape, too sudden to defend from. It had happened from the deaf kids at school, the pillows, again, again, until he was dizzy and sick and stymied into complete inaction, standing only because there was nowhere to go. Irwin had said things about the bar fight, his money, and Leda. Vague as bellyache was his separation from Irwin's children; tormenting and without recourse

294

was the fact that his father was alive and no one had told him. "Marie, where are the kids? I made a mistake last night — I wanted to say — " No answer. The children were now so afraid of him that they took every hint of themselves far from his power to perceive. They hid; they disappeared. And no one noticed, and of the ache he felt at their leaving, no one saw for all their seeings and seeings.

It had been his plan this Sunday morning to take Leda on a walk around Aureole, but that had been the old Aureole, town and river and the trail of his miracle. He'd wanted to say to her: here is where I thought I could see because these streets were where direction was begun in me — second sense. He told her this after breakfast.

"Let's go, anyway," she said, "get out for a while. I'll call your mom — we can meet in town, take her out to lunch instead of her coming here. Only a mile from town, anyway. I'd like to get by ourselves — Sunday morning — small town. Americana. Very quaint. A novelty for me. Besides, we are both in the doghouse around here because of last night."

So Leda told the others their plan and they set out. The first thing they discovered was that no one had intended the people living in Prospector Heights to go anywhere on foot.

There were no streets or walking roads leading to town. They had to make their mile on the side of the highway, a half-gravel, part-roadside-part-earth that was extremely difficult to walk on; John's cane kept sticking and snagging, and lips of asphalt caught at his feet to trip him. After stumbling and almost falling several times, John stopped and turned to her. "Didn't you see this as we came?"

"I didn't notice it."

"Seeing is believing," he said. It was the hardest criticism he could give. How could they say they knew so much because of that so important, so bragged about sense, and yet know so little? Leda, beginning to know Deaf-blind style, responded to the anger beneath the innocuous remark. Her hand stuttered impatiently. "I am sick of being responsible for seeing every problem you can run into. Seeing means seeing *everything*. You will never understand that. When I came out this way yesterday, I saw mountains, trees, road, sky, ground, cars, people, everything in one big . . . altogether. Nothing in your experience is like what seeing is. When a sight is new you get the whole thing. Why didn't you alert me about studying the conditions of the roadside? If you want to go back, we will, and get Irwin to drive up with us instead."

"No," he said wretchedly, "not that." He sighed.

"Think of it as an adventure," she said.

That was just the point, that adventures were not for this place and these people; competence was. He was here to be knowing, successful, competent at last. He had brought Leda to help him be this with Irwin and Richard and Mama, but he had also wished intensely, he now realized, that Leda also see him in the circumstances of his skill. This he yearned for because she had seen him hospital-fool-and-madman, bound to bed, filthy and stinking and crying like a child. Now he felt like a child again. Yet again. "OK," he said, "adventure."

So they stumbled on, lucky when they could go on the worn places off the highway, of which there were more as they approached the town. They began to pass places. Suddenly and intensely there were cooking and food smells, as though he stood in someone's kitchen, but humorously out of place in the roadway. It made him laugh. "Burgers and fries," John said, "and Mexican. Now more Mexican — oh, there are two places." They stood for a few minutes while John played at Signing the menu by the smell. It was actually making him hungry again, while he evaluated the places. "Old grease — "

"Yes, but truckers eat here."

"Sure, I can smell the diesel."

They had passed the restaurants and were walking along the road when John was hit in the head and went sprawling.

It had been so sudden and complete that for a long moment he lay there, belly and legs and chest and face and his cane arm twisted under him in some way. He felt Leda moving over him with her hands, trying to move him.

"Leave me alone. I want to rest here. Stop it. STOP IT."

But she had seized his hand and was spelling into it. "Cars are stopping. They think you are hit. It's getting dangerous. Get up. *Please.*"

"I can't. I need to get my breath."

"Cars . . ."

"Tell them I'm OK. Make them go . . ."

She was gone. Slowly he began to breathe deeply and his head cleared. There was dust in his mouth and his eyes felt gritty. He had skinned many places. At last he was able to roll enough to free his arm. He got up and began to brush himself off. She was back.

"It's OK, and we're coming to a sidewalk. How do you feel?"

"Dusty and sore, but I'm all right."

"Sorry — Sorry. It was a tree branch and I did not notice. We should have asked Irwin to drive us. I only wanted to get away, not to have to ask him again."

He laughed. "You are getting deafer, dear; you are getting blinder."

On the sidewalks the going was much easier, but John's right knee ached and his chest felt sore where he had slammed it. They came to a gas station and he went to the men's room and cleaned up a little.

"How do I look?"

"Better. Still a little dusty," and she beat at his clothing.

"I should get that new kind of cane, electronic, radar . . ."

"Yes, but now . . ."

"Now we go on." He consulted his watch. "It took me half an hour to fall down and get up. We'll have to go quick or we'll be late for lunch with Mom."

So they set out again, on John's pilgrimage to retrace the steps of the miracle he had had when he was twelve. They were past the old high school and on their way to where the road turned downward, a place of more mine dumps and tailings, which Leda said were now dotted with fancy old-new houses, remodeled from nineteenth-century cabins and carefully maintained. "The road — "

"Looks old, original."

It was not straight, windface-windback at

all. It was off true about fifteen degrees; it was, as the maps said, south-south-west. How could that be? How could he have thought that this street was true running? His miracle, the whole miracle had started from this, the moment of knowledge all of a sudden, of true direction and its veerings from true, of degrees of difference. "This is *off*."

Leda tried to explain how such a thing could have happened. He realized that the road turned much sooner than he thought, the walk being not long at all and the downhill part, two miles long he had thought, was only half a mile toward sunrise down the hill that Aureole was built on.

"Wait a minute — here's a place you can stand and still look out over the roofs of town and see the river."

"From here?"

"Yes, looking over. Nothing else is in the way."

John had never truly understood "looking over" or "looking under" or "in the way," although there had been careful explanations by people over the years. He did know about wind and shadow and on these heights nothing shadowed the wind, which today was sun-warmed and lazy-breathing in a summer doze from the sundown and somewhat wind-face, just hair-ruffle now and then and face-cool because it was still morning.

So they stood "over" the town for a while, and at absolute stillness of body, John rested and let his senses free themselves. His right knee had been badly scraped, and his elbow and his chest were tight where he had breathed out suddenly in his smash against the ground. He was smelling the dust on the shoulder of the road, the hot street and . . . the . . . *roofs*. The tar-shingle, a memory smell so balance-daring and balance-desperate and exciting that it still made his nostrils tingle. Corson had taken them up ladders once, to the roofs of the school building, balance training, he said. Corson, strange in his hate, his hate a foreigner even to himself, daring them to be slow or off balance and therefore to die, as he once said in anger they should have, at birth. But Corson's hate had taught them "shadow" — what Leda called "loom" or "presence" — and perfected John's direction until it was true as the fish he had read of who could remember the way to find again one stream out of a thousand. And now John's mind strained to capture an idea, and suddenly it bloomed words.

"We are," he said, "at the height of the roofs. I can smell them. Direction, which is an absolute, is absolute also as to up and down. We climbed the hill. We are at the level of the roofs — "

"Yes," she said, "so over which I can see *out*. I can see the river."

"Well, I can smell the river, but I could learn an absolute height as well as direction; why not, beginning from . . . what?"

"Sea level."

He began to ask her questions. Relationships that had eluded him for years began to make sense, and all from that rooftop tang, hot shingles and tar, almost palpable in the heavy heat whose radiations were like a thinner water. So, once again, in the place where he had first experienced revelation, more revelation came. "Hallelujah, the hills," he said.

She nodded, Sign in his hand. "It's time to go."

Mama expressed horror at his fall. Noticing the rip in his pants and what must be some stains here and there, she pestered them with questions. How? Why? Where? until John said, "If you had fallen and weren't hurt, wouldn't you want people to stop talking about it?"

"I'm your mother and I worry."

"I don't feel so Deaf or so blind as I do when I'm here."

"If you were here more, we could get used to all you do and everywhere you can go."

"There are no opportunities here, no other

Deaf-blind people."

"I suppose I know that," she said, Leda's hands beginning to give a feeling of her personality in their pauses and slow talk, "but I don't know why you would want to be with blind and Deaf people who couldn't help you when you got in trouble. We never thought to get an interpreter for our own son. Last night in all the family argument, I saw what a good idea that was. I know Irwin was out of sorts about it. I think he felt the family — it's hard to talk in front of a stranger about family things. I know she's not a stranger to you, but we've never seen her before and perhaps we overreacted."

"You did," John said. "Why didn't you tell me Dad was alive?"

"I suppose it was a selfish reason. I like peace and quiet too much. I hate it when the family shouts at one another and has bitterness. My years with your father did that, I suppose, made me afraid of family anger. He is so ashamed, so awfully ashamed of what he did to you. . . ."

"I don't want to be part of his shame. This is now. I am OK as I am — why should *I* have to be ashamed?"

"I don't . . . you shouldn't."

"Then why do all of you treat me like a child?"

"Pity," she said. "We can't help it. We think about being Deaf and blind ourselves . . . and . . ."

"And what?"

"If it were me, I wouldn't want to live," she said.

An idea ran before its words and was gone. Another idea came. "Is that why you are angry, why Irwin is angry; because he puts all those conditions on being alive and expects me to put the same conditions on it, too, and when I won't he feels guilty and gets mad?"

"He still resents you. . . . Things I did foolishly when you were children, your father leaving . . ."

The idea came winding back, like Fourbuds, wreathing. "Why is Irwin suspicious of Leda?" A long silence. No one moved. John went on. "Leda had lots of men before me, and all of them heard and saw. She did not want money from them or me, either." Again, no one moved.

They had ordered lunch. Now it came and John sighed. He had been taught in school how to order food when eating out, not as he liked it but as it was easiest and most polite to eat in public. Leda had learned to tell him, to show him where things were. Some day he would have the courage to eat liver and onions and mashed potatoes instead of hamburger on a bun and french fries, no catsup — kid food. He found he was very hungry, though. He told Ma about the Indian restaurant to which they had gone. "Leda said it was so dark it didn't matter what my table manners were like."

He was feeling the strain in Mama; her air jiggled. Now and then she reached out and patted his hand and he felt her trembling. Why? Was she afraid of his torn pants, ashamed of his face? He asked Leda, spelling into her hand for whispered intimacy. "Maybe it would be better if you stopped smiling," she said.

SEVENTEEN

The smile. He did not know from where it had come, or what had been its original use. It was habit now, like the room-walk, assuring himself before he left that everything was in its place, or the way he patted down, checking his appearance; it was a kind of safety, a defense, and now so much a part of him he could not tell when he started to smile. Sometimes his face hurt, with Leda and her friends, with his family, or at the workshop, and his cheeks would cramp and ache. Now and then he would rest his face and someone at the workshop would ask him if he was angry or sad about something. He had not realized his face was cramping with the effort of his smile. Now he let it go, slowly, part by part. They finished eating. He knew his mother did not want to talk about unpleasant things, but he had written letters to her for years and she to him and never mentioned that his father was still alive or that he was as close as Gold Flume, able to be written to or seen, with a new wife. Likewise, she had never told him about great changes in town or about Warlock dying. What then had she written? Like the cards, like Mr. Sherline's cards: spring flowers, spring rains, fireplaces, the birds on the windowsill. Gratitude and love. Suddenly that was doubling back on him.

"Gratitude . . ."

"It's nice to show those things but you don't have to smile all the time," Leda said. "Sometimes my face hurts just looking at you."

For a moment he didn't understand, since his mind had gone on alone, working on what had been said, moving away into other mysteries. Leda had wanted him to write about his father's drunken rages. He had wanted to be told things. John suddenly felt the world threaten to lurch off center. It might be all right for Sighted and Hearing people to be angry and bitter sometimes; they did not depend on one another the way Deaf-blind had to. If the world slid off gratitude and love it would be very hard for the Sighted and Hearing but a catastrophe for the Deaf-blind. And the smile was part of that, somehow. Even here, with his mother, for whom he did not have to smile.

Look at what unpleasant thoughts had done to the weekend, the special days he had worked so hard for and yearned so long to experience. Everything for which he had come was changing, going vague and unpleasant, like touching even favorite things when your fingers had gone to sleep.

They stood in the afternoon-oven, outside the restaurant, talking about plans for the rest of the afternoon. John knew Leda was tired of touching him with interpretation all the time. He felt her tiredness; her fingers stumbled more and now and then forgot their message, hanging in midword as her attention, fugitive as all Sighted and Hearing people's was, fled away, wooed by the butterflies and melodies about which he had heard so much. The flight to Denver was at seven. He felt the loss. He had expected . . . what? A celebration, a sharing of his success, perhaps. To Irwin, the poems were only failures. He had dreamed of understanding his family as he understood Luke and Swede. Leda had told him a great deal about her auditions and her parts. Bit by bit, day by day, he had come to understand the times and pressures of her special life. It was clear to him that Mama and Irwin did not want his knowledge of their work, their days and pleasures. His niece and nephews were still afraid of him. He sighed. Leda signaled him. They were going to walk.

They had already started along, eastward and down, meaning, he thought, to walk on the new walkway that kept the town from touching the river. It was very hot, and they walked slowly, John in front, caning along with a steady assurance. The way sloped a little more steeply and curved around toward the left, and John went along feeling competent and wise because here there were curbs and sidewalks. Leda and his mother were talking, no doubt. Maybe it was easier that way, letting Leda tell about their lives, though John would have liked much better to be part of it. He walked, envying how they could walk and talk of serious, intimate things at the same time. Leda said she and her friends did this. His mind was taken up with noting his location and direction and the messages of curbs and fire hydrants, of duration and change. Suddenly, there was a wall.

His cane grazed it and he came close and felt. Not a building wall; there was no shadow. He felt for the top; it was a little higher than waist high; adobe or concrete and painted, by the touch of it. He would have to wait for them to show him which way, right or left. He waited, moving his hand above the top of the wall about four inches to feel the heat-water above it.

He waited. Five minutes. Ten. Fifteen. He had thought they were right behind him. Twenty. Where were they? The heat was making him sweat heavily and loss of energy would soon begin to disorient him. He knew the direction to Irwin's house and the distance; if he followed the river, keeping, as much as he could, out of the open, the sunswelter, he could go there. It was an easy walk — no more than two miles. He turned upriver, following the river wall. The heat was relentless.

Suddenly the wall stopped and John stepped over into dirt and branches. He went back, caning the walkway; it was rough, unfinished. It would be far too dangerous to go in-country. He turned sundownward. Shadow. It was a wall, a building. He retraced his steps, upriver from this start. Wall ended. Foolishly, he realized, he had taken no preparations, no notification cards: I AM DEAF AND BLIND, PLEASE HELP ME TO THE HIGHWAY. He had depended on Leda or Irwin or Mama to be with him. Who knew where the new construction ended or what it was, buildings, bridges, roads? He knew Irwin's address and while the walk was not too far for him to do, it would take a long time, since he didn't know the way. Perhaps he might get a taxi somehow. He still had a strong sense of orientation: river in front of him, town at his back. Irwin's house would be at his left, upriver. He realized that if the "country" had been the edge of town, he would find it here, too, if he tried to go downriver again. His best chance was to find the road on which they had come this morning; that was maybe ten or twelve blocks turn-around from where he was now. He turned and struck uphill, away from the river.

Up. His new understanding, the miracle of the roofs, helped to guide him. Up from the river. Time and again, walls interfered. He followed one road that wound over on itself like a snake, dead end of walls. Retrace. Patiently, in the sun's mouth. Here and there, where he could find cool-side, he rested in it, and a few times he sought out the smell of lawns being watered and went toward them, felt the blessing of the water that he knew was being sprinkled on them. Going as close as he dared, he tried to cool himself.

He was now extremely glad that he and Leda had walked this morning. He could never have found anything had they driven. His only real worry was that he might miss the road they had come in on, passing it or turning before. If he passed someone he might ask — could you take me to the highway? Few people knew how to spell into his hand or wanted to touch him to write the words there, which he could also read.

Cars, he thought. Because it was a highway there were sure to be many cars and trucks, too, even though it was a Sunday. He was glad. He had learned years ago to notice the weekends and the holidays by the number of cars and the vibrations in the walks and ways of a city. Monday mornings shudder the streets. Sunday mornings at eleven, the air trembles with bells, but at eight or nine, the molecules are unmoving in the wood and silent in the steel and a man caning can feel against his own deaf ears, his heartbeat, his individual human vibration.

He had reached a level — all the streets were somewhat level, but this street did not produce the slight middle-buckle of the others. He passed it and went up one more block — level this time, and so he came back, wondering if it was the main street through town, on which they had come this morning. He waited for truck-shake, car-shake. None. He went across again. Perhaps the next street. He felt it to be close. He had crossed when he was suddenly grabbed, his shoulder and his arm. "Who?" "Who?" Nothing. He tried to cane away. His cane was pulled from his hands. He tried to defend himself and maintain his orientation. But he was pushed around and then turned again and pressed, tripping and falling, into a car. The car went, he thought, away from his wish. He kept saying, "Don't rob me; I have nothing." He tried reaching for door handles, but there were none. He tried reaching to touch something, to get back his cane, to right himself. His arms were held and then his wrists seized and he was handcuffed and he half-lay in the car, going farther from Irwin's home-going, God knew where.

Stopped, pulled, not violently but forcefully from the car. Flanked. Held by each arm because of the handcuffs and no step-warnings, falling up the stairs and hold-pulled-dragged upward into someplace, and in his panic and dislocation, vibrating his questions at them. "Stop! What is it? Stop! What is it?" until he was grabbed around the elbows of his still-manacled hands and Leda's smell and body broke on him. She put her hand over his mouth and spelled "stop it" into his shackled hand. Stop it. He stopped it. Everything. He stood still, abject. To keep himself utterly still, he began to recite, close-lipped, teeth tight, one of his own poems to himself, to keep himself company. All the orifices of his body shrank and were pulled in. His head was down. The poem didn't work. He began, without vibration or word, to weep with

313

shame. At his back someone was working the handcuffs. He offered neither help nor resistance. When the handcuffs were off he did not take his hands away from behind his back. He was too exhausted for anger.

Leda took his hand. He offered no resistance. "This was wrong — my fault," she said. "I got scared. We were talking — you ahead of us. Then your mother stopped — there was a little garden — someone's flowers — OK, because we could see you going down the street and it was only a minute — no more than three or four, and you were *gone*. We went where we thought — where you had gone. We panicked. She started crying, hysterical. We went one way — there was a three-way street; we went up one — down the other. You weren't in any of them. . . ."

"I was by the river, on the walkway."

"Which place? Did you know that there are three places where the buildings come right down to the river and there are arcades . . . "

"No, I didn't know that."

"Your mom went crazy. I thought she was going to have a heart attack. No one had seen you . . . we kept asking everyone we saw. We knew you would want to be in the shade. . . ."

"There was no shade, only sun."

"We came back and your mom made me get the police. While we were walking all that long hill back we were hearing sirens — ambulance. We were sure . . . your mom was sure it must be for you. They found you all the way up on Prospector. . . ."

"That's near the highway, isn't it?"

"I guess so." There was a pause. She was asking. "It's a block from the main street, which turns into the highway. You were way over on the west end of town — "

"I was going to Irwin's. I knew you had to come there."

"We were so frightened. We didn't know if you were hurt or lost. We thought — we came to the police."

"They handcuffed me," John said.

"You were fighting — didn't you learn anything in the hospital about not fighting?"

"I didn't know who they were. Why didn't they put my hand on their badges if they couldn't tell me — "

"I guess they didn't think of that. They said you resisted."

"They held my hands — "

"I'm so sorry. Your mom . . . we were so scared."

"Am I arrested?"

"No."

"Where's my cane?" It came into his hands. "Can we go?"

"Yes. The police know your family. The

man here says that two of them went to school with your brothers — not the ones who picked you up. They want to take us home, to make it OK."

"In a police car?"

"No. This is Bud Dieter — he used to know you when you and Irwin and Rich played softball up at Prospector Park. He says we can go in his car."

A hand, slowly spelling on his. "Bud speaking. We're all real sorry. Please. It was a big mistake."

"Where's Ma?"

"Here." There was a brushing against him from the left and suddenly Mama was embracing him, kissing him.

"I'm all right," he said. "You go home, now." The presence withdrew with gratifying speed.

"She's a bit upset and dizzy. Overwrought. She says she'll take a cab because she lives the other way," Leda said. Her ordinary speed and finger tension had returned. Her manner calmed him a little. "She'll be at the airport this evening to see us off."

"It's getting late, isn't it?"

"Yes. It's almost five and we have to pack and get ready."

"Could you — " John said this to Dieter whose arm he had been holding since his

316

mother had left, "could you not tell Irwin what happened, that I was in handcuffs — not Irwin or Rich. Or anyone."

"No one will tell," the words from Leda, "they're as sorry as we are."

They rode to Irwin's, back the way John had come, back over his talented, "sighted" way, a way that had become blessed with a richer understanding of the ideas of level and height, back over what he had won with his whole body and mind. They hadn't praised what he had done; they hadn't even perceived it. What were those grand senses of theirs that did not see him or hear him going through new territory to an approach from a new direction toward a place he had come from for the first time this morning and before that with only the crudest directioning of a car?

When they arrived at the house, they got out and John sighed and said goodbye to Dieter, who shook his hand again. They went inside to pack and get ready to leave. Irwin brought the kids again, stiff as trees, to say goodbye to their uncle. Marie, in Leda's tired hands, told John she hoped he would come back often, that familiarity would ease the kids and with a longer visit she herself would learn to spell to him and that Catherine and Ma would pick up their skills with the need. This house would always be welcoming.

"Thank you." They hugged. He was getting tired of hugging his relatives. Touch was healing, loving, but here there was only the goodwill without communication. Goodwill alone was, at this moment, too thin a mixture.

Their plane ride back was without talk. Leda was exhausted, John sad and feeling lonely. His new spatial knowledge, that height was an absolute, had been hard won. He had also gotten at the last minute his father's address in Gold Flume. He would write a letter.

Meanwhile, he had not made love with Leda all the time they were away. When they got home he said, "Let's go upstairs and be together — "

"We've been together all weekend."

"You know what I mean."

"Too tired, too . . . " she let her hand trail the word.

"What?"

"Tired of touching. Too tired of touching. In a mood. Want to be left alone."

"You rested your hands on the plane."

"Can't you understand?" she burst out at him, "I've been torn apart by all this! You were *lost!* I had to call the police and watch you come into the station handcuffed and screaming. I had to get accused by your chilly-ass brother and prissy sister and dippy mother of living off you. I was *responsible* for you and I never had a minute, not one minute, to myself. No more. No more to-night. I am going to read *my* mail, take *my* bath, be *my* self tonight. I'll see you at break-fast," and she was gone and he could floor-feel her going away, her air quick in the mustiness of the closed house.

He got coffee, breaking a cup she had mis-placed on the shelf, and, after drinking the liquid, feeling it touch none of his aridity, put his head on the table and moaned, wondering in that dust-eating dryness, from where tears could come.

EIGHTEEN

Bedrail, beaten, questions by police, and the questions not in his hands, since he was tied, but in fire on his belly, in letters of acid, questions without answers. He woke lying on his hands and tangled in the bedclothes, pillow in his mouth. He lay quietly, until his fear slowed and the blood-tingle was gone from his hands so that he could feel the time. It was four; early, early morning. He sat up in bed and tried to read *The Red Badge of Courage* for a while. The book did not take him. The young man in it was sitting at a fire with soldiers from another troop and they were describing their own battle and its chaos, but the words were only words to John and had no transporting power. His own fear still clamped at his inner organs. It was warm in his room, even hot. This house kept its temperatures longer than the place he had used to live, like an angry person remembering.

He went downstairs and made tea, the herb

kind Leda had taught him to enjoy, and took it upstairs with him, feeling daring and special since to do this went against all the institutional forbidding of years. It was wonderful to sit up in bed and drink the warm sweet-grass liquid which, paradoxically, cooled him. He finished it and lay back down again but still could not sleep, so he got out his Brailler and his paper and sat in bed.

He wrote a poem about Charles Darnay, the hero of Dickens's book, but it was about Irwin, too. The poem said that he knew all about Charles Darnay, Sydney Carton, Captain Ahab, and nothing about Irwin and Mama. It was as angry a poem as he allowed his poems to be. This poem was like going overland and not on sidewalks. There was no security in the validations of curb and street and curb again.

They always met at breakfast, even though Leda had only toast and coffee. Because of his poem he was happy and he felt once again a companionable air flowing in the room. They didn't talk much. Leda's show had closed; it made her sad and restless. She told him she would be working as what she called a "temp." "I have an audition later in the week," she told him, "a cattle call." She had explained this term to him. By now his contact with her friends and the little bits of talk he had had interpreted by her and by Bennet had begun to give him clear ideas of the problems of being an actor and the reasons for her anxiety about auditions. John had never been aware of competing with anyone else for work or a place in school. Decisions came to him and he accepted them or did without. Leda's life was full of pitfalls, a metaphor from the Hearing world that he well understood.

John's work had been changed again. He was now sorting and sizing secondhand clothing, and it was work he did exceptionally well. Mr. Bisoglio had explained it carefully, step by step, showing John how to take the bundles of clothes that came tied in fifty-pound bales and sort them by texture and form into men's and women's, boys' and girls', and then using measuring rods, further sort them into sizes, all of which he then rebinned for cleaning. Mr. Bisoglio said that the clothing went to outlets all over the Southwest and that what was not sold then or given to poor people was sent to the poor in foreign countries. When he told Leda about his new work she laughed and said that she and her friends often shopped at those secondhand stores.

"Your slave dresses?"

"Right."

"Those clothes are for the poor."

"Who do you think *we* are?"

"Poor people are cold and hungry."

"I'm so hungry I'm thinking of renting out the top floor of this mausoleum to some more acting buddies."

"If actors, why not Deaf-blind people?"

"I never thought of that."

He never had either, but now it had been thought and said, and became an idea between them.

He began his routine life again, work and home, and as the days went on his disappointments in Aureole eased in him and its hurting edges wore smoother. Now and then he still found himself arguing with their hands in his mind, words they had not said and questions he had dreamed of asking and had not asked, and praise he had merited but had not been given. Sometimes he walked the walk again and this time made no mistakes. Now and then he also relived, without being able to stop it, the capture and handcuffing, but even that he felt would slowly lose its pain, the hands that gripped him would soften, the nausea at the memory diminish, watered away by the other memories only to be evoked in bits now and then in dreams or smells or other anguish. His "saloon brawl" and hospital time were too painful for him to think of at all, even after four months. He wrote another poem, this one not begging.

My shins are sore with sudden chairs
And sometimes dueling shadow with my
  cane
There is surprise of tables, shock of edges,
That dog-bite my legs;
I am one hell of a Deaf-blind man!

Where is he, that certain-stepper
Whose cane is a quick kiss,
Whose hands here, here, here, are fingers
  down a page
Reading — knowing — eating the facts
Of word and wall and doorway,
Master of sidewalks through thick-soled
  shoes,
King of roast beef and gravy;
Where is he?

At school I was always in the year behind
  him,
Sleeping in his bumpy bed that lay due
  north and south
To teach us east and west; I tried to touch
  him,
To pull him closer than my clothes.

The teachers said he left before I came;
The counselors say he is expected any
  minute;
Is there stimulating work, love making, a

> *dinner plate with peas*
> *That do not roll*
> *For that gifted man?*
> *Until he comes, world, world,*
> *Make do with me.*

One Thursday at work, John was sitting at lunch when he idly began to imagine the people who had worn the clothes he was sorting. He had to do the work too quickly to think of this while it was happening, but sometimes a special garment would make him aware for a quick moment — pregnant — a dress with pleats from the collar, a little woman because the dress was so short. A fat man and one who sat a lot — the seat was smooth and worn with his sitting. Maybe a judge, steady and powerful as he presided in these vast pants to which there was no jacket. A judge would not want to wear a jacket under his robes. John had learned about robes from his reading. He thought of the robe as a bathrobe, but not made of bathtowel-material. A little girl was here, busy as her ruffle, amazed at a world in which there were buttons on a dress that didn't button anything; and later her sweater, all pilled with wear. It came to him that if he were to study a garment and describe the person in a poem, it might be interesting and would not plead or explain or defend. Someone said "Clothes make the man." In his poem, the people would be proven by their clothes.

Impulsively he got up and took the judge's pants out of the pile he had not yet bundled and began to study it with his fingers. Smoothness at the pockets, a road worn there by the hand two or three thousand times. The man had been right-handed, but maybe not a judge, or if a judge, one who suffered pain. The wallet back pocket was worn and enlarged. If he sat a lot, as the threadbare seat indicated, it must have been forward or the wallet would have pressed against the place where the joint in the backside was. John knew this pain from his own experience. He smiled. He held the pants up. A short man. The top of the man's head would be at the level of John's nose. The waist had been taken in one time, let out and taken in again, at another place, the stitching cruder the second time. His wife had left him and he had to do the sewing himself. John felt the vibration of the bell and went back to work, but the reality of the judge and his goodbye wife continued with him into the afternoon.

It was this circumstance that later made him think he might learn Leda more through her clothes. He got this idea riding back home in the van. Had she been fatter and then thinner like the judge had been? Was she messy or precise in the way she sewed her buttons? How did she walk? Alma bounded when she walked, and while Leda's steps seemed smooth, she was a stopper, coming abruptly to a thing and stopping suddenly with no slowing down. What part of her foot first met the ground, and when she was away from him, not guiding, did she grind or glide or come down like Fourbuds, all the foot at once?

When he came home, he telescoped his cane and put it in its place, greeted Fourbuds, and checked her dish, put his lunchbox in the kitchen and then went up to Leda's room, to the closet where her clothes were and her shoes and the fragrance of herself, essences of the soap she used and the oils and of her own body and hair, well known and well loved. It was the loss of his mother's fragrance that had given him the keenest pangs of homesickness when he had been sent away to school and it was in her closet that he had hidden himself most often from his father's angers.

This closet was jammed and messy. The soft fabrics she favored, the gauzy cotton blouses and skirts, were bulging off hangers or being held by the press of other clothes. Some had fallen to the floor and lay almost in bundles, among them, shoes and slippers, sandals, mukluks, boots, all single. At home often she wore long skirts; he used to laugh at the clinginess of them and the denim and coarse muslin slave clothes, all unironed. He had offered to iron them many times as he ironed his own shirts, carefully, having been taught to do it by Mrs. Pfansteihl. Leda always laughed and said no. He found a skirt, rolled up in a ball on the floor. He unrolled it, wrinkled and without body, insubstantial. These were not at all like the judge's clothes or the clothes of the little girl or like most of the clothes he came across at work. The waistband was limp and stretched. The woman who wore these things did not like confinement or stiffness, crisp collar edges, no smooth, tight-woven things, but she liked embroidery, ruching, smocking, soft lace collars, and wide, loose fabric belts. Her shoes, even there, hating what was stiff and confining, the sandals, which . . .

Her hand was on him, angrily. He was being turned around so that he had to scramble up. "What are you doing here?" The speed of anger. "Why are you here? This is private. This is a private place!"

He stood without defense. His idea of learning her led back to the clothes he had been sorting at work, a poetry idea then linked to love. He saw this now as a progression so complicated that it was beyond any explanation. "I thought . . ." and then he felt the truth of what he had been doing. "I know all of your private body places. We make love all over our bodies and you taught me to do that. Now I wanted to know you better — things from your clothes . . ."

"No. First because . . . it's asking too much. We don't do such things. It's . . . it's *obscene.*"

"Obscene?"

"Well, too private. Second, when we make love, I'm *there*, giving permission."

"Yes, I see that, about permission. Will you give me permission then, and . . ."

"No!"

"Why not?"

"It's my *closet.* My *clothes.*"

Why? What was this mystery? To what had he blundered in? Clothing on the body — clothing off the body — surely when clothing is off the body it is *less* personal. . . . He had learned some of her clothing secrets already; that her straps left ridges in her shoulders because her breasts were heavy against them; that women have to struggle more than men in dressing, putting their hands behind their necks and backs to button blouses and snap those harnesses; that they wore all kinds of metal clips and plastic clips and sliders in

329

their clothes — all those personal things had been wonderful to him, connected as they were to her own warm secrets, her body planes and folds, warmths and coolnesses, odors and incenses. "I don't understand."

"You don't have to. This is private, personal, mine."

He left her room and for a day or so there was a coolness between them. Again it had not been explained to him; again he did not understand why she felt the way she did.

Tuesday of the next week, Leda came home soon after John had put his things away, ringing the vibrating bell to alert him. He came down and into the circle of her arms, moving air, an energy that was almost current.

"A call! A wonderful opportunity!"

"What?" He knew she would not tell him at first. She always started to explain at an unexpected place, so he smiled in himself as he read her beginning.

"I've been a bitch since we got back from Aureole. Felt out of work so long I can't even remember my last *theater* job. It makes me angry and scared, bills coming in and this big house to keep. I've been worried sick."

He started to say, "Why didn't you tell me?" but she was going on, and as she did, he realized that her spelling and Sign had improved enough so that she was now almost able to keep up with ordinary speech.

"You know I went for an audition last week — "

"Cattle call."

"Yes, and nothing happened. At these things people are around, standing around, who seemed to have wandered in off the street. So — one of those stand-around people had come in from *Gray's Anatomy*, which is a New York play that's been running here. . . . Well . . . "

Of all the things John loved about Leda, this dancing, jumping, pound-the-hand excitement was the thing he liked best. Her joy was that total, spontaneous thing he remembered having once had in hearing. He loved this sudden example of it, unrehearsed. "Yay!" he said.

". . . and *I'm continuing the tour!* Phoenix, L.A., and then up north, San Francisco, Portland, Seattle."

Sudden knowledge sometimes opens on a fall. "It means you won't be here — "

"Not for three weeks or so, but I'll tell you where I am and what's happening all the time. I'll send you postcards, and I'll call you at work, when I can . . . "

It sounded so happy off her hands and he felt as though he was receiving it all in the rain. "And when . . . "

331

"With holdovers, three or four weeks. The leads have commitments in September."

"September!"

"Don't be difficult. I didn't *say* September. This is money for us and very important for my career."

"But . . . "

"I'll take care of everything before I leave — lights, phone messages, all of it, and it will only be for a few weeks at the most and I know that with you here, I'll feel secure about the house. . . ."

He stood in the rain, letting it chill him.

"Stop doing that."

"Doing what."

"Looking stark and tragic."

"You complained about my expressionless face — "

"It's your whole posture, Beaten Boy Number Six."

"I can't act glad when I don't feel it and *you* said I never should."

"OK, OK."

They sulked. Dinner was spiritless. Leda asked if he had any new poetry, and he was suddenly shy about giving her the one he had written. Perhaps she would get angry, thinking he had criticized her. She had slapped his hand with eagerness, saying be honest, show feelings, show anger and impatience, weep for the beating of years ago, but not the leaving that will be . . . when?

"When will you go?"

"The day after tomorrow."

"OK," he said.

"Mary Margaret Martyr."

"Sad, that's all," he said.

"OK, it's allowed."

So she left, and the air in the house closed over where she had been. Nothing moved but what he moved and what Fourbuds moved at his ankles. Nothing was said but what he said.

For the first few days he took revenge. He cleaned and arranged the cabinets in the kitchen in decent order. He ordered the refrigerator as it should be, so he never would have to putter about and wonder. Cans and dishes were marked and God bless the many shapes of plastic. And he violated her express directions, murmuring about it as he did so, by going up to her room and hiding himself in her closet among her soft, cobweb clothes, most of which she had left, having told him that theater people learned to travel light. Even Fourbuds seemed to go ghostly and insubstantial, weaving across his feet in her old gesture of comfort.

NINETEEN

John was writing things — he could not call them poems and he no longer even tried to show them to Mr. Sherline, but they were things about being Deaf-blind:

Sam told me that for the sighted, things get bigger as they get nearer and smaller as they get farther away. The opposite is true with us.

Name any year you will, and someone in our group will say: That's the year I became Deaf-blind.

He wrote a series of haiku about the seven senses and for the first time in his poetry, concentrated on each. It made him feel happy to read his own reality back to himself.

One evening after work he went to his print typewriter, set his hands carefully on the keys, and typed.

Dear Dad. How are you? I am fine. I am very happy at the news that you are not dead but live in Gold Flume and are in business there and that you see Irwin and Mom, and Richard and Catherine. I would like to see you, too. I work, did you know that? I write poetry, too, and I am living independently. I wanted you to know those things about me.

I was in the hospital because of something that happened in a bar. Irwin may tell you and if he does, please let me tell you my side. Also I am in love with a Sighted and Hearing woman. Irwin and Mama may tell you something about that. Please let me tell you my side.

Please remember that I am a good person with many talents and there are special things about me that even most other Deaf-blind people do not have. ~~For example~~

Continued good health to you and your new wife.
Your son, John Moon.

Then time slowed. It went back to the speed it had been before he and Leda had moved in together, but now John found he could barely endure its slowness. It was like a dying pulse, clogging and stopping as it fought death to a standstill. His work seemed

335

more routine than ever. Poems stopped at the brain. Food lost its flavor.

Twice a week Bennet came and played Leda's message tape and asked John how he was and went through the house checking for leaks and other problems. The first two or three times, John offered him coffee, but Bennet refused in a way that made John unwilling to ask him again. John got the mail every day and Bennet also went through that for significant bills. After two weeks Bennet read a postcard for John from Leda. The play was not very good but had a good cast and was getting pretty good reviews. They were being held over in California, where the weather was wonderful and there was always the possibility of getting to the beach. In Bennet's hands the words sounded cold and ritual and John found himself feigning a happiness in them that he did not feel. After another week there was another postcard. She was on the road. The heat was miserable, she had had no sleep, and there was a lot of dissension in the cast because of bad accommodations and the habits of the leads. Bennet's hand made her message and then pulled away.

"What is it this time? Why are you angry this time?" John asked him.

"I'm not angry; I'm busy. I have to go now." The letters snapped away, unforgiving.

"You can spell, even Sign a little. What do you have against Deaf-blind people?"

"Not Deaf-blind people, you. Leda and you. I think you're using her."

"How? You mean making her do things she doesn't want to do? Cheating her?"

"Yes."

"I pay rent here and there are things I pay for that I didn't have to in my old place. We are together because we love each other."

"Love. Since you've been here I've seen her always worried and nervous. Even before you moved in — all the time — taking you around, running to help at the hospital after that brawl you got into — I know it's her propensity for picking up — uh . . . She came back from that 'weekend' of yours looking like a ghost."

"I know the weekend was hard for her. She told me. It wasn't supposed to be like that. It was supposed to be fun for both of us; some interpreting, yes, but fun, too, it was supposed to be . . . " John found he could not say what he wished. It was too complicated.

Bennet spelled so quickly that the letters broke and it was hard to read them. "Take advantage . . . used her . . . exhausted and worried and you lost and wandering around . . . "

Something evil-tasting rose in John's throat; something he had not eaten. "I wasn't lost," he answered, fearful of vomiting over his speech. "I wasn't lost once. They were gone and I began to go back home." Even as he spoke, vibrating, which meant he was too loud, defending himself, he knew that the accusation was not the cause of his pain. Leda had told Bennet, had confided John's secret; she had walked, Deaf-blind, past his triumphs and his accomplishment and told all about his shame and humiliation, *her* embarrassment. Was there more, too? Had she told about his handcuffing, his being pushed into and pulled from cars . . . how much more? The anguish of remembering was made more bitter in John by the memory of being held by the metal and held down by the men. He began to moan. He couldn't help it. It overwhelmed him so quickly that he had no defense against it. He stood before Bennet in Leda's living room, to which he had come as a sharer, and let the vibrations go. After he had quieted and apologized and gone to get some tea for Bennet, he came back to find that for some unknown period of time, he had been alone. Bennet had gone.

His loneliness was becoming obvious to people at work. Mr. Bisoglio mentioned it and Bernard hit him in a different way, pityingly, he thought. If Deaf-blind people were so bad at showing their emotions, how was it that everyone now knew so much about his feelings? Even Alma came from the fourth floor one lunch hour, and having found him by striking his shin with her cane, stood before him and began to talk right away.

"I — Luke said you in bad trouble now. We Leda don't like. You come us weekend, stay over Luke, eat, talk, have fun good way."

He asked her if she had moved into Luke's room together. She shook her head wildly. "Weekend. Saturday night only. My family get minister. Swell boom-boom Signer, like hell but he bite his finger skin all rough like little boy, tell me bad about make sex in bed me-Luke. We go Saturday night. Luke brother say OK Saturday night. Big bed. You come I — Luke." The Sign was not her old babyish fingering; it used to be like someone with gloves trying to tie his shoes. She was quicker and the words, though still babyish, had a form to them in the lifts and falls of the hand. Luke was teaching her as John had hoped, a while ago, that Leda would teach him. How he had ached for that world; how he still ached, although it had proven infinitely more complex and baffling than he had dreamed, blooming with angers and envies he could never decipher. The acts of seeing and hearing seemed to scatter the intellect, not focus it.

"Wait — " he said, and came over a rim on

to an idea that was waiting there. "Leda and I have a place. It's a whole house. Kitchen, living room, bedroom upstairs. Why don't you visit *me* for the weekend?"

Even as he spelled the words, he regretted them. He liked Luke a great deal but he still had trouble even tolerating Alma, and if the two of them were lovers the way he and Leda were, it would be difficult to suffer their joy as it ground against his loneliness. There was also the sudden clutch of nervous anxiety. Maybe they would fight. But the words had been said and he fought the desire to change them. This he knew he could do easily by confusing her with more, or by burying her in language she did not understand. Then he could claim she had been unable to interpret him. He hung for a breath or two on his wish and then let the breath go. "Well?"

"Me-Luke talk. Tomorrow come you tell."

Through the day he alternated between feeling better about what he had done and feeling worse. Living with Leda had, in some ways, reminded him of his school days, the time when his social life had been at its fullest, though it had also been at its most savage, ridiculed for his blindness by the deaf students and for his deafness by the blind. Did he prefer arguments and even savagery to the nothingness he was feeling now? The years working alone had been bearable only because he had so few expectations beyond his work and because reading and creating poetry had occupied him so fully. Leda had torn John's world open while turning it inside out, and now, as occasionally happened with his clothes, he did not know which way his life was to be worn.

Still, it was his house and he would be able to say what went there; when he was to be left with his reading and when he could be available to them.

Alma returned the next day. "Deal," she said. "We come Friday after work Saturday Sunday stay. Go work Monday. Home us."

"Deal," John said.

It was nice showing Alma his house after work, then waiting for Luke, Luke's arrival, walking the house, cooking, sitting out after dinner in the junk-perilous backyard. Slowly, hour by hour, John was beginning to see beyond Alma's crude and sometimes incomprehensible Signs to a kindness and humor that had no words to frame them. Struggling to give birth to an idea, she would often pick up any word at all, so that the more words Luke taught her, the wilder she flailed away among them and the further she got from being understood. When Luke and John didn't understand, she sometimes got frustrated and hit their hands away in a rage of impatience and sometimes she cried, but John could see, beginning to be born in her, the first understanding of the power of words to carry meaning from far off, like the scents, pleasant or unpleasant, by which he could tell the days of garbage collection on the block. He could also recognize that Alma's love for Luke and her wish to please him were the reasons she was so dutiful at words and meanings. In some way this disappointed him. For herself she would have been happy making her needs known, easily as Fourbuds: being soothed at irritable moments with caresses, food, water, and the warm corner. Love had thrown her out of Eden into worrying about the distinctions between steal, take, borrow, and lend; between wish, want, need, and hope-for.

Or had it been an Eden? When the pain of thwarted communication was on her, Alma could tear at them like a wild thing, and on Saturday she vibrated so badly that on Sunday afternoon a neighbor came and told them through his eight-year-old daughter's spelling that the neighbors thought a woman was being kept and tortured in their backyard. John told Alma that for the privilege of being with him and Luke outside, she must never, never vibrate at all. She sulked but complied.

They left Sunday night. It had been friendly and happy and even exciting. John invited them for the next weekend and they accepted.

Wednesday evening. Bennet again. This time his Sign was made like chopping cotton. "The neighbors talk about wild parties here. The man next door was out in his yard now. Told me they nearly called the police. You and your friends."

"Only two friends — Deaf-blind also — " John stood, his mouth open to speak, and realized he had no way of showing Bennet what had happened or Alma's history in wordlessness. John had been fortunate, and he told this to Bennet, that he had been a special student, that he had had interpreters and teachers helping him since childhood. He tried to say this quickly, feeling Bennet's position change and change again, the foot-weight going from one to the other as though the impatient man was miming his departure already: walk away and be gone. Then John said, "When I moved here, Leda said that she could have her friends and I could have mine and that whenever I wished, my friends might stay over and visit. And before she left we talked about having no rooms here that weren't also for Deaf-blind people staying. To help with the rent."

Bennet did not answer and then he said

slowly and with his chop-anger slowed with contempt, "I don't like you. I think you're moving in on a good thing. Leda is a sucker for hard-luck stories. Her husband was a hard-luck story. Walter Kadama was another one. You. They smell it, some way, that she will take care of them."

John wanted to hit Bennet but he said, "I pay rent here. She told me you had said this to her. I do the dishes and the cleaning and the wash. I clean up after parties I'm not invited to. I love Leda."

"Keep the neighbors from having to call the police," Bennet said. "The man said next time they would." And he left. John sat thinking for the rest of the evening.

John waited the three weeks Leda said she would be away. Then there was another week. Held over, Bennet said. Then another week with no news, and still another. Held over, Bennet said again. John knew there were many means for Leda to reach him from miles away. She might get in touch with him through Mr. Bisoglio. Why didn't she? Even the postcards read through Bennet's unwilling hands had stopped.

And at last, suddenly, she was here again, all of her at once, smell, arms, the hair struggling against the ribbon, the whole body, shattering his loneliness, complete as though she had never been away. And she was full of talk. The producer, the other stars of the show, the city . . . cities, the reviews, the play, its writer. They talked for an hour and Leda went up and had a bath and they talked in the bath while John soaped her back and she draped her bath-warm, soap-hand, wet in his to talk as she lay in the tub. Then they went to bed, to meet one another face to face and hand to hand and all his body to all hers. She pulled his pain from him.

He lay in the bed, drunk with joy and sated in the middle of the day and marveling at it. Leda had gone downstairs to look around and make them some coffee. She was gone a long time, so long that he got up and washed and got dressed. He was almost finished when she was up to him. He heard her speed pulsing up the steps and across the bare floor. The words were quick and efficient but the sense was missing. "Bennet. Messages. My phone messages. Two weeks. TWO WEEKS! Bisoglio. I called him at home. Emergency flight, if you want."

"What?"

"We can take two days . . . I can, that is."

"What, what is this?"

"Your brother. This is about your mom. Two weeks ago she had a stroke."

TWENTY

Between the arrangements, Leda told John something of what had happened.

The messages had been sent to her telephone tape. Bennet had come twice a week to play the tapes and call her if there were anything professionally important for her to know. He had chosen, why she did not know, to understand this favor in a very narrow way, and when the message had come two weeks ago, for John, Bennet had ignored it.

"My brother could have gotten me at work — "

"Yes, that was *my* fault. When we were in Aureole, I had told him to call here instead, because you had not gotten some of his messages before. We had made that arrangement and he had followed it. He had called twice. I suppose he would have called your work number if things had been worse, but I talked to him as soon as I found out, and in that conversation he said things were much better than they had originally thought. Your being there was never urgent — your mom was not in danger of dying. Now, she's better than they first thought she would be. Irwin wanted you to know. What I can't figure out is why Bennet would be so stupid about not telling you."

"I don't have that problem. Bennet thinks I'm living off you. Using you, he said."

They got a car this time. Leda said it was Bennet's. They drove the up and down way to Aureole, a way of traveling so different from the plane trip as to declare almost a different destination. Now the westward sundown nature of the route became obvious and the subtle windward pull, by this trustworthy road, had something witty about it. The town had come, must have come, before the road, or else the road would have been straight and would have turned at ninety degrees, the way city grids turn, cornered like sheets of paper, cabinets, books, windows, houses. City people love corners; John loved them, too — a corner is a great truth in location and direction, a thing such as Hearies described in their music, and the pleasure they got from their music was built on the same recognitions and relationships that John experienced in space. He wanted to think about this as they rode westering, now straight at the sundown, now rounding something so that the curve went north or south for reasons he could not see but could sometimes feel, the way music must be felt rather than known. He thought he must know this because there had once been music in him and he still repeated a song he had been taught years ago when he had his hearing:

I had a little nut tree,
Nothing would it bear
But a silver nutmeg
And a golden pear.

He had long since forgotten how the song went up and down and where it changed its notes but he had not lost the sense of wit and direction in songs, one that agreed with his learned truths about location and direction, as people made their roads. The roads were made by man, after all, with the same emotion with which they made their music — going away and coming home.

John was working a bit to keep thinking of his idea because he did not want to think about his mother, hurt and suffering; his brothers angry at him; and his ineptitude. Whenever he was not actively seeking another thought, the worry, sadness, and anger would be there, as obstructing as the turnstiles at the zoo.

The trip took five hours. They got out at

Windom for coffee and again at Chinaman's Creek, where they walked around. Campers were there, Leda said, but none of them came near him so he had no perception of them.

And suddenly, because it was summer and the car's windows were open, the memory burst on him, and he flinched with surprise and then joy. The air had changed. The quality of the air and its temperature and pressure had changed. They were in the canyon of the Ute. "This is better than the airplane," he said to her, and she told him, one-handed, a little of the look of it, the black cliffs made of slick rock that broke cleanly, as though chiseled and built into dream cities. Even the trees seemed dark — fir, mostly, and blue spruce. To the left of the road, sluggish and unwilling, the river, at its autumn level. "What is your reality of this place?" she asked. He knew he could not tell her, but the way the question had been put made his lungs crowd his heart with pleasure. This was shadow in its richest manifestation, a difference in some body touch, air against the face, pressure in the hollow bones in the face, and one that intimated that the world was there beyond the farthest reach of finger end or even cane. Smell did that. Shadow did that. He grinned into the wind of the car's speed and repeated to himself "coming home . . .

coming home." For once, the proof did not need to be brought to him by someone's telling. There were moments when he was sick to death of people's telling. This was as evident, as palpable as eating a ripe peach. John remembered then that this trip was not for pleasure, but he could not forget the joy of coming-home-canyon-shadow and Leda's knowledge that his was a full reality, one of a number of equally valid truths, and he resolved to write a poem in praise of it.

Stop and go. Stop and go after they had emerged from the canyon and gone into the town. Leda had to find the hospital. Vision had been described to John many times. Why didn't they see where things were and then go closer to them by the streets until they were there? He had learned, however, not to ask Sighted such questions, especially in the process of this going and stopping. Both Martin and Sam had given explanations, but John still had no real understanding of what they had said.

At last Leda came to a place; the slowing and turning ninety degrees against true direction made John know that they were in an entrance and parking place and they were at the hospital. They got out and went into the strange cool of air-conditioning where all odors change and the breathing slows and

thickens. With the odors of the air-conditioning were also many, many others, all alarm-
ing, drawing on memories of accidents and
illnesses, a hibernating sleep-body smell, the
smell of the sweat sweated in pain, of urine,
medicines, starches, and buffing wax for the
slick floors. Elevator, hall, hall. For the second time John felt the bite of fear. This fear
was not of what he knew, the way one fears
beating or burning or familiar losses, but of
what was not known and, as such, brought
shame with it and self-impatience. They
walked in the hall. Leda was hesitating. He
had hold of her arm because wide-sweep with
the cane was impossible with so many people
around.

"What's going on?"

"Just trying to find the room . . . " she said.
They turned and went through a door, which
she held open.

John's cane hit . . . what? . . . a chair. The
room was small; he could feel the loom of the
four walls and the trapped-air vibrations that
said the space was full of furniture or equipment. Ah — the bed. A big bed — high and
heavy. He put his cane away, telescoping it
until it would fit into his pocket. He moved
hands over the bed. No hand came to guide
him until Leda's did, putting his hand on a
hand that lay almost at his thigh and through

bars. He began to struggle to pull the bars away, feeling for a hasp or bar to move, in growing frustration. "Stop," she said. The Sign was forceful in command against his hand, "I'm getting the rail." There was a long pause while she struggled to move the bars. When she did and he felt them go, he reached for Mama's hand again. It was small like Mama, but there was no other resemblance. It lay uninterested and unresponding in his and too hot and with none of the old importunity and enthusiasm. John leaned in. Her smell was foreign, alien, enemy, even. "Is this my mother?" he said out loud, and again, clearer, "Is this my mother?"

Leda's hand was quickly spelling, "Stop that. She may not be able to speak, but she can hear you."

"I want to know — "

"Of course she is — "

Nothing was the same. The strange smells repelled him, bathroom and medicine smells warned him away, but he could not explain the absence of the smells he had always associated with his mother. It was as though she was already dead. He was, all this time, standing very close, in confusion. Leda said into his right hand, "Kiss her." John didn't want to, but he leaned in closer and put his head down against the woman's cheek and finding it, turned his face to find her cheek and kiss it. He did not feel anything familiar.

Someone behind him. A hand, not Leda's. He got up and turned around. Catherine. Her Sign was rough as ever, familiar and loved. He fell into her arms. She led him out into the hall. "Mama's very sick, but she will recover most of her motion." Leda had come out, too, John realized, and was speaking to Catherine. "Even now she can move both hands," Catherine said. The Sign was very clumsy. Leda took over, straight interpreting. "She has motion and strength in her legs. The stroke was an unusual one in an unusual place in her brain. Mama can't talk now and it makes her frustrated and angry. Part of her mind has been affected and she gets angry for no reason. I think she was angry just now and that's why she didn't want to show you that she *can* raise her hand and use the other one."

"She was angry because I didn't come to see her."

"Leda called me and explained all that. I told it to Mama. She knew about it."

"But she was angry. She was angry because I didn't come."

"I don't think so, Johnny. I think she was mad about something we can't even guess. She was so sick those first days I don't even think she knew where she was or who we were. Please don't feel bad, and don't think it was Dad's visit that had her so upset."

"Dad's visit?"

"Because of your letter."

"*What is that?*"

"Shhh . . . you're yelling." Leda's special gesture. "Too loud."

"Oh, God — please . . . " he said.

Leda went on quickly and efficiently. Dad had gotten John's letter. He had called from Gold Flume and talked to Mama and they had argued again, Catherine thought. The argument might have been about John, but it might not. Mama was crying and Dad still guilty and ashamed at what he had done and saying that he could not see John because of the shame. Catherine had not been there, neither had the others, but she had pieced this together, after Mama's stroke, from Dad's new wife, Colleen. Mama had been talking to Dad before he left for work. She had gone downtown to work herself but had come in staggering, and people thought she was drunk. Then she had collapsed at her desk and been taken to the hospital. There they said she had had a stroke. Irwin had called John. Two times, to Leda's message tape. They had waited out Mama's more dangerous days, and the effects of the stroke were beginning to pull away like a glove that thickens the fingers being slowly removed to allow motion and recognition, life again. Day by day more and more was coming back, Catherine said. One thing was not returning — speech. Mama heard everything and she could point to words on a board to express her wishes, but there was no sign of returning speech and the sounds she made were unintelligible.

As Leda took Catherine's words and smoothed them out for him, amplifying, an idea woke in John that Mama might, if the speechlessness continued, learn — be taught to Sign. The idea was suddenly real as a taste in the mouth. He became excited and began with his free hand the fanning motion that Leda so hated.

"Now what?"

"You see — I think — Mama might Sign now. *Use* Sign. I could teach her spelling and we could get someone else to teach her, too, because if she can use her hand to point, she can spell, and she wouldn't have to use her voice, bypass her voice problem entirely, and after spelling, she could Sign, and if she practiced . . . " He was making ideas one after another as he often did when he was excited. He felt he had learned this from Leda, in the Hearing world, to be creative, as she said, full of ideas and plans. He thought not all of the plans might be good, but the important thing, she had once said about what she had called brainstorming, was to get as many ideas as possible. This had happened in her Improv class and she had told him about it. Now as he was telling her all of his ideas she stopped him abruptly.

"What are you doing? You are getting all excited."

"I am brainstorming."

"This isn't the time." He felt her impatience, a cording in her hands, sweat, something hurried and angry in the word-end-flip. "No one knows what her condition is; now is not the time."

Again John was puzzled-thwarted. He had questioned Leda carefully about this brainstorming, first because the word had suggested so many things to him and then because, when she had explained it, it seemed really to have been a Deaf-blind idea. Deaf-blind tried one thing and then another, made one explanation and then another, trying again and again for what was sensible and would answer their question, guessed and guessed again when people's words seemed meaningless, when door and wall were not where they were expected to be and the cane hit empty air instead of the welcome landmark. Leda had said that people used this brainstorming any time an answer was needed;

he remembered the conversation clearly. They had been outside at the time, in her cluttered little backyard, and he had been standing facing windward and sundown and it was not yet night; the sunwarm had survived after the first breezes of the evening against his face. The sun had also warmed the rust-roughened tools so that even as he remembered, he could almost smell the old brass and iron and the pimpled rust. She had said: "You can use this method any time you want and it is very creative."

Not now. He felt the anger wake again, that same anger that sometimes shot up from his belly and out his mouth as vibration. He bit it back. She was saying, "We — they — don't know what her brain will be ready to do; it's too soon, too early to know if she will be able to use that kind of help."

"*I* would help her," John said, "*I* would be the one this time."

"Yes, we know that's what you want."

At certain edges corners meet severely. Sun-facing and sun-siding truths close on one another to a knife-edge. Other corners come from sides that begin, long before their edges, to state their truths. Like aromas they come, a whiff, a hint, more and more surely so that a hand or foot can never tell precisely when the turn is made. Ideas were like these two kinds of edges. Some ideas make their connection thought-to-thought at that sharp, perfect meeting. Some come hint by hint, bending into form without any single moment's consciousness: here it is. Some ideas are like falling a sudden sprawl; for some, balance loses itself only after a long struggle.

The idea about teaching Signs and finger-spelling to Mama had been a knife-edge, a sprawl, but sudden falls are as total as slow ones and the idea had claimed him. Back in her room, John reached again for Mama's limp hand. This time there was a little motion in it, a waving as though to wave to him, or wave him away. Slowly, gently, he Signed into her hand, "Mama, I love you and now I want to help you to speak."

There was no response. He did not really expect one. Someone else was there then, and Leda was saying, "Nurse says there are too damn many people in here. She told everybody our visits had to be one by one."

"Did you tell her there was a special reason — " but John was cut off and shoved somewhere and before he could think, he was being pulled out the door.

There was something of a family conference at Irwin's in the evening. Leda had told John that she could stay only Saturday and half of Sunday. Either he drove back with her

or he would have to make other arrangements; she had a performance on Sunday
night, "and interpreting you and your family
is no vacation. They are nice people, don't get
me wrong . . . it's just . . . draining."

"Why?"

She paused a long time before she answered.
"You want so much — descriptions of the
place and people's movements and locations.
What is put in? What is left out? Which of all
the sensory truths gets included? The choice
— it's the choice that's so wearing and difficult."

It was hard to understand what she was saying, even harder to believe it. In the end, he
didn't. He didn't think she was lying but he
put her statement into the place where his fiction was, where Mr. Micawber lay in jail and
Sydney Carton substituted himself for Charles
Darnay.

That night John had a nightmare. It was a
memory of something that had happened
when he was a boy, only the happening was
ugly with dream-fear and without its real end.
It was the Junglegym dream. He was in a Junglegym, bars here and there. He climbed
over, under; there was no end, and no form.
His left-hand — right-hand guide made no
sense because there was no solid wall, no end
or edge or limit, only climbing and crawling,

and he had also lost all his sense of direction and had no idea if he had cornered somewhere and was now moving toward an edge or the center, if indeed there were those things. Exhaustion and terror built in him. The ground was hard on his hands and knees and no one seemed near. He began to perceive a wobble in the ground, first faintly and then with more sureness as the wobble became more pronounced. The Junglegym was on an island in either air or water. Its middle, therefore, was the mass of bars and the hard pavement; at its edges, death. He woke vibrating and strangling in the sheet; he had thrown his light blanket off and was now shivering with the dream and the cool of the mountain night. He wondered if he had cried out. He hoped not. He had done so when he lived with them years ago and disturbed people; they would remember and criticize him for it. He waited for them, feeling his watch; four-thirty. They did not come. He spent the time before seven reading.

John and Leda left the next day after seeing Mama again. She was a little better this time. Her hand came up and stroked John's face as he bent in to kiss her, but she still had no identity for him and he had been made ashamed to say so; her smell was alien, her hand vague, its gesture unlike her. Nothing came out to him. Even her hair seemed different. Only the little mole on her neck provided identity. As he was being led away he said to the nurse, "She can learn Sign language, she can learn to speak — "

"OK, OK," Leda said, "they know."

But did they really? No one had acknowledged his idea. He felt hurried away and he pulled back. "Wait, please — "

"They've told us to go."

"I want to talk to the doctor."

"He's not here — it's Sunday and we have to start for home. You have work tomorrow and tonight I have to be at the performance."

"We have to come next weekend — "

"We'll talk about that later."

"We have to help Ma — she can't talk."

"I know, but John, I am not your interpreter or your driver; I'm your friend. I have my own work to do and my own weekends to look forward to. We have to leave *now* or I'll be late for my performance. If you don't come with me now I am going to have to leave without you and you will have to take the bus to Denver."

They were angry with each other, driving back. John had been pulled here and there and given no word from the medical people about the foreigner his mother had become, and Leda was angry with him for wanting to come back every week. On the ride home he brooded, at first sitting on his hands in the old school way to avoid striking something in anger and being punished. He wanted to hit the places he could reach. He couldn't help hitting with his foot, and then with his hand, the unresisting floor and the side of the car. After a while Leda nudged him and he stopped for a few minutes and started again. He wanted . . .

She had been moving the car, as she had once described it to him, around the other cars so as to go faster than they did. He had a sense of going faster but he could not tell how fast. There came a vibration in his head as of a storm, but different, located behind him. Leda slowed down and went to the right, on rough-ground, off highway, and stopped. "Police," she said, "and stop kicking and making noise or you'll get him as crazy as you got me."

A long time. What were they doing? He found his feet going again, walking the floor while he sat there, as though he would walk or run away if he could. What were they doing? Why was it taking so long? Twice, Leda spelled "shut up and wait" into his hand. He said, "What's happening?" and she began to interpret, her own hands greasy with nervous sweat. "I was speeding. I'm getting a ticket."

"Why is it taking so long?"

"I have to show him proof of this car, which is Bennet's, that I have the right license things, and that the car isn't stolen."

"Why were you driving so fast?"

"I have to get back to Denver because I have a performance, as you know, and because you were driving me nuts with the noise you were making, and because of certain other things. Now, let me deal with this cop and get on our way again, and *quiet*. No tapping, bumping, knocking, or clicking. The World of Deafness is too loud for me!"

He knew she was angry. He had been angry also, but after what she said he kept himself silent and let the tired part of his feeling come up through his body. He found the tiny, hard-stump at the side of his fingernail and pulled at it until he made it hurt. When the trip was over she left him at the house and went driving away to the theater. He went in, hating the musty heat of closed windows and unmoved air. Fourbuds's greeting pushed him to the kitchen. It felt as though they had been away for years and that now, years later, they had changed the house and all its contents had gone strange.

He started to make himself some dinner, feeling restless and annoyed. The routine of his weekend had been shattered. No lunches again this week. The upsets of the weekend had exhausted him and he found himself without energy or concentration. He fell asleep waiting for the oven to warm his food and woke to it half-burned, dried out, and unpleasant. His clothes had twisted on him. He gave Fourbuds most of the dinner and stood, bereft, assailed by sorrow in the middle of the floor. He knew he should concentrate. He decided to make himself a sandwich and Leda a sandwich for when she got home. She liked the bread that came in loaves not already cut. He had learned to cut bread very well and to make nice sandwiches. Hardboiled egg and cheese and canned hot peppers carefully dried on paper towel and lettuce — one of her favorites. Again and again as he was working, his mind drifted away to the hospital bed, its bars, Mama as stranger to the denial of his help.

A part of him wanted to move back, to be a good son and do what a good son did, to visit Mama and make her real and familiar, to get his brothers' respect and even their praise. Part of him wanted to stay here, to concentrate all his life on his poetry and on trying to get a better job so that Leda would respect him more. He knew her friends would never respect him. Bennet had kept the news of Irwin's calls from him out of anger and meanness, and now Leda had had to borrow Bennet's car to go to Aureole. The knife with which John was cutting his bread cut into his left forefinger. He felt the slight stitch of first-pain and then the increase of the pain as his finger accepted the truth of its injury. By that he assumed it was bleeding.

The worst part of bleeding for him was that he would sometimes bleed all over his clothes and the floor and whatever he touched; he couldn't tell where the blood was. People were horrified by bloody clothes and hated the bleeding of other people. John made for the kitchen sink and the paper towel rack. He could feel blood-slipperiness down his hand and he tore two towels from the rack and held them on his finger for half an hour until he was pretty sure the blood had stopped.

His hand was throbbing but there was no way of knowing how bad the injury was or how much blood was in the kitchen. The towels were now stuck to the cut, so keeping the hand away, John began to sponge the counters where he had been working and the floor, also. He had been making Leda's sandwich for when she came home. When he was finished with his work, he completed the sandwich and put it on the table. He would have to do with canned sausages for his lunch tomorrow, or cold beans.

Leda was tired when she came home. He was waiting up in the living room. He felt it in the smell she had, even as she touched him. "I . . . practically fell asleep on stage. What happened to *you?*"

"Cut myself."

"Show me."

"Tomorrow. I can't unstick it. Go to the kitchen because I made you something. Snack."

"I thought I'd skip all that, a bath and then sleep, but you were sweet to make it. Maybe I will go in."

"There's herb tea — Sweet Dream tea."

"I'll take it all upstairs and eat it in the tub like a Roman Emperor," and she went away to get it.

After she went up, John read for a while and then returned to the kitchen to make up his lunchbox and by chance found a plate in the sink. For a minute he did not know how it had gotten there and then he thought — Leda. Perhaps she had eaten standing up in the kitchen the way she often did. He smiled. If she used the garbage, she would not close the little lid he had made and Fourbuds . . . so he went to the garbage, which she had not closed. He checked it for things hanging out of it and found the sandwich there, the one he had made for her. He was shocked and hurt, so much he felt it gathering in his belly, like sour stones. He swallowed hard, trying to swallow them away. He couldn't, after the awful day they had had. He went up to her room and knocked on her door and went in. "Why did you throw it away like garbage?"

She couldn't answer because he had not come close enough. He wasn't even sure she was there. She had said she was going to bed but maybe she hadn't; she might even have gone out to see her friends. He went to the bed and asked again. Then, there was her hand. In his misery and confusion he was struggling to be glad she had not lied to him. "Why?" The hand was tired and stumbled with exhaustion and a kind of sadness. "Sorry, I thought I could get away with it and spare you. Lost my appetite . . . blood all over the bread."

TWENTY-ONE

For three weekends John took buses to Aureole, for which he had to leave home at six in the morning. Leda took him to the bus station until he became familiar with the place where the tickets were bought and the place where the bus waited and then left. Then he was able to use a cab that she called the night before. Marie or Richard's wife, Judith, met him at the bus, and they went from there to the hospital and after the second week to a nursing home where Mama had been taken.

Without Leda these visits were empty of meaning, uninterpreted and full of long silences and forlorn waits, hours during which he read as much as he could but found he was unable to write. A restlessness was possessing him, a thickening of mind. He was unable even to work on poems for Mr. Sherline. All the Deaf-blind Man's Prayers he tried ended up as love poems or yearning cries or as poems in Leda's style, which was becoming his own and never mentioned starry nights or lovely flower gardens on dew-fresh mornings.

Whenever he could see Mama he tried to teach her fingerspelling — cat, bat, rat, mat, as he had learned it years ago. She weakened so soon and so completely that it was only for three or four minutes that he could command her attention. Her fingers moved slowly and unwillingly and then suddenly dropped and could do nothing.

During the fourth weekend, Catherine said, "Don't come next time. Mother is speaking now. Only confusing her when she tries to spell. They give her physical therapy; she will soon be moving again."

"When can I come to see her?"

"Come around Thanksgiving. Then she may be ready to learn some more."

Careful words. He felt more voices in them than Catherine's alone. "Does Mama say that, too?"

"Yes, she does."

"She told you?"

"Yes, and the doctors and nurses same."

"She's improving then, and she speaks?"

"Yes, she speaks and we are all very hopeful."

But when John went to kiss Mama goodbye, he leaned in close and said to her, "If you can really speak, Mama, say something." Then he held his hands near her jaw and spread them over her throat the way Tadoma readers do. Vibrations came, but he could tell they did not create words, because the locations of the vibration did not start and stop, long and short, as they did when people were speaking. He had never learned to receive Tadoma, but he could tell that much. He thought of Irwin's evasions, Catherine's, Leda's. There was nothing he could do. They had all the decisions on their side.

So, John came back on the bus, wishing he could understand them, all of them or any of them. Had Mama improved? When he touched her she still seemed a stranger and her periods of concentration were only moments, her grasp and smell still foreign and unsettling. Had they only told him of her improvement to get him to go away?

He had not eaten before he got on the bus. The bus would not stop for hours. He lay back and tried not to think about his hunger. A food idea came to him, blending into his misery about Mama, and it began with something Marie told him yesterday evening when he had come from the nursing home. Marie and Catherine were cooking for a church supper, what they called a covered-dish supper, and Marie, in Catherine's slow hands, had described it to him, how everyone brought the

370

dishes of which they were most proud. John began to form a poem in his mind, and, as he thought the words in it, the idea came clearer — equivalents between hunger and his loneliness in a way he had never thought of before.

He wanted to write about the covered-dish supper as an idea of the way his life was, as though he had come with his contribution, the product of all his wit and labor. The last lines were:

> *"No one," you said on the back of my*
>   *hand,*
> *"Not even the starving,*
> *Will eat what you bring."*

He fussed with his poem, words out and words in, but by the time the bus stopped to let people eat dinner, John felt some kind of content with it. Using the ideas of food, he had met another idea that was not about food at all but about hunger of a more secret and hidden kind. He sat over a burger and fries. What had he written — "Not even the starving" — and reached into his memory for what someone had said, someone in school, about poetry like that.

Whatever had happened, John felt he had crossed some kind of border into a place he had not been before. Nothing in any of his poetry had prepared him for this. Only in individual lines or words had he described one thing by means of another. There had been a hint of this in some of his recent poems — he had come to the border but not crossed over. He sat thinking hard about it until the driver tapped his shoulder, and it was time to go on the bus again. His sorrow at their refusal of him was still there, but now the poem was there, too, not more real or less real than the sorrow itself.

He wanted to spend the rest of his time on the bus thinking about it or about how he had been sent away from Aureole, but he fell asleep instead, a sleep so complete that for a while after he was awakened at the bus terminal in Denver he didn't know where he was and had to wrestle in his mind for it, since there was no one in the terminal to tell him and no other way to know.

The driver who woke him got his overnight off the rack for him, and checking to see if it was his, John awakened enough to realize he was home again. He began walking through the terminal feeling the familiarity of the wall on his right, a much-longer walk, he had told Leda, but surer. He had left the space where there were seats against the wall. Sometimes there was trouble walking there. The flow, movement, purpose, was through the building in the middle, as he had read of rivers, and once, of blood in veins. At the sides, water, blood, and people flowed slowly. Some people removed themselves from the flow. They went to the side. Sometimes there were people waiting there, or asleep, or confused as he had been, and it was easy to hit their feet with his cane as he went, using the wall as his guide, and sometimes one or two would be sitting on the floor against the wall as he went, and he would touch them with his cane or even trip over them.

This time he made his way well and soon stood near the taxi stand. Then he felt someone close and took a breath, saying, "I am Deaf-blind. I can speak but I can't hear you. Can you help me get a taxi?" Whoever it was didn't wait for the last part but took his arm and pulled him across the street, resisting his words and leaving him on the opposite side. He felt the vibration of much traffic paralleling, and he had to wait a long time before another pedestrian came to take him back.

This time he was happy to get into the routine of his days at the workshop. Alma had begun coming down at noon to eat with him. He still found her conversation limited; it was hard to understand and only about the driest and most daily things, but because she was seeing Luke so much, John was able to get some news of his friend.

Luke was getting SSI as John had, but somehow, even though he was obviously Deaf and blind, whenever the grants were reviewed his money was stopped, pending proof of need. He lived in a constant state of anxiety about the grant and was unable to plan for anything. Luke's brother, with whom he lived, was trying, Alma said, to get control over this money by getting himself made Luke's . . . "like his father," Alma said. All this would improve if Luke were able to get work. "I wish he job beggar," Alma said, "beg good money. Easy job."

"That's bad for self-image and for the image of Deaf-blind people," John Signed to her, "and it would help Luke's brother get his hands on the money."

On Friday, Mr. Sherline came. John had none of the poetry he had planned; none of the Deaf-blind prayers they had talked about. Instead, he showed Mr. Sherline the poem about the covered-dish dinner. "I know you can't take this poem because it is angry . . . "

"Our cards are supposed to make people feel good — "

"I only wanted you to see . . . the idea of the style . . . "

"Too fancy. People don't want to have to sit

374

down and figure out what you're really saying. They want it said for them. You used to be good at this. Remember the idea of the Deaf-blind prayer. People need to feel that there are those less fortunate than themselves. It helps them live with what they've got."

"Less fortunate means worse, doesn't it?"

"Whatever it means, it doesn't mean smarter. Be simple, not fancy. Don't get poetic except in ways people can recognize right away."

"I guess I'll try again."

"I'm sorry I can't pay you anything this month. Royalties for 'God's Braille' don't come until the next quarter. You'll be doing very well. We figure one year, maybe two, for 'God's Braille' and then we'll need another big seller. People get tired; the market gets saturated. Why not write a poem about a Seeing Eye dog. People love dogs."

"I don't have a Seeing Eye dog."

"Why not?"

"It's hard to give them the attention they need, impossible to exercise them and care. Soon autumn will come, then winter — wind and ice and snow. We can't go out for their exercise then. It's also hard to praise an animal if you don't know what it has done. Especially, in bad weather, we can't feel — "

It suddenly occurred to John that the world

he shared with Leda was of a season also. Like marriage, they had made love; like marriage, they had bought some things together, a charcoal grill was the most recent; but the relationship had gone on changing in both of them; he had not been accepted into the world she occupied and she had not done well in his. She was angry at having to be his eyes and ears with his family. She wanted things he could not see or hear. He wanted a world she was perhaps unable . . .

These truths hit him like a wall in a park or unexpected water. He stopped. His mouth was open, and he was forced to breathe hard because his head went suddenly empty. There was also no feeling in the hand in which the interpreter was speaking. Location-direction left him and for what seemed like a long time he simply stood up struggling to endure the estrangement of knowing where he was but not feeling any of the reality of it.

At last his attention returned. He felt aware again. "Are you sick?"

"No, I was having too many thoughts. I'm fine, now."

"Well, please remember: the public wants nice thoughts. There's enough misery in the world already and enough people are scared of poetry they can't understand. I don't want to stop coming — we need poetry for our cards but not what you've been producing."

John left the office and walked hard into the back wall and went sprawling. He lay in a heap for a moment, trying to imagine why it had happened. The route was to go out of the office, steps, one, two, turn right, take the cane out, pulling it long — he had not done any of it. The cane, a very nice telescoping one, was God knew where, but he had not even gotten it out, and though he had turned — he couldn't have turned. He lay still for the space of ten breaths and then began to move his legs and arms. Most of the force of the fall had been on his forehead and knee. He reached up and felt his head. A lump was beginning. The body wasted no time in announcing its complaints. The knee, aching badly, was not broken. Perhaps there was a whole circle of people standing around watching him move and feel here and there and breathe hard with pain. At least they didn't do here what they usually did outside — pick him up before he was ready, pull him and stand him before he had his sense of location back. Were they watching? What would they see? Does seeing include knowing how it feels to fall? Had they seen him smash against the wall? What kind of sense was it, seeing? Why did it shame those who were seen?

John pulled in a long breath and sat up.

Then he got to his knees and began to search the floor for his poem-papers and cane. The poem-papers came first — one, two, three of them. The cane was . . . he began to hunt for it in the widening half-circle out from the wall. It was . . . here it was, against the wall two yards from where he had fallen. John stood up. He felt vulnerable and ashamed without reason. He pulled the cane out long and went back up the stairs to work, not using the elevator because there had been enough of a show for the day; enough mistakes had been made. By the time he had walked up all those stairs, his knee was wobbling with pain and weakness.

Question: Why did falling hurt so much more now than it had when he was a kid? There had been bad falls then; he remembered some of them, but since he had come out of school they seemed to hurt more and they took longer to feel better. He went to his work table and cut the heavy string around a bundle of clothes. He was glad for the work he had to do, even though he still felt a little sick from his fall. Sorting clothes, women, girls, boys, men — now he was sizing also, using a special measure. The job filled his world with people. He had no time to think about the sudden thoughts and realization he had had in Mr. Bisoglio's office, the idea of the change in his relations with Leda and the death of his dream.

The next Monday, after work, he was waiting at Alma's van. "Will Luke be home this afternoon?"

"Yes."

"You live walking distance from him. We could go together because I want to come with you and see him."

As John spoke, a hand, someone, grabbed him and began leading him away. "I want to go in the other van." The someone left him. He made his way back the way they had come, to Alma's van. The people were boarding. He was about to get in when he was pulled back again. "I want to go with Alma," he said again. The unknown person pulled him along again and then left, and in a minute Mr. Bisoglio put his Sign into John's hand. "I want to go with Alma, to see Luke — " John repeated.

"Sorry, that van's left already. Better luck tomorrow."

"Make a law allowing me to go in the van I want."

"There's never been a policy against it."

"They wouldn't let me . . . "

"That was just a misunderstanding."

"*Tell* them."

"They thought you had made a mistake, that's all."

John didn't have the money for a taxi and the buses were too much of a hassle. "I want to go tomorrow," he said. *"Tell* them."

"I will."

That evening Leda didn't come home. At eight John remembered how they had planned a system by which notes would be left taped to the refrigerator. He went to the kitchen and ran his hand down the door. There was the paper. She had left him a note typed on his Braille machine.

Audition. Washington, D.C.
May be break I need.
Back Friday. Love.

It made him feel odd because he had opened and closed the door on the refrigerator ten times and missed the air-fluttering of the note that he now felt as he expected to feel it. Inattention, said Mrs. Pfansteihl, is the enemy of all Deaf-blind people. Did Mrs. Pfansteihl know, did Sam, whom he still missed, did Martin in jail, know how it was to have to pay attention when the soul and mind were being torn ten ways? He still lived with the anguish at Mama's stroke, the pain of sudden truth that his own family would prefer him gone and Mama speaking no speech at all rather than his. Leda said may be the break she needed. The meaning he knew of the word *break* did not yield him joy.

But Leda's absence made him easier at the same time, and the consciousness of that further confused him. He loved her. He could no longer feel real joy or sorrow without wanting to bring it to her, to rush from the place where it had been given and tell it, laying the words upon her while her held hand said its listening, "yes, yes." She and her wishes, opinions, angers, hopes, filled his days and he would still, whether she liked it or not, go to the closet where those soft-cottony-limp dresses hung and bury his face in them to get the tang of her, a pleasure of aching intensity. Yet, her presence made him need to behave in ways that would give her pride in him and not shame. She was messy; he was neat. He had to learn to clean up after her without showing his annoyance. She was able to change all the surfaces and textures of his life and so were her friends. Bennet, for example, was still coming around. Leda had forgiven Bennet, she said. She had discussed his problem with him. Bennet had always been "immature" about some things. He had had a terrible childhood and that had afflicted him.

So now that she was gone, he picked up the clothes and cleaned the smelly ashtrays and ordered the rooms, and they stayed orderly

and then he could walk or sit down or go any-
place in the house easily without falling over
things or upsetting them or getting tangled
in her jungle-bathroom, where she hung her
pantyhose and underwear.

He was ready the next day to go home with
Alma after work, but there was trouble again.
Again he approached the van and again someone came and began to lead him back. This
time he grabbed Alma and said, "If I can't get
in her van, she's not going in it, either." Alma
recognized his touch and began to laugh and
they clung to each other until at last he was let
go. Mr. Bisoglio had obviously not told the
van people. Did they think John was retarded
and didn't know one van from the other? Getting in with Alma was a kind of triumph, but
John realized it was not one of intellect or will
or creativity. It was like the triumphs at
school, getting even.

To John's great surprise, Luke was not
sympathetic. "She's a tourist; we told you
that. The Deaf-blind world was a vacation for
her and now she's got to go back to work.
Hasn't that happened to you before? They see
us as novelties. Some of them pity us, some of
them use us to get to heaven. It's a game."

"You used her too much," Alma said. "You
want mother child friend wife interpreter
driver. Our trouble Deaf-blind. For them

382

maybe, for us *everything.*"

"They should . . ."

And Alma hit his hand away, arguing, "Should, should, should. Don't. *We* always come *we* need. Them never *from* us." She began hitting his hand in a kind of joy-frustration as something happened in her which was difficult to make words of.

"Overflowing," he said. "Do you think I overflowed her?" He said it first to Alma, then to Luke.

Luke answered, "That's what Sighted say about us sometimes. I don't understand why, but it's what they say."

"I think it's what my brother Irwin thinks," John said, "and my mom."

The words he spelled into his friend's hand made John's emotion fill up and spill. His eyes began to run and there was the familiar presence of filling body liquids in his face, nose, throat. They grew and burst in him and he was crying before he knew it. It took Luke and Alma a moment to be aware. John had to go for a handkerchief, and there came a tremor in his hand that Alma perceived and then told Luke. John was happy that it was here and not with the Sighted that his emotion had spilled this time. He did not understand what they approved, what they pitied, what made them impatient. Perhaps they would have called him a coward or baby as they had when he was a kid in school. Here he was safe and neither jeered at nor given false comfort; they left him alone until the leaking stopped.

"The problem is that I miss her more than she misses me."

"The problem is that you *need* her more than she needs you," Luke said.

"Yes."

"That will be a problem until God gives us the senses He has."

TWENTY-TWO

Mr. Bisoglio stopped John on his way to the van. "Word from D.C.," in his slow, clumsy spelling. John became suddenly sweaty. "There is a telegram and they read it over the phone: 'Got the part. Back tomorrow. Break out caviar and champagne. Love, love, love.'"

"Could you call someone for me, to take me shopping?"

"I don't know if she really means that . . . "

"I would like to do it."

Sue, one of the secretaries in accounting, took John to the stores. The clerks were good and helped to get the things he wanted. It astonished John that the prices of these things varied so much. Sue wrote into his hand. She told him to pick the cheapest, but Martin had said people who could afford it should get the best, so he got the middle-priced things, a bottle of that wine and, at the market, a tiny jar of caviar no bigger than a jar of salve. Sue explained slowly what caviar was and said people ate it with cream cheese or sour cream on little round crackers. They got round crackers, too, and the cream cheese.

John was elated. Leda would be home tomorrow, but coming from D.C., she probably wouldn't be in until late afternoon or evening. He would come home from work and fix the cheese on the little round crackers — four apiece? — and put the caviar — just a very little, Sue said — on top. Glasses . . . wine glasses . . . in the . . . where? He remembered Leda's party where they had had wine in special glasses, and she had told him where they were when they had gone through everything. Yes, the pantry, cabinet shelves, up two. Two glasses; they would have to be made cold. Martin had told him. He had said he put his in the freezer after running cold water over them.

Of course, the names of Leda's records had never been Brailled. She liked things on the record player, and sometimes in some of the selections were vibrations he could feel in various bones of his body and face. Now he wished he had learned those names and had Brailled them so he could have her nice music waiting for her, the music lights-are-low as he had read of, and the caviar things and the champagne in the glasses, announcing what?

Toasting, it was called. Leda had gotten the thing she wanted but it was in D.C. and what would that mean? John sighed and consigned his fears to the long future. There were party plans to plan.

Champagne and caviar and lights-are-low and then they would call a cab and go to the Indian restaurant. Next they would come back home and he would have incense to burn upstairs and he would have — her body oil cooling just like the champagne, so if she wanted it, it would go on cool in this heat. They would have the fan on upstairs — he would put that on early so they could make love in her room because it was cooler there and there was the double bed. Flowers — these evenings have flowers that the woman wears. Learned from . . . Rahner, of all people. Tomorrow he would ask Carol to call the flower store and have the right kind ordered. The corsage. The house in good order. He would have to make sure.

So during the evening John went over the floor barefoot. All was smooth. Each surface he checked. All smooth. He took the dusting stick and cloth and moved it on the walls around the rooms where they met the ceiling, rims of doorways for cobwebs. He vacuumed the rugs and couch. When he came from work tomorrow he would set out the glasses —

neighbors, conventional people, thought she was not a good woman. She had introduced an unstable element, they said, and her new lover was Deaf and blind.

The yard seemed all right. It was hard to tell when the kids used toilet paper because there was no way he could cover the yard completely and now he did not want to get on his hands and knees.

He went into the house and opened the windows to circulate the air. Then he burned two sticks of balsam incense to freshen the rooms. It was 5:35. He got the round crackers and put cheese on one, having very carefully washed his hands and measured the amount with a measuring spoon, using a little scoop. Then he opened the caviar and smelled it. It was not like fish, not like food at all, but like a place he had been once — he tried to remember where — it was near the sea, a watery place in a storm . . . or . . . it also had somewhat the smell of boiling cloth at the laundry at Deaf school. He tasted it cautiously. Soft — if beads were soft — a sudden explosion of salty brine filled his mouth. He shook his head, disappointed. He had been hoping for a new flavor. This was only salty. Still, he was glad he had tasted it. He would put only a very little bit on the cracker. With great care he dipped the knife-tip in, measuring with his finger at its edge. He tasted one. Better, much better, but still too salty. Two or three crackers and he would have it right. He had sampled himself into a mighty thirst. Aha — that was when you drank the champagne.

He had just finished arranging the little round crackers when he felt the air-change of draft. Someone had opened the door. Leda would have used the buzzer. Who was it then? He rinsed his hands again quickly and dried them and rushed to the front of the house not touching wall or doorpost as he went. The one stopping him, holding him, was not Leda. There was another and then another. Who? "Who!" he cried into the bodies. Then she was there. "Party," she said after a quick and impersonal hug, "for me. They met me at the plane."

Bennet again, the hated Bennet. "Great day for Leda. Big part. Equity production. A big break."

There was that *break* again, that word theater people liked to say. John sat on a chair while the room-air vibrated with unheard voices. Now and then there were the stronger vibrations that meant music and the voice vibrations in his head grew stronger. He had learned that this happened when people tried to shout at one another above the music. Someone gave him a plate with cake on it and later a glass with wine. In an hour, Leda came to him, a little sweaty and nervous-excited. "Sorry. Couldn't be helped. They met me at the plane. It was a dear thing you did — caviar and champagne. I saw it before they got to it. It's been eaten. They were starved. Later, when they've all gone — " But they stayed until three in the morning. John left the party at twelve, going upstairs and finding lovers in his bed.

He had to leave before she was up. He didn't eat breakfast because the kitchen was a mine field of balancing plates and open cabinets. Luckily he had packed his lunch before preparing the caviar yesterday afternoon, when he had been so eager and dumb and joyful. Now, he was able to find the lunch in the refrigerator. On an impulse he opened the freezer. The two glasses were no longer there. He sighed and went to work.

"We need to talk," she said that evening.

"Yes."

She had cleaned up some of the mess. "I'm really sorry — "

"It's a quick world. I can't keep up in your world." She did not answer. "Nobody has to plan for anything," he said, "you just jump up changed so often. Now I wonder what life is like for you. I never did that before."

"We're frustrated, too — we can't call you

up and let you know. Even if you had a Tele-braille . . . I'd need one on the other end . . . "

"I know," and he knew what he felt, the rushing feeling pouring away of himself that he had experienced in headlong falls, the feeling he was having now, the feeling he had had days ago in Mr. Bisoglio's office.

He wanted to defend himself against what was coming but there was no way, so he sat silently and waited. She, too, was having difficulty. She started, stopped, started again, stopped again, the letters falling out of her fingers half-formed. The ideas were dribbling away in the middle of the words. "I'm going to . . . I'll have to . . . there won't be . . . "

He took her hands into his and said, "You're going to D.C. To live. I can't come along because it's no world for me. You would be doing this all the time, sticking me in a chair with a cake plate and a glass of wine while you talked with your friends and they thought I was clinging on to you."

"You're being cruel," she said.

"I'm being true."

"I want this house and I want you to live here," she said. "Maybe D.C. will be bad for me, three months, six . . . and I want you to be here."

He thought about it; then he said, "And the rent would be the same?"

She said, "I'd have to ask for more, I guess — you'd have to pay all the utilities instead of half and all the repairs and the taxes — that's where your rent would go. I wouldn't expect to make a profit . . . "

"How much do you think it would come to?"

She was out of his orbit for a while, figuring. When she told him, he felt stunned.

"I can't pay that."

"Maybe you could get some of your friends from church . . . "

"Deaf-blind people?"

"Why not?"

He felt the cold finger of unwillingness touch his viscera, slowing everything. But she had said . . . and he wanted with everything he had to please her. "And it would keep the house for you, here."

"Yes."

"I will ask people."

"I think you'll like to be with other Deaf-blind . . . " She said this because she believed it and because it was convenient.

"And you will be back . . . "

"I'm not dumb. Theater people are homeless; they have to be. With this house *I* won't be like that. I'll have this place to come to, for which I have Granny to thank."

"And me," he said.

She took him in her arms. He was too sad to follow, and raise his arms to hold her. He took her embrace passively and allowed it to embarrass her. "You know there are Telebrailles in D.C. We could — when *you* have one we could talk and it would be like the phone conversations Hearing people have . . ."

"You'd be closer if you were farther away," he said. "That's a good trick."

"Don't make me ache over this and feel guilty. I want to be your friend, to love you and still be free to do what I do, to go where I have to go to get work."

"And Bennet will be coming here and taking messages and telling me what you say . . ."

"I'm sorry about that, but it's the way things have to be. Bennet knows how to spell and he's here and he'll do it. Not many people fill those requirements."

"If someone hates you, you don't have to deal with him."

"I've talked to him. I won't be here to complicate his feelings."

"You were lovers."

"Yes."

"And you still . . ."

"He can spell."

John felt he was arguing about the wrong things. The true things, the real points of anguish, were beyond his finding, his naming, or his power to correct. "When will all this happen?"

"I got the part. Rehearsals start next week. I have to find a place to stay."

"So you will be leaving in five days?"

"Four maybe. I'll really talk to Bennet. He's doing me a big favor."

So she began to pack and to tell him things about the house in between, about the heating and the water heater. He put it all on the Braille typewriter and ended up with a list of what to do and check that was longer than what she had given him when she went away the first time.

He went to Alma the next day at work and told her about what Leda had said. The next day Luke came with Alma to work and they talked. That afternoon Alma went with John in the van to his house. The workshop would not let Luke ride with them because he did not work at the workshop and the insurance company forbade it. Luke had to ride in a taxi, which meant he could not afford food the next day. John agreed to give him the money to pay for the cab ride.

Leda and the three of them stood in a circle and interpreted to one another. Luke's questions made John know how quick he had been to wish them with him, so quick he had forgotten how inconvenient it might be. He knew, as Leda did not know, that the reason was not their all living together, but Luke's living with Alma, which both their families had forbidden. "Maybe the play will not last long — if it lasts only a few weeks we will be here and then we will have to move again."

"No," Leda said, "there is room enough in his house for you to stay whether I'm here or not. If you pay the same rent as you have been paying — "

"We don't pay rent. Alma lives with her foster parents and I live with my brother. I have SSI grant and she has her grant and her pay from the workshop. My brother charges me to live with him. I will move out and pay you instead."

Alma said, "Mother father no-no Luke and me together. They tell Mr. Bisoglio. What is law?"

"Over twenty-one."

"Luke has caseworker; I have caseworker . . ."

Leda said, "I think you are both still citizens of the country. You can move if you wish. Good idea to discuss with your parents and caseworkers."

John had led them through the rooms before when they had visited. Now they went again with the idea of living in the house. The tour took until late into the night. Leda called Luke's brother and Alma's foster mother and they came. John had met Luke's brother several times; he was a man who had Irwin's impatience about him. Alma's foster mother was gentle-handed but did not know how to spell except by writing the words in Alma's hand. John told Leda to introduce the subject of Luke and Alma's moving.

"Too late, it's too late." John wasn't sure what she meant. Later she said, "They were impatient to get home; too impatient to listen."

"But you will talk to them — "

"Of course I will."

Again there were friends and friends of Leda's coming during her last days, Saturday and Sunday, to say goodbye. There were the drama people and friends from other places. Bennet, too, and a girl named Kitty who said she would interpret for John when he got a Telebraille and the new line had been set up at the Deaf center. Then he could call in and ask for her. Her fees were. . . . John said thank you. He was about to walk away when he thought that even though this was a social time he might be honest. "I rarely need an interpreter. I need a person less trained who does more. I need a shopping helper and one to help with clothes shopping and a person who can help with the bills."

Her hand was rapid and competent in his. "I do all modes; ASL, Signed English, SEE Signs, and of course fingerspelling — "

"Yes," he said, "and I think — " he tried to select the words carefully — "you feel plain handspelling is a little bit of a waste of your time."

"I have had two years of ASL."

"I've learned Deaf Signs from my Deaf friends," John said, "but not their language. I was born blind and became deaf later. The wonderful language of deaf people is as foreign to me as Japanese is." He felt her impatience.

"I'm only offering my services," she said. She handed him her Brailled business card. It was larger than the ordinary card because of the Brailling.

He patted her hand. "I need a sweet-smelling flower in my window," he said, "not the botanical gardens." He took the card and slipped it into the pocket of his shirt, then reached for her hand.

She was gone. It was one of the problems of his having learned to speak before he became deaf. People could understand without the touch and while he was speaking, could walk away without his knowing it. He went into the kitchen to try to find Leda.

And then it was Monday and Leda was gone. This time he had been nerved for her absence. She had not taken most of her things. The presence of the clothes she had left, winter ones mostly, comforted him greatly. Every day he touched them before he left the upstairs to begin his leaving for work. John worked hard, obeying the lists she had made. Even Bennet was milder and said he would deliver any message John received.

Twenty-Three

Four days after Leda's departure, Luke came with his clothes and possessions in suitcases. He had argued with his brother. A day later, Alma came. She brought electronic equipment. Various timers vibrated a little box attached to her waist. John gave them Leda's big front room. Then, happily, all over the house they modified things to suit them, and chairs and tables were oriented to John's strong axial sense, which neither Luke nor Alma seemed to use. When Luke walked upstairs they could feel his paces thrumming slightly. It was possible to feel a person moving on the stairs by touching the bottom of the banister and to feel the water pipes in the kitchen and know if someone was walking in the bathroom or using the tub or toilet. John installed Alma's devices. "In a few weeks," he told Luke and Alma, "we'll have to show the neighbors we're not crazy or retarded, but want to be neighborly. We'll have to walk to each house and introduce ourselves. We'll have to go with an interpreter. In my old place the people were very friendly to me. Here they are not, but I think that's because we are mysterious to them." Luke's idea was that he should keep house for John and Alma, clean and cook. John reluctantly agreed.

The third Sunday came and they were picked up by one of the church people in her car. This was a new volunteer. At church she got an interpreter to tell them that she would be glad to take them back home after their social hour. "Church parking lot at one-thirty."

Everyone was excited about what Luke and Alma told them, that they were living with John in Leda's big house. "At least you'll have companionship." Why had they not said it when he was with Leda?

Coming out of the church to wait, the air of the warm afternoon had the lifting breeze of autumn and the sun's direction had changed since spring. Standing in the lot, John felt its most direct warmth at his cheek instead of his ear; it was also lower in the sky at this hour. Summer's freedoms would soon be over; already the autumn's cold nights and warm days were being announced by this sun's changes from what he had been told were millions of miles away. He was suddenly wrenched from his position. Luke, being pulled, was pulling him. He had to plant his feet and bend his knees quickly to avoid falling over. The pull of all of them was toward the car. The woman did not know how to let John feel the doorway for himself. Hands were pushing him somewhere, and before he could protect himself he had smashed his head into the door frame. The contact freed his hands and while he wanted to hold his head in pain, he reached out instead to feel the opening into which he stepped and sat down. In his head the pain flowed with a pressure like the river, and for a moment he felt sick. Someone was spelling something in his hand that he could not read. After a minute he read Luke saying, "She's sorry. Tell her you are OK so we can go." John murmured the appropriate words.

They were home. The lady must still have been feeling bad; she wrung his hand in farewell. Leda had done that when they had first met, a way of yelling, at that time, forgive me. Later it was her way of yelling I love you. The homesick ache came again. He had had the feeling often. What he hated most about it was its sudden and inappropriate presence. No way to predict it. "Like dog shit in the street," Sam had said. Now it gnawed a hole in his wonderful day. He had been looking forward to a nice lunch and an afternoon of reading and working on his poetry. It's still there, he said to himself, trying to comfort, all still there.

John finally wrote a poem for Mr. Sherline, but it didn't touch his feeling about Leda's being gone.

Love and Loss

Because my love for you is deep
And you have gone away,
The pain I have in missing you
Is more than I can say.

The sunshine on the roses,
The sky of deepest blue,
Are hidden from my spirit
Because of missing you.

He wrote another for himself that did a little better.

In an office I know, there is a computer
Whose memory is not like mine.
It waits in a button, top bank, next to the
*   end:*
R, I am told; it stands for Retrieval.
Press this button and with no warmth
*   and no heartbreak*

Memory will tell you what it remembers.

In an office I know there is a computer
That would remember you not by touch of
*   skin or hair*
Special hair that springs away as though
*   it was excited*
By being on your head;
And not by smell, warm rose on warm
*   body;*
Not by wit Signed small on my hands, a
*   secret when others are talking;*
Not by the shiver you shiver in ecstasy,
But by a number which bears no sense
*   of you.*

In an office I know there is a computer
Whose memory, no warmth and no heart-
*   break,*
Can spell your name to another computer
That puts it into Braille, another kind of
*   number.*
Now comes the mystery: touching that
*   number*
My heart pounds to breaking, my eyes fill
*   with tears.*

The three of them had been living in the
house together for two weeks when Madonna
and Swede asked to come. There had been

some kind of argument with Madonna's family. Swede had lost his temper. His speech was poor, and he could not make himself understood. John never understood the argument, but it had something to do with Swede's doing too much socializing in the Deaf community. He had been seen, apparently, with Deaf people at bowling and in a bar, and then Madonna's brothers had begun to follow him after work. This he got a bit from Swede and a bit from Madonna. They came one night, angry, and asked John if they could stay. There was still the large room on the warm side of the house. Since Swede could see, John thought he could do the things that might take vision — finishing touches on the cleaning and yard work, maybe. The money, with three of them working, would pay the taxes and utilities and there would still be some left over for repairs and the purchase of necessities for the house. Swede's deaf friends could visit as often as they liked. Luke and Alma were happy. Madonna and Swede moved in.

John, Luke, and Swede had all been to Deaf residential schools. Their first argument came because of John's idea of assigning the household chores the way they had been assigned there. Luke couldn't do everyone's housework. John wanted to type out the schedule in Braille for who washed the dishes and who cooked and who did the morning and night checking of the house. Luke said he had had enough of lists to last him the rest of his life. Alma could not read Braille at all. Luke wanted to take the home-repair money and buy a Telebraille. John joked and said, "To talk to who? All our best friends are here." The joke went hand to hand and they all slapped at him gently in acknowledgment.

Things were difficult for John's discipline as a poet. It was harder now, with the lure of friends and socializing, not to go short on his writing. They came to him too often with ideas and arguments. He decided to set a time for work in his room, door closed. The closed door was his signal for privacy.

At first John avoided Bennet when he came in to get Leda's phone messages and check her mail. Bennet did this Tuesday evenings, and John was always upstairs or busy in the kitchen. Luke met him, Alma, then Madonna and Swede. They reported that he was nothing like the angry savage John had described.

"He's older," Swede said. "He's almost bald, too. Some of what you feel as dislike might be clumsiness. You can tell he's not tall, but he's like a very big man and a very small man bumping into each other on the street and the top halves changing places. He has a big head and shoulders and big heavy waist and then little hips and legs and little tiny feet. He's like . . . like a buffalo."

John, who remembered and cherished his memory of the afternoon with Leda at the museum, laughed and understood. He hit Swede's hand. "We'll all go to the museum and see it,"John said. "I can write a letter. They said come again." It amazed John that suddenly the danger of Bennet had been lessened by this comparison to a buffalo. The next time John encountered Bennet, he remembered the great head and neck and the little body of the buffalo and thought that the buffalo's head was hairy and Bennet's was not and he smiled to himself.

Something had changed about Bennet also. His spelling was more relaxed, his hands no longer stiff with dislike. It was difficult to tell the motives of the Sighted. Only with certain Sighted-hearing friends — Martin and Sam — did one have the privilege of asking, not even Mama or Irwin, not even Leda all the time. You could only accept, minute by minute, what they did or said, and hope that some day the reasons would be made clear.

When John thought about Leda, he was unable to understand much of what motivated her even after these months together as friends and then lovers. When he thought of her at all, the pain of his loss returned, sometimes still so strongly that he had to fight tears.

And there were arguments in the house. Alma and Luke fought and John could feel it in the floor because they stamped and vibrated, and Alma, who had never heard her own voice, made vibrations so strong that John could sometimes feel them when he was in the same room and close to her, a buzzing in the bones of his face. Sometimes Alma and Madonna argued, hit out at each other, slammed and stamped and sulked, and John wanted to hit both of them, and once there was a fight and he pulled Alma's hair hard and spelled "stop this mess" into her hand, kicking her in the shin until she stopped. Madonna cared only for Swede. She would fix breakfast for the two of them and afterward wash only what the two of them had used. Alma was accustomed to being served because she had always lived with people who served her, however badly. She expected Luke to tell the others that she couldn't do the things the others did. Swede, too, got angry because as the only one who was not blind, his communication had to be slowed into tedious spelling most of the time instead of the rapid, graceful language of Signs. He found it vexing and slow, so there were arguments, hurt feelings, sulks, suspicions. He still wanted to spend lots of time with Deaf friends; his Deaf-blind "family" needed and depended too much on him. Fourbuds liked them all differently, but Alma was afraid of her and Luke didn't like cats and would not feed or brush her. They were a strange family, John thought, and not the one he had foreseen. They were less comprehensible, more complex. There were sudden resentments, brutal as stubbed toes; rages broke over them like the sudden-hot sudden-cold water of the school showers. This was not a pleasant truth to face. He had assumed bad manners, anger, and stubbornness to be Sighted-Hearing qualities. He did not know from where the anger came.

But there was not emptiness, and everyone knew it. Their days were full of activity and new kinds of meaning. They were beginning more varied, richer lives and they reached to touch the changing shapes of new realities every day. Sometimes the contact was frightening and they drew back. There were times when the five of them kept to their rooms feeling raw and miserable, but they were beginning to learn how to cooperate, and there were other times when they took on projects together that none of them had ever dreamed possible. They went on shopping trips with Swede and they learned to cook from John.

Laughter grew in them, humor of shared trouble and common challenge. They were alive, more vividly than they had ever been.

John, who had imagined everything differently, who had begged Luke and Alma to come, still preached the possibility of a life of peace and harmony. It was books, principally, which had given him this vision. He loved the home as harbor, the family warmth of Dickens, the friend-created groups in *The Three Musketeers* and Mark Twain's *A Connecticut Yankee in King Arthur's Court*. He preached it like religion, argued it like politics. The others, nonreaders, had none of his models; they bore his preaching with polite incomprehension. He realized he had been, even to himself, the object of action so often that initiating action was strange to him and full of unpleasant surprises. "I didn't know it would take so long," he said to Luke, "to learn the ways to do things together."

Habit had to rescue them when philosophy failed. The varying of the jobs became a kind of calendar and the work became part of Alma's life and Madonna, while not thinking much beyond Swede's existence, was slowly learning to do the jobs for everybody that she was assigned.

People came to the door selling things. Swede wrote a note on cardboard that said NO

SALESMEN, and they had to get rid of lots of papers people shoved under the door to advertise. In the beginning Swede looked over all the material, but after a while he only gathered it up and threw it away. Bennet's visits began to change from once a week to every two weeks. He said that the mail, which they saved carefully for him, was not important and there were few telephone messages. He said that Leda's play in Washington, D.C., was doing well and that she had "opened" and gotten special notice for her acting, that there were other possibilities beginning for her. Some of the times he came he was busy and taken up with his own concerns and barely said hello, but at other times he was ready to chat a bit about Leda and once about himself. His theater group was, he said, his real interest in life.

One afternoon Swede led Bennet around to the side of the house to where lower parts of the siding had rotted away. There was also some foundation work and a lot of caulking needed around all the window frames. Swede, who worked in construction with his brother, knew how to do it all, and they had gone over the jobs to see how many could be done by Deaf-blind people. He decided that with teaching, they could do all of them. "If we can touch a thing, we can do it," John told Bennet. "We have saved the money for the job. Swede's brother has ladders and we will only work evenings and weekends under his guidance."

Bennet would not believe they could do such work, but said he would watch them do the parts they could reach without ladders. If he was convinced, he would write to Leda, praising them and describing the repairs. After the house was fixed, they told him, they planned to get a Telebraille. "Then we can use it the way the Hearing use their telephones."

"End of privacy, end of peace," Bennet said. It was his first joke.

TWENTY-FOUR

Now and then there was toilet paper and garbage thrown on the front lawn. Swede said it was neighborhood kids, thinking none of them could see. He brought rakes to the house and the five of them were able to get the mess cleaned up. They had cleaned out the backyard, too, and made order there, and a nice place to sit. It was October and the weather was still fine for being outdoors. On the weekends they ate their meals in the backyard, even though it took a long time to bring things in and out.

Bennet came by on the Sunday they had set and watched John fit the caulk into the gun, cut the end off the tube, pierce the protecting layer inside the tube, and begin to lay a trail of caulk against the meeting place between the wall and the window frame. Swede had done work like this for years with his brother and uncle and he had taught John carefully. It was not difficult. Going over the window and frame first with his fingers, he located and understood. Swede had explained the entire process very carefully to John, who used the gun around the whole window and then walked to the next and began again. They did patching with concrete and some painting. Bennet was impressed enough to say that when he talked to Leda he would tell her that the repair fund was equal to the rent she would have charged, and that their maintenance was increasing the value of the house. John wrote to Leda often but he was always too shy to talk about the money they were using and how much they were doing.

Swede said it would take them all the nice weekends of the year to do the necessary repairs. Madonna wanted to call repairmen. It was difficult to convince her that such people would want to be paid. Luke wanted to work on his own while Alma, John, and Swede were at their jobs, but Swede said it was too dangerous. They argued again. John sighed and said, "The Sighted don't argue like this. When I visit my family in Aureole, everyone knows where to go and what to do. Why can't we be like that?" He wanted them to be shamed, but they only shrugged and went back to their argument.

There were days of rain and fog. John now had to wear a sweater when he got up in the morning, and Alma's hands were cold to the touch as they waited together for the van that took them to their jobs. Luke and Madonna stayed home. Luke said that they would learn to cook and keep house. Swede said the yard had slowed down on the toilet paper; school had started last month and the children of the neighborhood were no longer summer-idle.

Busy, exhausting, with too many arguments and too many surprises, life went on, but John found he was missing Leda less because his energies were all spent on the new adjustments in the house. He found himself sleeping in the van to and from work, and sometimes he even slept through poetry. Mr. Sherline liked "To a Friend," and wanted a series of new holiday poems. Thanksgiving and Christmas were coming. At work the summer garments he sorted and sized gave way to the heavier winter things. The season's wheel was turning — people were going through their winter wardrobes, getting things ready, and John was part of that, belonging to the process. Sometimes he ate lunch quickly and tried to think about his poetry in that time because he was alone in a way he no longer was at home. He realized that this was a psychological thing. There were doors for privacy, but his mind was not free of the other people. That would have to be learned.

When Bennet came again he didn't stay but took the mail and messages and went quickly, a thing John ascribed to his busy life. It was another feature of being Sighted, apparently. Bennet's hands were nervous. John had been in a train with a sighted guide named George and the train had been side-to-side a lot, and George had called it "rattling." Sighted people rattled come- and-go.

John and Alma came home on a Thursday and found the door open. They walked in, feeling strange. People? Who? John said into the strangeness, "Where is Luke?" Perhaps there were no people. After a minute or so Luke was there. "There are people. They say from the city. They have a law. We have to be out of this house in ten days."

John felt weak. He thought he might have misunderstood because Luke's fingers were upset and now John was so upset himself he was having trouble receiving. "What? What?"

A strange hand took his and wrote words into his palm. "Sheriff. You have ten days to VACATE. Eviction notice served."

"Why?"

"Zone. No group home or halfway house here. INADEQUATE SUPERVISION."

"No supervision!" John cried. "We live here on our own. I am independent. Three years I have. I have been here since June without trouble."

The hand withdrew and was gone. John reached out for the body. He fumbled and found nothing, then a confused and fumbling Luke. "What?" As quickly as he could he passed the message and together they reached out for the people who had been there. No one was there now. The door was closed. Who had done this? Why? What supervision was needed? What was a halfway house? And why had they been accused? Ten days. No one slept that night.

Bennet came in the morning. John and Alma were just going to work. "I don't want to go," John said. "I'm afraid they'll come and take my rights away while I'm gone."

"I've been down there trying," Bennet said, "at the court. Leda got a notice because she is the owner of the property. She thought it was a mistake and didn't pay attention right away. When she did she told me to take care of it." John interpreted this to Luke. The others were close. They had never trusted Leda and now their anger at her lay like a cobweb on John's face. He opened his mouth to speak, but Bennet shook his hand interrupting him. "I've been down there twice. It's this: because you are all handicapped, the neighbors say this is a group home or halfway house and the area is not zoned for that."

"What is it, *zoned?*"

"I have no time for that now. I have to go. Welfare people will be here today or tomorrow. *Make them explain.*" His hands rested a moment and then said, "It isn't your fault. The neighbors never liked Leda. She was too . . . free for them. Parties, drinking, different lovers . . . They were only waiting for a way to get back at her. . . ." And then he was gone and John and Alma had to go to work exhausted and overcome with nervous heavings in their bellies. They had not been able to eat breakfast. The sheriff and Bennet's visits had upset their routines both evening and morning. John had prepared no lunch.

At eleven, John fell asleep on the sorting table. Someone woke him, shaking him none too gently. It was noon. At four-thirty, Bisoglio stopped him as he left to go home. "You were sleeping."

"I'm sorry. There's trouble at home and I didn't sleep last night."

". . . mustn't let outside things interfere with work."

"They told me that when I came here."

"You are a good worker."

"Yes. They are throwing us out of our house."

"You live independently, don't you?"

"Yes."

"Why not go to a group home, then?"

"They said that about my home, now."

"Talk to the social worker."

"I want to fight, to have a lawyer."

"Hassle, money, bad idea."

"The neighbors didn't like Leda so they are against us."

"It's time to go for today. Do you want to talk to Mrs. Favilla tomorrow?"

"Yes, please, maybe she will know."

But that evening, Alma's foster parents came and took her and said their living idea was bad, police coming, the law brought in. The next day Luke's brother came for him. Alma lived too far away if Luke was here. "We can arrange it — "

"When you get a real place, I want to come — my brother hates me for having failed."

"Why don't we make a legal fight, maybe. . . . This isn't fair."

But Luke left, and three days later Swede and Madonna returned to Madonna's parents' house. They had lost their little waiting-listed apartment and were bitter and angry at John.

He was now alone again. He roamed the house in a long, deep rage that sometimes broke out of him in vibration. It was a curious rage, sometimes set against himself. He left doors closed or opened without noticing and got a strange, guilty pleasure in slamming against the butt ends of the opened ones or head on into the closed ones. If he was still a man, he was of mankind and punished mankind by hurting himself.

Bennet came a few days later. "The neighbors have to refile."

"File again? They've filed away four of us."

"I mean, if they want *you* out, they will have to say something else against you, and that will take time."

"I'm alone now, like I was. We had plans but now it's . . . it will be OK."

"I would see a lawyer if I were you. They want you out."

"*Why?*"

"They say they don't think you can cope with — well, clean your part of the street in the winter, for example, keep the house up. There's toilet paper all over the front yard again and some kind of powder — it looks like cement — on the lawn."

"All this to hurt Leda?"

"I think most of it, yes."

"I wish I had a cannon here that I could fire and blow bad sound to all of them."

"Leda's going to call me on Sunday. We'll talk this over. I want to help you. What should I say to her?"

"I'll write her a letter.

"I'm sorry things didn't work out."

"Yes."

"Leda is a wonderful woman but she . . . she has enthusiasm."

"Yes."

"She wanted to be your eyes and ears — she really does love you, but she wants all these other things, too. She forgets . . ."

"Yes. Can we get the rakes and clean up the lawn?"

"Yes," Bennet said.

They cleaned up the front yard. From the feel of what John took up on his rake, the paper had been there for some time. He called to Bennet, trying to keep his voice right, not too loud or high. In a minute, Bennet was there. "How long has this been here?"

Bennet began answering and then his hand stopped and then a lie, patently and obviously a lie by the starting, stopping, and the too neat spelling. "I drove by yesterday and it wasn't here."

So for days, since Swede left, it had been there, advertising his weakness and his difference from his invisible, inaudible neighbors. He had heard years ago a joke about some blind people whose house had been decorated by Halloween trickers, so it was Halloween at their house until Thanksgiving because they did not know and all the neighbors laughing. Was Bennet laughing behind his lie? No, maybe not. Maybe only pity and impatience, common mix, ordinary as morning grit in the eyes, as kitchen grit under foot.

Later, Bennet said, "I drive by and see that the yard is OK. I talked to two of the neighbors. They know this isn't fair — they know now."

"I should have gotten an interpreter. Gone house to house like I did in the old place. Things happened so quickly — it was all so quick — "

"You know you did make a lot of noise — especially one of the women yelling out in the yard."

"We would have made her stop. Luke was teaching her to stop."

"I can't come in every day, but I'll be back for messages every week — not your fault." A pause, then, "Oh, here's a letter."

"What letter?"

"It's from the city."

John sighed. "No more," he said, "no more — "

Bennet's hand again. "From the city, yes, but not the parts that are bothering you now. This is from the museum. About a visit. Did you write to them about a visit?"

"I forgot I did . . . a . . . this . . ."

"You can still go. I'll tell you what: I'll take you, all of you. We'll go next weekend."

"I can tell Alma. She can tell Luke. You'll have to call Swede and Madonna, though."

"I will. Saturday OK? I'll check at the museum."

John knew the families wouldn't want to see him again; he himself had lost the spark to go, the idea of the fun of going. The others would tell Bennet; let the others do it for once. . . .

Then, he dreamed about it, going to that big room where the air seldom moved, going carefully through openings, carefully along a very precise trail, sometimes inches at a time. There was the sudden touch of the animal, like furniture upholstered in fur. The animal could not breathe and be warm to his fingers, but as he touch-trembled, delicately over its surface, its form — its outline, as it were — was clear to him. It was a tiger, a Fourbuds gone huge and menacing. He read the Braille sign: TIGER. Then there was a bear and its sign: BEAR; then a wolf and its sign. Another walk, another animal, smooth, this one two-legged, hairless, fists clenched, head back, mouth open, face wrinkled in anger or pain. He groped for the Braille sign, got it, it said: DEAF-BLIND.

Leda came. She came with that sudden

embrace of hers, quick, the lip-brushing, forehead, cheek, then lip and lip, while her hands held his and her secret, more-herself scent, hers, hers, hers, home at last.

"Hit show," she said. "Raves for me."

"Big break," he said. She told him she was here because of the uproar of the neighbors, that it was for the day only. They went to agencies instead of going to bed together. He was a concern now, not a lover. They had an interpreter from the agency for two hours. She explained about the zoning and group homes, which he had already figured out. He spoke about his position now: a single, Deaf-blind man was not a group home, but the neighbors apparently had the same anxiety that he could not care for the house or the street outside it. At the end of the day they were tired and went somewhere for coffee.

"Easier than home," she said, "less hassle." That hurt him, too. Everything was hurting him lately. "Has Bennet been a good friend?" she asked.

"Yes. He surprised me. He comes by and rakes the lawn."

It seemed to puzzle her. "Are you trying for a lawn?"

John realized that she was not aware of the attentions of his neighbors. He said, "Cleaning it off for the winter." He felt sophisticated, Hearing, and desolate.

"How is your mother?" she asked.

"Fine."

"Has your dad ever written back?"

"No. Irwin's wife, Marie, writes now. I like the letters better. More real news. She does not . . ."

"Predigest?"

"Yes. She does not predigest everything to spare me. She writes almost every week and Mr. Bisoglio's secretary reads the letters to me. They have to write so I won't come up."

Her hand trembled a little. "I have to sell the house," she said. He did not answer. She said, "I did the figuring — Washington, here."

"We could have paid."

"Not you alone. Renters? It's no good to be in another city when you have renters. I couldn't have others. You five were the best tenants I could have had and you couldn't make it alone — "

"We could have. It was the neighbors who — "

"For whatever reason, it didn't work out."

"*Your* friends, then; I could stay here with your friends. You have so many."

"They're like me, coming and going. I thought — I didn't know the money it would take to live in Washington. I have to sell the house."

426

They sat quietly for a while. Then he said, "When do I have to go?"

She jumped. Then she said, "Not until the house is sold. You can stay till then. Forget about the money, too. Use it for going back to your old place."

He saw-felt his old apartment, mind-memory, the coziness of it, neighbors who touch-greeted him, the kitchen arrayed to make him competent. He would miss Leda, but the dream of putting on her life as his garment had long ended. The garment was like it was when he worked sorting and rebundling clothes.

"I'm sorry," she said. "None of this was what either of us thought it would be. I'm so sorry it didn't work."

"*We* worked ourselves out," he said, "until we were too tired."

"Bennet told me a bit of what you have been put through — the way they served the papers. He admires your courage."

John knew Bennet had not told Leda much of what had happened. It comforted him because it was not pity. He was still a little angry at Bennet so he said, "But when I move he will not come to visit me, I think."

"People get busy with their own lives."

"Can I ask you for a favor — to call my old place?"

"I'll be leaving tomorrow before anything is open. Maybe Bennet — "

And she was too tired to make love that night. He was too dispirited. He felt a hundred years old, someone who had lived longer than everything he had ever wanted. He certainly had outlived his friendships. Luke, Alma, Swede, and Madonna were angry and bitter at what had happened, blaming him. Luke had said, "You read too many books; everything with you is story, story." It was true. Somewhere he must have read about a happy family living cozily together, each doing some special necessary thing toward the success of the whole. He would, he knew, in months or years, be let back into the good circle of his friends. If Deaf-blindness had any bitter truths, it was that no one could afford to be choosy. The boys who had used him in school were boys with whom he had spent the next two years. Bennet, who had been cruel to him, was kept on until he became a friend. The Deaf-blind world was as small as an embattled frontier family. They would take him back, no matter what, at last. Meanwhile, the story would go all around the Deaf-blind community, and because of Swede, into the Deaf world also, Signed and spelled everywhere, about how he had gotten his best friends to risk everything, gamblers' odds.

Like the stench of burning rubber, the shame of what he had done would drift on the wind of his community so that time and time and time gone by, strangers would remember it, and for the rest of their lives, events would name themselves by it — it happened the year John Moon got his friends . . .

Leda was gone, nothing like the way it happened in books, no final words to make him weep as they did there. She dwindled away like breezes on a hot day, or day by day, like the pain of an injury. Letters now and then, Bennet delivering messages. Then Bennet didn't come anymore because Leda had made arrangements about the mail and the phone.

John wrote a few poems for Mr. Sherline. Sometimes he thought of something about Deaf-blind gratitude. He wrote a good poem called "Friendly Fire," which Mr. Sherline rejected for a reason he couldn't understand. But he was writing more of his own poetry as Leda had taught him:

I wash and shave, the acts by which I call
  you.
Are you going through the door, getting
  into your car and turning the key?
Preparation is my call; under and outer,
  shirts and pants,
I dress to bring you closer; it is my magic.

429

My tie begs you to come as it slips into
   place,
The same place around my neck that
   your arm should go;
My socks and my shoes, a hint about
   walking.
I move and the clock moves; are you
   moving too?
There are binding spells in the tying of my
   laces
To bind you and bring you in the tying of
   my tie.
I have wished you through my button-
   holes — come through and come in;
I pace in my shoes the space between us.
I strike Braille commands with my
   fingers, tapping
Morse code with my foot up and down as
   I sit.
Bring her here; bring her here.
The clock runs in circles.
What magic have I forgotten? What end
   is still loose?

John's apartment had been rented. The
social worker said she had called. The people
put him on a waiting list. In the meantime,
she said, it was not wise to stay in the place he
was now living. The mischief against him
might increase; parents who hadn't controlled

their children before were unlikely to do so now. And now he was alone. This was told him by an interpreter very professionally, spelling quick as water. Time is money. The words sped on almost too fast for him to think about. Other apartments — they could look. He was fortunate to have money for a place of his own, the social worker said, although it would take three months' rent.

"I want to stay where I am."

"The house is to be sold."

"Until it is sold. How many days, how many weeks does it take to learn *where*, learn *how*, in a new place, the walls, the doors, the bathrooms? I want to stay where things are familiar."

"We think a move would be wisest."

"Yes, I know."

"We'll find you a good place."

"I have a place now."

"The neighbors don't want you there."

John stopped talking, answering them. He was perfectly still and suddenly words came from somewhere, from his new knowledge, Bennet, Leda, wisdom he didn't know he had. "Tell the neighbors if they want the house sold, to stop putting out toilet paper and cement powder on the lawn. No one will buy a house that is so ugly." Then he took his hands away from the interpreter, a thing he had also learned without knowing where. Perhaps it was learned from shreds of conversation he had been given by Leda and her friends, maybe bits of a freer, wilder world. Then he groped for her hands again and they were still. Nothing moved.

During the first week in November, John went on the bus to the prison to visit Martin again, this time with Melvin.

"Where's the ripe tomato? This guy looks like his underwear's too tight."

"Gone," John said, "to Washington, D.C., career."

"Loved and lost?"

"Yes."

"So you did get in. Last time you were wanting to."

"I thought I could get in to her life, too — to be part of — " The idea was too big for him. He stood like a statue for a time, hand up for Martin's spelling.

"You got the blues," Martin said, "the lonesome blues, and that's got nothing to do with being Deaf-blind."

"It feels . . . "

"I know. Man, if you could hear, I'd tell you to go to some nice old saloon and play all the woman-gone-blues on the jukeboxes, heartbreak stuff."

"No more saloons," John said.

"Well, you're a poet. Poets have been crying the blues for a thousand years."

"Crying the blues . . . and the Hearing understand? The Sighted?"

"Like a nail in the shoe."

"Sherline wouldn't want me to write that blues. Deaf-blind people are not supposed to feel those things."

"Oh, yeah?"

"On my own, maybe."

"Maybe you'll get famous and I'll have to stand in line to be with you."

"I'll have a business card in Braille, like the one of an interpreter I met."

"There'd have to be a hell of a lot on that card," Martin said.

John felt warmth in his face. " 'John Moon. Reads Braille. Speaks and receives in three modes.' "

" 'Former coconut,' " Martin said.

" 'Can love. Can cry the blues.' "

" 'Is competent with foot, hand, and cane over parts of three cities.' "

" ' — and a mountain town both before and after its changes.' "

" 'Identifies everything in the air from stench to fragrance, and by touch, everything from silk to sandpaper. Works a job.' "

" 'Worries about his taxes and since spring

has been surprised by his capacity for grief, but has also known every kind of joy.' "

"That card would be the size of a dinner napkin!" Martin hit, funning, into John's hand.

"It's not finished. Down at the bottom it would say: 'Is twenty-six. Is not just waiting.' "